# SOULED OUT

ELL CLYNE SERIES: BOOK ONE

BLAKELY CHORPENNING

This is a work of fiction. Names, characters, places, and incidents either are the product of the author's imagination or are used fictitiously, and any resemblance to actual persons, living or dead, business establishments, events, or locales is entirely coincidental.

ELL CLYNE SERIES: BOOK ONE
SOULED OUT



PRINT ISBN-13: 978-0-9847010-2-5
EBOOK ISBN-13: 978-0-9847010-3-2

Cover design by JJ's Design & Creations
Formatting by Inked Imagination Services

*DEDICATIONS*

*This book is for my parents. Though it is not my first book published, it's the first one I finished. You have been there every step of the way, and you know better than anyone that my dreams may have begun here but they started taking shape so many years before this. And dreams are only as great as the love we give them. Thank you Mom and Dad for giving me enough love to fuel all of my dreams.*

*This book is also for our newest generation: Milo, Ivan, Asa, Zora, Charlie, Ellys (my baby love), Ares, Noah, Austin, Ben, Grace, Naomi, Devin, Andy, Garrett, McKenzie, and Coming-Soon-Audrey. Don't be afraid to run to the edge and dare it to give you everything your heart desires.*

*And, of course, this book is for everyone who has traveled into the darkness without a flame and created your own fire.*

# Prologue

I never expected eternity to feel so damn long. The real shame is that it's barely started. I took the vow four years ago to become the Cypher, but hadn't figured on life losing its patina until I was at least a hundred, maybe two hundred years old. And the prospect of eternity, especially in this town, will drive a girl unequivocally mental.

It seemed like a sweet deal, at first. Live forever without becoming the undead. Possess a bank account that can support a small island. Days and holidays subject to my whim. And all I do in return is a little soul searching. But it turns out that reading souls, which saved someone very dear to me, has left me with one dangerous mother of a secret. Oh, and a hole next to my heart where my own soul used to be.

I learned quickly what my world was... And more importantly, what it could never be.

My life isn't normal because I am no longer normal. I'm twenty and already put out with the world. And now the monsters are growing wise to my conspiracy.

Am I ready for what I've started?

# Chapter One

It was Friday night and because everything was blooming in the early stages of spring, hibernation in Mission, North Carolina was officially over. The evening sky was open, the light waning as fast as legs scattered. A few languid clouds tried to shield some of the billions of stars. I wished they would fall to the sidewalk and hide the people who were, no doubt, meeting with friends, finishing last-minute chores, or just enjoying life. For a mediocre-sized town, it sure acted like a big city—not that I had firsthand knowledge to compare.

Living in Mission was not my first choice, or even my choice at all. The Allegiance, the eldest vampires and, consequently, the ones in charge of my status as the Cypher, had decided this modest town at the base of the Smoky Mountains was the perfect headquarters for our little operation. And by little, I mean worldwide. Why not a fun ride like Reno or Hollywood? Why some sedate, no-dot-on-the-map place? Because I wasn't in charge. That was my answer, anyway, when I asked four years ago while packing boxes in my hometown of Somerset, Texas. I had no room to argue their decision, so Mission became my new home.

Being a Cypher is fairly simple. The vampires bring the prospects to me so I can "read" their souls—which consists of sucking their souls into that empty space in my chest—to gain insight into their future actions. The vamps want to know whether or not the prospect in question will jive with their particular cause. If it's a bad date, they go their separate ways. Even the prospects are left ignorant of their fates. If they're destined to do something great or horrible, to become an asset or hindrance, they may not be aware of it. Their souls, however, know what storms and blue skies the future holds.

To vampires, I was the Cypher. Among humans, I looked like a withdrawn teenager. To myself, I was no longer sure. Was "undecided" even an option?

Walking down the street, I was invisible in the crowd, *to* the crowd. Voices swarmed, mixing with millions of rustling sounds. Along with the cacophony, people bustled so close their body heat grazed my skin and disappeared, only to be replaced by the next and the next. It was a living maze, constantly shifting, altering, swaying. Between the human chaos and the steep rise of tightly clustered buildings woven to create the cityscape, I was overwhelmed and dizzy. Unable to stomach the mist of humanity a minute longer, I resolved to escape the heaving streets.

What was a soulless girl to do?

# Chapter Two

The best thing was to hang out at Danny Lynn's sports bar, Two Cents. I know, sad. But it was only four and a half blocks from my house when I cut through a few backyards and skipped down a dark alley.

I never found much solace at Danny's, though it gave me a place to be openly bitchy, which had become my brand of socializing. So I wasn't winning any congeniality pageants. It saved me from barricading myself in the house. And it gave me a reason to get dressed, even if that only meant thin T-shirts and ratty jeans.

Two Cents may have seemed like an odd choice of hang-outs, especially with its overdose of Southern décor reflecting Danny's North Carolina upbringing, but it was the first place in town that ever caught my eye. As a sixteen-year-old fledgling in a grownup world at the time, it fit the bill. There was always a good meal waiting for me, and I never felt like I was eating alone. Danny must have taken pity on me in those early days. He never turned me away, even when a large group of people came in on a crowded night eyeing the booth occupied solely by me. They waited their turns like anybody else. But as soon as I was struck with the genius idea to suck it up and buy a fake ID, Danny "upgraded" me from booth to bar without formality.

I was content sitting by the wall, hoping no one wanted to talk because I had nothing to offer in return, especially of late. But karma is a funny thing. A bitch, really. At the height of my most antisocial rut yet, I could have sworn the universe was giggling at my expense. Why? A simple glance to my right.

It really wasn't my evening.

The same damn vampire who'd robbed the corner mart the weekend before happened to be talking to Danny. Looking. Right. At me.

I prayed Danny was on his game. He knew my presence was just for show, although investing in a No Loitering sign would have closed the gap for speculation.

Danny was a good man in his mid-forties who knew how to work a bar. I guess from years of paying attention and seeing people for who they were and how they wanted to be treated. He made a place for every type of customer, making each one feel at home, accounting for Two Cents being the oldest bar in the neighborhood: seventeen and counting. So many catered to popular crazes, disappearing faster than it took the crazies to find the new *It*. Not Two Cents.

He must have been too busy to cater to little ole me, though. The vamp worked his way right through my safety net. What a shame. I secretly wished he had been ugly. Easier to reject him that way.

As he got closer, I could see his eyes were a striking hazel dowsed with golden and olive flecks, and the blond surfer look was in my top two. His hair was about three inches long and as controlled as a natural disaster. Waves intermingled with straight, both simultaneously fighting to flee the catastrophe. For some reason, it came across as more tousled than scruffy.

He wore tattered jeans, a semi-fitted white shirt that strained against all the right places along his slender muscles, and a pair of brown flip-flops that were new... maybe five years ago. If I'd been looking, he would have been the one to jump on. I mean, to find. But there was no point in wasting his time or, more importantly, mine. I knew how that story ended—me watching his ass disappear faster than the speed of sound when he found out who I really was and what being a Cypher truly means.

Apparently, he didn't get the hint from my glare because he sat next to me. I could tell by his smile that he thought he was something special. Confirming my suspicion, he exclaimed, "I sensed that you want me, so here I am."

"What?" I choked on my tongue.

"Just kidding. He warned me you weren't in a good mood." He nodded toward Danny.

"Perpetually, but thanks for your concern. Bye-bye."

"Wait. I just wanted to meet the woman who needed a caffeine fix bad enough to interrupt a robbery."

I *knew* that would bite me in the ass.

This guy caught me on a bad day last weekend. On top of the shit storm that was my day, I had waited in line everywhere, and what should happen when I was right around the corner from my house? Numb-nuts here, at the head of the line, decided to rob the place. What can I say? My patience snapped. I started yelling, "What is this, the 7-Eleven or the seventh ring of Hell?" I pushed my way to the front of the line, which wasn't difficult considering patrons had started scattering from the store—some taking unpurchased items with them, I observed.

When I reached the counter, I stared the vamp down. Don't get me wrong. I'm not a hero waiting for that pertinent moment to save the world. I've just always had a very short temper when dealing with idiots. This particular idiot just looked at me, glassy-eyed. As I pushed his gun to the side, pointing it at the door instead of the counter, I couldn't help but subtly point out the obvious. "You know what you are.

Of all the things you could be doing, screwing my night over was number one on your list?"

I would never have called him a vampire in public. They only existed in films and literature as far as the poor kid on the other side of the counter was concerned. The knowledge of vampires is far from mainstream, unless you're in the secret "Yeah, I might die a freakishly horrible, bloodless death after all" club. The pointy-toothed robber knew what I meant, though. Catching him by complete surprise, I saw that *"how did she know?"* look stall his face.

I've been able to tell a vampire from a human since my inauguration into the club, I guess. I don't think it's a particularly uncanny ability, though. It's more about knowing the basics, like traits to look for. A normal person—someone who has no idea they walk among us—might look at a vampire and see a pale, exceptionally veiny person with slightly exaggerated canines. I see that, too, but I also notice the extra shimmer in their eyes as they size up the buffet of people around them, and the subtle growth of fangs once they choose their platters. Not unlike two-for-one night at the Golden Corral. I also notice the way they move like river water rippling over the rocks, even as they try to abide by human gravity.

Maybe Danny and I had something in common after all. Like his years behind the bar, my time spent in the company of man-eaters enabled me to know who and what I was dealing with.

Anyway, after the vamp started blinking again, I had the attendant reluctantly ring up my soda. I started to hand the poor kid my change but stopped. What would be the point, right? I shrugged, turned to this vamp, and dropped the coins in his hand. "Have better timing next time. Like when

I'm not here, dick!" Turning to the attendant, I added, "I hope this ends amiably for you."

I walked out and finally made it home. But I could have sworn I saw this vamp's sly smile as I left the store. His ego over-shadowed the Statue of Liberty.

Now, he was sitting next to me, feeling chatty.

Honestly, I had been plagued by the feeling of loneliness lately. More so than usual. However, considering getting close to anyone meant telling said person about my life, I remained as closed off as a Ziploc bag. So I sat on the barstool, staring at him staring at me.

When the silence threatened to continue, I blurted, "Well, you've met me. Feel free to sense that you're unwanted."

He leaned closer, invading my biggie-size circle of personal space. "Did they hold a beauty contest when they chose the North American Cypher?"

"Oh, you found me out," I muttered, not caring to hide the sarcasm. "Broke my secret identity all to hell. Guess I should have left my pageant sash at home." Leaning in, I added, "Like every vampire on this side of the continent doesn't know who I am? If you're trying to impress me, finding a brain before speaking again might be helpful."

He chuckled as if I had told a joke, killing the bite I was hoping to take out of his ego.

"It's a little early in our relationship for pet names. Lucky for you, I'm into that."

Why do people feel the need to talk just because we're in public? I needed to stop his awful attempt at bonding, but all I managed was, "What the fu—" before he interrupted.

"Hey, I'm just trying to share a conversation. Is that too bizarre to process?"

Actually, it felt nice. Which immediately led to an empty

feeling in my gut. So instead of playing twenty questions to learn obscure yet endearing qualities about him that would inevitably land us naked together, I opted for, "I can see you're one of those outgoing people. Bad luck for you, I'm not." For the record, though, my heart chose "naked." It was out-voted by my brain and the hole in my chest.

"I'm not a person, I'm a vampire. But you already knew that."

Give me a break!

"Person, vampire, same thing. Only, one sucks the life out of you with fangs and the other with company. You must be a hybrid because I'm about to die, but you haven't bitten me yet, just talked me to death. Slowly, I might add. Just get it over with." Holding the collar of my heather-gray T-shirt away from my neck may have been a bad move, but how could I take this guy seriously? He robbed the corner mart, of all things. I didn't think he had it in him, but if he did, I was the dumbass for offering.

Sensing his proximity, I couldn't help but wonder whether he was savoring the aroma of my DNA. Or maybe he was asking himself whether he had the balls to bite me in public.

Danny seemed unmoved. A tad amused, to be honest. He knew about the secret world of vampires. I had no idea how or when he had gotten his first dose of reality, but I guess it would be impossible to run a bar in this town and not know. He also had a resident vamp on the payroll. Gotta give him credit for being progressive.

I trusted Danny's instincts. He didn't think I was in danger; therefore, I was probably safe, which left room to linger on other things—like the vamp's broad shoulders and the light touch of aftershave reminiscent of fresh running water under the moonlight. A stream touched by a spring night, to be exact.

After allowing myself to fully indulge, I concluded that he wasn't bad. Not in the least. His features were smooth, but masculine—a boyish face with a kickass physique to counter it. His voice played between smooth and hoarse, as though he had spent too much time at a concert. That voice had the power to turn a whisper into a lullaby. If a better mood had been on my horizon, I could have given him a run for his money. Then again, maybe he would have had me running.

The quirky vamp leaned back on his stool. "Brazen little blonde, aren't you?"

"You didn't do it." I tried to sound nonchalant.

"No, but you've talked to me longer than anyone else, by his count." He nodded his head in Danny's direction.

The air skipped out of the room and my heart stormed against its ribbed prison with three jarring whacks. My cheeks flushed with that feeling of being watched like an ugly bug in a distorted jar. It called up embarrassing moments, like the time that dear in algebra class pointed out that the shit smell enveloping the room was coming from my shoes. Or the day I was hoping to get a cute guy's phone number before school started. I ran up to him and let out a fart that could have been used by national security. Never talked to me again.

Nothing pissed me off more than being embarrassed in public.

"Well," I smiled artificially, "I'll have to buy you a first-place ribbon." My words were heated through a clenched jaw. Was anyone ever truly interested? Guys just have to see who can catch the tough girl first. The elusive prize.

Degraded in my own little corner of the world. Wonderful. I was reduced to a conquest to a guy in a bar.

A sports bar! My evening was complete. No Zen place for me.

I acted tough but letting some two-bit vamp hurt my feelings hadn't been on my to-do list. After all, I was the Cypher, damn it, not a footrest for the undead.

Our bodies were in sync as I stood. Had he realized his insult? Didn't matter. His chances with this girl just melted faster than an ice cube in the afternoon sun. It's always annoying when guys stand to follow you out after you've shown no interest and they've proceeded to mortify you, regardless.

I stopped, spun around, and extended my hand. "I owe you a ribbon, but I didn't mean right now. I guess you have bragging rights, though." My hand, I observed, had landed right on his tight stomach.

He was taller by a few inches. On a good day, I'm five foot seven. On a day I don't wear heels, I'm five four. I hadn't taken the time at the corner mart to notice the difference. I should have, though, because he had been standing right next to me.

*Why was I even thinking about that?*

An observation. Nothing more.

The warmth exuding from his body clued me in that he had fed earlier. Also, that I was *still* touching him. Willing my cheeks to stop blushing, I removed my hand.

He smiled like a man who knew he was attractive, but spoke like someone who held doubt.

"I haven't told you my name."

I breathed deep and released it. "That's okay. I'll just cry myself to sleep later when I think about the chance I just passed up." With that, I rolled my eyes, turned, and walked away, saving at least a tidbit of self-respect.

My exit would have been much sweeter if he hadn't

winked, effectively causing me to run into the door on my way out. That'll teach me to look back. Aggravating as hell. More aggravating was my self-treachery for ever allowing myself to think he was something worth having.

What a night. And it only promised to get worse.

# Chapter Three

I worked from home. I didn't have to but it turned out to be a personal advantage. It was better to be home when the supernatural festivities ended. I never let anyone stay because I didn't want them to see what happened afterward. How I felt after a reading made me laugh. Not in a hearty way, but one of those sick laughs that creeps to the surface when you're so depressed there isn't anything left to do. It was disturbing, especially when I thought about how distinguished being a Cypher is supposed to be. I rarely felt distinguished in those moments, if ever.

My consolation prize: physically, I will age slower than God. Luckily, I had a growth spurt right before I became the Cypher, thinning out my round cheeks and adding a spark of skepticism to my glare. But my body will always be susceptible to the wild nature of the world, like lethal accidents or foul play. A vampire's body is able to heal itself if the damage is not a killing blow, like a beheading or being torn into confetti. I will heal the same way, as long as there isn't major damage. If I were in a nasty car accident, however, my chances might be the same as any human's.

I asked around. The oldest Cypher looked thirty. That's a long time to live with memories and information that was never ours in the first place. I don't know what this Cypher looked like, but she haunts me. Her age haunts me.

*That's a long time to live without a soul.*

A person can never possess more than one soul at any

given time, so the Cypher must be soulless. And considering a soul is never exactly willing, it's like one string remains attached—a kind of otherworldly equivalent to Silly Putty. It won't give up completely, but the Cypher is allowed to borrow it with one string attached—ha, ha.

So I borrow souls and take into myself their information, obtain their future possibilities, and give them back. The downside, other than being the equivalent to a karmic rat, was that it's getting harder and harder to give their souls back, even ones that are tainted or belong to vampires. And yes, contrary to popular belief, vampires and souls do mix. None of these souls, however, fit as well as my original because every soul is a personal puzzle piece. But I'll be damned if I couldn't feel my body trying to break the Silly Putty, remold every soul, cram it in, make it fit, call it my own. And it was time to go through the whole process all over again.

They were due any minute.

The evenings I saw Gabriel Vertiline were loathsome. That covered most nights of my life. Supposedly, Gabriel used to be feared by everyone, maybe even by the monsters. I only caught a glimpse of that vampire when I first started working with him. Now I was stuck with an upper-management, pessimistic, dead-and-hating-it vampire. His demeanor was as distasteful as the sound of a bug being squashed under the heel of a new shoe and as inviting as the idea of cleaning it up. Sometimes, I thought I might prefer him evil rather than discouraged, but I didn't get to choose. And if fashion were a sin, he was the devil's idea of a businessman, right down to the tippy-toes of his couture socks. If I dared look close enough, I'm sure the label would read Evil Bastard.

I used more restraint when I dealt with the prospects.

My dysfunctional relationship with Gabriel aside, the readings held a sense of professionalism as well as ritual. There was nothing more intimate than rolling a soul through my body and learning in a few seconds more than I could in fifty years of marriage. Admittedly, it was a spectacular rush, the power buzzing through me, the prospect, and the universe as it happened. It reminded me of a giant switchboard, temporarily connecting me to the world. I felt awake. Awake to so many emotions aside from sadness and pain. It forced me to remember that I was capable of so much more. And that, ironically, was what snared my heart, caging my happiness deep within.

The muffled slamming of car doors let me know they had arrived. Every time I heard Gabriel's footsteps in the gravel, an overpowering olfactory memory of his cologne swept my nasal passages. I swear it had its own directive: seek and destroy all that is good. Gabriel reminded me of an overly ripe buffet. He needed a tattoo: Surgeon General's Warning: save the whales, save Easter, save the tatas. Run!

"We're here, Peaches." His voice could be so sweet, it was in danger of drawing ants when he wanted it to. Not very flattering, however, since I had come to the conclusion that he only used it to agitate me. And he only called me Peaches to irk the ever-loving hell out of me.

"Come in!" Under my breath, I added, "You son of a bitch."

Gabriel glided in. His six-foot-two frame always moved with calculating precision, giving the constant illusion of authority. He was accompanied by a brown-haired human and Ben, a Member-appointed bodyguard whose overly developed muscles left me cringing in revulsion.

Ben was a dark-haired, blue-eyed version of what happens when frat boys and weight-lifters consort. Being a young vampire of only five years, which was like being a newborn baby in the nursery, meant he tried twice as hard to prove his worth.

Ben had key goals from the start to maneuver his way into the Members' graces, and I gave him kudos for his devotion, but something about his candid plan made me nervous. Every time I saw him, I wanted to hold my breath and wait for some impending failure on his part that would destroy everything he had built. I hated to admit that, in a business capacity, he should have taken notes from Gabriel, who kept any career moves closer to his chest than a winning hand of poker. He could have been planning to breed alpacas, for all I knew.

Gabriel, unlike Ben, had striking shoulders that managed to be muscular, yet understated. Well proportioned—not that I made it a habit to ogle. His hair was midnight brown, like the darkest shadow in the deepest pit. However, in certain lighting, it adopted the ghost of highlights that made me wonder how vivid they must have been when he was human. It was too long to stay out of his face completely and too short to successfully tame with a hairband. It didn't detract from his emerald-green eyes. His Italian mother and Irish father had done a good job. Not bad on the eyes, though useless for anything more due to my previous points, and because of his most important flaw: the man couldn't stand me, either.

"I've missed the place." His smile remained unmoved.

Flatly, I noted, "You were here yesterday."

"And how are you?"

"Asstastic. Thank you for inquiring."

Returning the tone, he looked around and said, "Every minute away from this oasis is like a year in Purgatory."

"Really? I feel like that every minute you're here."

Give a girl a break! My home wasn't dirty, but far from "insert photo on cover of magazine." It maintained a playful balance between coziness and junkyard chic. The only real eyesore was the pile of boxes turning mutinous in the doorway between the living room and kitchen. Each vendor had taken care and forethought in the exterior wrapping, but clustered together, they looked, well, muddled and possibly a little dispassionate about the products concealed within.

I had started ordering products online a few months ago as a means to pass the time and it got a little out of hand. Too many late nights spent with overzealous infomercials and the Home Shopping Network. It had been in my planner to stop, but once Gabriel began observing the growing pile with an air of distaste, I decided to not only keep my new hobby but contribute more time to it, as well. Three more were scheduled to arrive by his next visit. It made my inner brat smile.

Overall, I liked my house. It was a modest two-bedroom ranch. The living room and kitchen were divided by one of those half-wall things with pretty rails up to the ceiling. It offered the illusion of privacy between rooms and left the space feeling open at the same time. A few colorful prints of fruit hung in the kitchen—a thrift store find. And a stressed brown tapestry hung on the wall to the right of the couch. It had been rolled up next to a dumpster when I found it and took pity. Someone had loved it enough to set it beside the bin rather than chuck it inside, hopeful that someone would discover it and drag it home. I was the sap who fell for it.

The hallway to the left of the front door led to both bedrooms and a bathroom. And through the kitchen to the right was an inconspicuous door leading to a really big perk: the basement. At one time, I had used it for the prospects, but the atmosphere seemed to freak people out. So I moved my computer and desk downstairs, and cleared the spare room out so people would stop feeling as if I were going to hack them up instead of read their souls. It wasn't a bad exchange. The basement felt more private anyway—not that privacy was in short supply. None of my neighbors lived too close. I was on the edge of the city, so the lots were spacious.

There was only one personalized touch to my entire house: my junior class photo. My last photo. It hung behind my bedroom door, out of sight to visitors. At any time, I could inspect my white, strained smile. I could count the different hues of blonde that made my long hair look dusty. I could recall my worry that the concealer would fail, the imperfections frozen in time for all my classmates to point out. I could see how my brown eyes were haunting next to the listless gray shirt I wore. Gray has always been my favorite color, which accounted for my twilight wardrobe. And I could laugh at the bad tan my sister made me get, which had long since faded, leaving my naturally rosy skin exposed. Most importantly, it was a reminder that my life before this did exist. I had a family. Once upon a time.

*I needed to focus.*

It was time to repress my baggage and be the Cypher.

My line of vision rested on the guy in front of me. He looked pale but unmistakably human. Hey, I liked knowing what I was getting. Vampires have souls, but they're kind of encrypted to not show up on supernatural radar, and they feel different because of that. I wondered if they could feel their souls and just didn't recognize them. Probably not, which was where the whole "no soul" myth came from. How could you argue with an accuser if you weren't sure the person was wrong? But their souls are there, although the vampires thought I used the body to hone in on the soul in question and pull it from wherever it resided, like Hell or Purgatory, or an elephant's ass. Vampires just assume they've flown away somewhere, gone because they're legally dead. Not so, but why be the myth-buster? Not in my job description.

*Focus.*

The guy had a geeky air about him, from the institutional haircut and manicured hands to a reasonably branded office suit, though he seemed as if he had enough will to hold his own if forced. He looked close in age to Gabriel, who died when he was twenty-three, but Gabriel towered over the poor guy, who was five eight at most. Truthfully, in any other setting, I would never have noticed the prospect because next to Gabriel, he wouldn't have had a chance. And not just because of Gabriel's looks.

Gabriel was dressed in relaxed, well-tailored black slacks, his favorite blue-collared shirt, and shiny black loafers. In dress alone, he appeared more professional than almost every person in Mission. But what did it really matter? We weren't there to size each other up. We were there to analyze a soul.

Gabriel snapped his fingers in my face. "I have other things to do tonight besides watch you daydream."

Ignoring him, I tried to seem amiable as I asked the prospect, "Are you ready?"

The guy looked as though he could readily pass out or throw up. Or both. He was seriously scared. I guess it didn't help that there were so many horrid rumors about the Cypher. Started by people who had never met me, no doubt. Rude. Or maybe some of the past Cyphers were extreme bitches. *Thanks, ladies.*

I could hardly hear him mumble, "I guess."

"Okay, then. It won't be unpleasant, no matter what

people have told you. It's like being placed in a type of sleepy, suspended animation. You won't feel it. You won't know it's even happening. Cool?"

He looked a little less like vomiting. An improvement, I guess: somber, but not fatal to my carpet.

"Uh, cool."

I could tell he didn't use slang very often.

"Good. Let's move to the guestroom."

Once there, I told him to sit in the baroque chocolate armchair covered in an electric-blue leaf pattern positioned in the middle of the room. The chair was a leftover from my sister. Her affection for all things baroque knew no bounds.

"Sorry about the choice in furniture."

He shrugged. "It reminds me of home."

Scrunching my eyebrows together, I decided not to ask who his decorator was.

I purposely had as few pieces of furniture in the room as possible. Didn't want it to look like a junk room—plus I used a lot of incense, so fire safety was always in the forefront. The long wooden side table held the incense and a lighter. The incense wasn't an official part of the reading. I just thought it was soothing and added a nice touch to the ambiance. A small hunter-green lamp with a dim bulb sat next to it. Matching green curtains with chocolate accents hung on the single window, masking the outside world. The soft material looked nice against the eggshell walls. I chose that color because it reminded me of my grandmother's house, which always felt calm and free from the boundaries of time.

Because I had just started using the room full-time, the carpet was still a crisp, creamy hue. I supposed it would have to be changed when the traffic started to crumple the fibers, leaving pathways through the room. At the increasing speed people were being brought over, I would have to invest in new carpet sooner rather than later. There was an absolute urgency in the air lately. I would find out why soon enough, so I felt no desire to ask Gabriel about it.

Ben, who had recently started accompanying Gabriel everywhere like a good bodyguard posing as a lesser evil, helped the guy find his seat. After looming for a second, I asked both men to leave.

Voyeurs have never been favored in my book. They weren't a distraction to me, but they had a knack for making the person in the chair very tense. It took longer to read a soul when there were spectators causing fear. Cooperation wasn't necessary, just a means for it to be over quicker for everyone involved.

Gabriel smirked, pausing at the door after Ben left. "Always wanting to be alone with them. Makes me wonder what else goes on in this room."

I scowled. He got the message and left, shutting the door with a pleased expression. Bastard.

Offhandedly, I said, "Ignore him. He's just hurt because no one's cared enough to stake him yet." I recaptured his attention and smiled. "Are you ready?"

# Chapter Four

Funny, Gabriel was sort of right. I always found myself alone with a stranger. In a nutshell, my life was one long line of strangers. I had no friends, only countless lifetimes of unfamiliar people in my future.

If I ever decided to be social again, to have close friends, I didn't think I could maintain relationships with regular humans. They would just die, leaving me alone and depressed. Again. That left vampires, because there couldn't be more than one Cypher on each continent at any given time. That was a pity, both because the vampires hadn't proved to be very chummy and because another Cypher could have been a healing presence. Someone to count on, even.

I had a best friend once. We had such a bond. I was always happy, even when bad things happened. And we always had secrets to tell each other. Granted, we were just kids. The secrets were not that important. The point was having someone to tell anything to and knowing no one else was allowed in on it. She was gone now, and I was left with one very big, looming secret with no one to tell, or to trust.

*Back to business.*

My thoughts and hurt feelings shed away as I focused on my job. "Calm down. I didn't lie to you. This will not hurt."

I gave him credit for trying to relax. The lines smoothed around his shallow brown eyes. He leaned against the chair back and stopped gripping the armrests. He even did that neat speaking trick.

"Do a lot of people who come to see you end up dead? Are they going to kill me?" Spoken by a nameless stranger seeking comfort from the axman—er—woman.

"No. They just want to know what kind of person you are. If you're someone they can trust, I guess."

"And you're going to tell them to trust me or not?"

"I'm going to tell them what your soul tells me. If it's not what they want to hear, they'll leave you alone."

He smiled nervously and whispered, "Then I hope it's not what they want to hear."

All I could do was shake my head to show that I was listening and that I understood. I could have kept talking. I could have tried to tell him that even if they wanted to turn him into a vamp, he'd probably love it. Right now, he was just ignorant and scared. Being a vampire wasn't that bad for most. There was the whole "what am I supposed to do for eternity?" dilemma most vampires faced once turned. However, very few strolled into the sun for an afternoon suicide.

He nodded, as if to relay that he had found strength in some inner corner of his mind and was ready to proceed.

Finding a soft spot in my armor, I offered one bit of advice. "There's no point in worrying yourself over things that haven't come to pass yet, or might never." The words made sense, but that familiar twinge of guilt had already begun winding inside me. No matter how I justified this with strangers, at the end of the day, the blind eye to good and evil bugged me. Sometimes, I wanted to tell the prospects how lucky they should feel, or ask whether their mothers would approve, or tell them to run as fast as they had ever run away from a bad, bad future. But I was reduced to clenching my jaw shut like a trap.

With a sharp nod, I said, "Okay, I'm going to lean close

now. Don't talk and don't hold your breath. You might feel a slight pull next to your heart, and then you'll wake up and go home."

I closed my eyes, stopped thinking, and felt for his soul. My palm rested on his chest as I found that invisible weight. I breathed in the sandalwood incense. Probing through the physical realm, I slowly called his soul out, almost free of his entire body. Just that one string hung on.

The feel of a soul was very humbling. It's more like a feeling than an actual thing, like the comfort of visiting a place and knowing that you can shut your eyes and identify every part of it in your heart. You know it inside and out.

Suddenly, I could see him from the interior instead of just the exterior. He was honest and candid because no one was allowed to defile that inner sanctum. *Except me.*

I was viewing previously classified secrets his soul dared not whisper to anyone, least of all to himself. And there was that familiar sense of euphoria mixed with the jitters. An odd combination I would never get used to.

Bumping into metaphysical roadblocks like a blind person in an unfamiliar room, I scavenged through curiosity and overabundance, fear and laughter, excess and shortcoming, love and hate... So much emotion threatened to overtake me when I had to steer for my purpose. Why was he here, in my chest, in my head? Who was he to them?

In a few short minutes—sifting through the smell of homemade cookies, the feel of his mother's laughter warming his heart, the emptiness when his grandfather died at his feet—I learned that this man, whose soul I cradled behind my ribs, was going to be one of the most noted scientists in history. He didn't have the nerve to fight in battles, but he had the brains to come up with some very interesting theories that would manifest into hard facts.

This man would change eternity for all vampires and alter medical science. He would help mold vampire and human communities into one organism. This man was rare, profoundly unique. In the span of every Cypher, one crossed very few with such deep-rooted purpose. This was my first. I never asked for names, but I would have to. This man would be a scientific hero.

If the powers that be allowed it, that is. If not, he would just be a mortal man, and I would be left feeling the loss for the world.

I couldn't be greedy. It took all of my strength to gently lay the soul into its proper owner. How could I think to keep such a wonder when I could never live up to half of what he might accomplish?

He awoke slowly and stood, uncertain. There were questions he wanted to ask. Would it be wise to answer? No, but I never had to make the decision. He refrained.

I held my hand out to shake his. "What's your name?"

"Nicholas Grant."

*A name to remember*. But before I could finish bathing in the presence of Mr. Grant, the shadows of pain began to creep through my body like a hunter stalking its prey.

Oh God, it was starting!

# Chapter Five

Why were they still here? Mr. Nicholas Grant had already been hauled outside and stashed in the car. So why were they in the doorway, staring at me?

"If you hadn't noticed, your presence is no longer required." My voice sounded slightly strangled. I was trying my best to remain calm as the pain flipped every switch in my nervous system. If only my body could understand what my mind knew, I wouldn't have to experience such torment after every reading.

Gabriel always left immediately when a reading was finished. This time, he took a step closer. "Feel like dancing?"

"What?"

Without breaking eye contact, he spoke over his shoulder. "Ben, leave us."

My nerves fluttered. He sent Ben away. Ben was gone. Just the two of us left. This was not good. Then again, good things were reserved for other people.

*Leave!* my brain begged.

I couldn't mask the growing agony much longer, the pain that would constantly plague my future, forever chaining me to the past.

His face was void of expression. "Dancing. I asked if you wanted to go dancing."

"No."

"I didn't think so. The past Cypher used to go out afterward, as if this whole process energized her."

"Maybe she was too outgoing. I'm not a good dancer."

My pained heart scrambled to calm down, which only caused it to beat more furiously.

"No. You struggle." He took a step toward me. "I've been watching. I know this is abnormal for a Cypher. Your soul is gone, and it should know its duties, why it's gone." He claimed another step. "Your body shouldn't crave the loss as it does. It should accept its freedom."

This man—no—this *vampire* was about to figure out a secret that could not be told. Not yet. Not ever. The sting in my heart couldn't grow much worse than the squeezing, irregular thumping it had adopted from the impact of his words.

Was Gabriel really that observant? I should have known. He wasn't stupid, and he was definitely malicious. I should have been nicer to him. Why couldn't I ever just be nice? Maybe because my soul had been pried from my body, leaving me with an uncertain afterlife and a hollow space next to my heart. Things like that tend to leave a girl a tad bitter.

If I acted normal, he might leave without the knowledge that anything was wrong. *Stand up straighter. Make the usual disagreeable expression.* There. Everything was fine. I could do this for a few minutes, if it would be enough to make Gabriel slink away, unsuspicious.

"Why are you wasting my time, Gabriel? If you couldn't tell already, I'm not social. I don't like company, especially yours. I don't enjoy it and I sure as hell don't invite it."

"Oh, I'm all too aware of your stunted social skills, Cypher. But I'm not talking about etiquette. Be a bitch for five hundred years for all I care. It turns me on."

As he leaned in, a kind of peace filled me as I realized I would choke to death on his cologne long before he ever discovered anything important. I breathed in the fumes, willing it to surround my organs and stifle them. That had to count as foul play, right? That smell made him a walking assassin. Actually, it wouldn't have been half bad if he toned it down to a national threat level of yellow.

"Are you smelling me?" His posture turned rigid.

Damn! He thought I was coming on to him. His wild green eyes were brighter than they had been two minutes before. A good or bad thing?

I did not want to get into this with Gabriel, but I had no alternative. Protecting a vital secret makes you do crazy things under scrutiny. A slight suicide attempt mistaken as inept flirting wouldn't kill me, but I had my limits. And like I said, he was not a stupid vamp.

I tried to act sly. "You'll have to drag me to court to find out, Gabriel. Are you done with your conspiracy theory tantrum?"

An empty expression filled the space usually reserved for a nasty comeback.

This was the nicest I had ever been to him. He didn't know what to do. Ha! He was utterly and openly confused. A first, and I liked it. I should have tried to kill myself more often. When he was confused, he was amusing, almost likable. And much cuter.

Dark hair veiled his face. He was too stunned to push it behind his ears, though I doubted it was tame enough to stay if he tried. Cute was not a description I had ever used for Gabriel. Then again, my body was wracked with pain I was trying to hide, so I was sure my mind was escaping through the means of a sick fantasy. Good distraction. Bad choice. I didn't like Gabriel. I would never like Gabriel. And he tolerated my existence because, in comparison, it made his seem much livelier. Finding company together was a disgusting fairy tale. So why were we standing in my front hall like we were on a first date?

Bad decision-making. I shouldn't have been nice.

Out of discomfort, I blame-shifted. "Are you hitting on me?"

"What? No! What the hell is wrong with you tonight?"

A flustered vamp really was the best gift.

"Then stop standing in my living room, eying me like a nerdy teenager! Jesus!"

"Are you hitting on me? Are you blushing?"

*No, and yes.* I blushed as my heartbeat sped due to a spike of pain. It must have been a sure sign I was about to pass out. Great. But I could use it to my advantage.

"No. It's from the pain of watching you leave. Let's not keep doing this. Stop taunting me with your body. Just get out!" And with that shameful act of self-exploitation, I pushed him out the door, not missing the look of absolute shock on his face.

I locked the door and ran to the basement to hide from my shame.

Could the evening get any worse? How do you surpass excruciating pain, self-loathing, and embarrassment? Ah, yes, tomorrow night. I had to see Gabriel to plan the next month's prospect scheduling. Should have thought about that before my theatrical outburst.

Double damn.

# Chapter Six

I spent the better half of the day wandering through town, trying to forget the shameful moment with Gabriel the night before. My mind was unforgiving. It was a loss I'd have to accept.

Nothing had caught my interest lately except the two-bit moron at the bar. Caught my eye was more like it. I might have been experiencing a personal permafrost, but that part of me that was pure female enjoyed the occasional eye candy, as bitter as that candy might turn out to be. That's why I had a personal rule to look but not touch. The guy had turned out to be a complete douche, anyway.

A small park was close by. Luckily, it was empty, giving me a chance to rest my feet without interruption. I sat down on a bench between the yellow slides and metal monkey bars, overlooking the tennis courts.

Could I ever be as happy as the rest of the human population in Mission seemed to be? Doubtful. The first step involved being happy with myself, and too much had transpired for that to happen.

The bench was hard, but I stretched out to see the stars better. It always stunned me how brilliant specks of light were able to silently tell the history of the universe. They held a special power, the same way ancient lore breathed mysticism into an unsuspecting, overcritical world.

Allowing the night to consume me completely, my eyes shut before I could stop them. In a matter of minutes, I was coiled in dreams. The feeling was unpleasant because I knew they would be vicious repeats. Nice things had disappeared from the menu months ago. Only a chosen few filled my sleep now, which was why I usually said a small prayer to no one in particular to not dream at all. It worked most of the time, but not tonight.

It felt so real, as always. Although the visions changed, the root of my heartache remained constant. My sister and I were jumping on our parents' bed. They never allowed it, but we were young and didn't see the harm. The comforter was plush, wrapping around our forms as we fell time and again. Even in the dream, I could smell my mom's flowery perfume in every thread of the cobalt-blue monstrosity. We knew it well because sneaking in and jumping had become a ritual in our youth. Before leaving, we would always straighten the comforter, giggling that we had gotten away with it yet again.

In reality, those times seemed to last forever. In my unconscious state, it was a fleeting image as the hallway from our parents' bedroom turned into a slide. Our laughter echoed down the slippery slope until we landed in mounds of cotton. It surrounded us until we were huddled in a cocoon, whispering secrets so close I felt the warmth of her breath on my cheek. It was safe and warm, and we were happy.

Timeless.

All of a sudden, the cotton disintegrated and I fell onto the road in front of my childhood home, smacking my elbow on oil-stained concrete. My fingers tingled, and I found myself alone.

No longer a child in my hazy memory, I struggled to cradle my elbow and stand at the same time. That is, until I saw the broken charms of my bracelet on the concrete in front of me. They lay crushed, surrounded by a delicate, desecrated silver chain. The road had eaten away at it, eternally greedy. The pain in my arm was suddenly gone, replaced by a new ache in my chest. It felt as though my heart were crying. Because that was impossible, it imploded. And then another shift occurred, entwining two separate incidents into one emotional mess.

I stood in a circle. It was the circle signifying the ceremony which marked me as the Cypher. The Members enclosed me. I was staring at the broken charm necklace at my feet like I had done when I was eleven. The portly male vampire said a few words to jump-start the ritual, as he truly had when I was sixteen. Actually, it had sounded more like a verbal agreement.

"As the Cypher, you honor your predecessors with your devotion to an elite link within the chain of time. In return, this gift will link you to all. You will disclose futures and act as a guide to the light of knowledge. With no bias for good nor evil, you will encrypt the world with the ability to meet its greatest potential."

No pressure at all for a sixteen-year-old, right?

Countless faces stared from outside of the circle as his words collided with my body. Uncertainty and dread numbed my limbs, just as it had that night. I searched the strange crowd for my parents, but they hadn't been allowed to attend. Only my sister was there. Unlike true events, though, I found her on the outside of the circle...smiling.

I woke with a start, falling off the bench. On hands and knees, I ordered myself to stop hyperventilating and slowly sat back down on the bowed wood. I hadn't been asleep for long, but it felt like years. After taking a few deep breaths, my heartbeat resumed a regular pace.

A crumpled envelope in my pocket demanded attention. I had been obsessed with it ever since it arrived three days ago. It was still unopened, of course, though I'd taken it out of my pocket a dozen times to toy with the edge of the flap, working it ragged.

Honestly, I wasn't sure I wanted to read my sister's letter. But I refused to leave it closed, abandoned like the others. Maybe this one would be different. After the nightmare, I willed the thin letter to be a savior in my dark existence.

Slowly, I ripped the paper and unfolded an anorexic letter on dainty stationary.

Dear Ellenore,

I have been busy since the wedding. Nick is expecting a promotion and we are buying a house. Mom and Dad love it. I would have sent photographs but my life is so full, I rarely have time for the small things. I'll try, though. I know how much the small things mean to you.

Regards,
Myranda

Regards? I think the letter was meant to stay wrapped in the pretty envelope or framed and hung on the wall, where I could look at it any time. Where I could hold it and hope that its contents resembled the sister I used to know, who I jumped on the bed and shared harmless secrets with.

Regards... A sentiment to one stranger from another when every other farewell seems awkward or too personal. When had we reached that point where too personal was inappropriate? Recently, I guess. We were always close until now. My being the Cypher had never bothered her. Did it now? Something was definitely wrong. My parents hated what I was. So much, in fact, that they hadn't talked to or seen me since half an hour before the ceremony on my sixteenth birthday.

Happy birthday to me, right?

Snide remarks aside, Myranda had left out so much. There was a time not long ago when she would have asked my opinion on decorations—sending one boring wallpaper swatch after another—all the while wondering why no one else on earth shares her love for purple baroque embellishments. And I would laugh.

I wanted so much from these letters. I wished for notebook pages full of good stories and memories rather than snarky, strange comments so unlike her. And these precious pages were not in my imagination. They shouldn't have been beyond my reach, because I had kept them all. Every letter she had ever sent. They used to be the only things that made me smile and laugh without fearing that such moments would ever end.

And to bring up Mom and Dad without saying more... How were they? What had they been doing other than visiting Myranda? Had they asked about me? It was as if she had done it on purpose. Tell me enough to goad, but not enough to quench.

I didn't even know Myranda's last name since the wedding. A wedding I was told *nothing* about until it had already transpired. The envelope was only signed with her first name. And the address was a PO box for a town I had never heard of.

In another life, maybe I could have salvaged a shadow of optimism. In this one, it sent a lonely chill through my bones. Wishing for nothing more than to be with my family, I couldn't help but let a ball of spite choke my tears. I was the Cypher. Other families might be proud of that so-called honor, but mine ran from it. I imagined my parents visiting

Myranda: Mom making dinner, Dad talking to Nick like a son, talking about the future. One I was no longer privy to. I had become an outsider to my own lineage.

For a split second, I wondered whether they kept any photographs of me in the house or whether those had been banned along with the memory of my existence.

I folded up the letter and slid it back into the tattered envelope. As bad as it was, I would keep it. I always did. I couldn't bring myself to throw it away because that would be giving up hope that they still loved me. Bitterness stole a piece of me every day, but it was anger that threatened to fill me up until I was no longer myself. No longer human at all. Hope kept me from turning into the vengeful monster my traveling soul fought to reflect.

After regaining some mental composure, I laid down on the bench to watch the stars again. There was no chance of dozing off a second time.

Tall tree branches swept the sky. The wind blew a little above a sigh, tickling my eyelashes. My eyes closed, and I listened to my breath as it pushed and pulled, becoming one with the wind. I had to calm down before I went to work. No, I had to calm down before my heart shattered and I dropped to the ground to invite death.

*I shouldn't have read the letter.*

Some people might have thought I was wasting a good thing, too busy caught in a hail of self-pity to enjoy the Cypher perks. But that didn't change the truth that nothing was free when dealing with vampires, especially when your soul was involved. My price was more expensive than I understood when I accepted my fate with a sweaty palm and a fractured smile. I didn't realize what type of life I had accepted but, as I said, it saved the life of someone very close to me. So, as much as I had grown to hate what I was, I would accept it again and again because I could never condemn someone I loved. Even when I woke up every day wishing to die but too afraid of where I'd end up if I did.

I had unlimited resources at my disposal, but it was clear that money couldn't fix what was wrong with me. Something needed to change.

*I* needed to change.

# Chapter Seven

The only immediate thing I could think to do was hang out at Two Cents. It was the best place to think. Of course, it complicated things when I couldn't seem to get away from my number-one vampire stalker moonlighting as a thief.

He wore a loose, long-sleeve black shirt, baggy green cargo pants, and the same ratty flip-flops from the previous evening. On anyone else, those shoes would have been unforgivable. But somewhere in the recesses of my mind, I had already established that he would look attractive in a rain poncho and a fanny pack. Didn't mean anything. So he was cute. So what?

Why was he here? I wanted to *feel* more social, not *be* more social.

We made eye contact before I could look away. Had I woken up in another nightmare? It was the only explanation. If vampire pigs flew through the bar, I would be certain.

He hopped onto the barstool beside me. "My name's Seth."

I stared at the bar. "I don't care."

"You should."

"Not really."

"You're supposed to ask why."

I sighed. "Why?"

"Because—wait, did you say why because I asked or because you don't know why you should say why?"

"The former."

"Oh. Well, you ruined the pickup line."

"That's okay. I like being well-grounded."

I could almost hear him trying to think of something witty to say in return. Why was he trying so hard? There wasn't room in my life for a guy. I worked. I came and went whenever. It would be unwise to have someone around, asking questions that had no answers that I wished to share.

On the other hand, I had been so depressed. It might help to talk to someone else without being hostile. When all else fails, try something new. Being chatty was new. Taking a chance was new.

This was the change I needed to make.

Taking a deep breath, I asked, "Why did you rob the store?"

An interesting conversation never killed the cat.

*Hopefully.*

"Wow, jump right into it. A second ago, you didn't care what my name was and now you want to know my personal motives?"

"If you knew me, you would take this as a miracle. I'm more content to sit here by myself. Then again, if you knew me, you'd probably leave me alone."

"You don't scare me." He was almost offended.

"That's not what I meant."

"What did you mean, then?"

"Never mind. Nice talking to you."

Well, I just earned my first-place ribbon for failure. Conversation killer, that's me. Sitting in awkward silence just drove it home. Why was I trying to be anything other than what I was? I mean, who I was.

You can't live as a shadow because there's nothing real about a shadow. There are no defining details, no real essence. It's a mimic. And that's all I could ever be. My emotions mimicked something real that didn't belong to me anymore.

"I was bored."

His soothing voice broke my thoughts. He was still there. Most people would have fled the second they saw my eyes glaze over.

Confused, I blinked rapidly. "What?"

"I robbed the store because I was bored. It was just something to do. Sorry to disappoint you. No hidden motives."

"Normal bored people don't turn to crime for giggles."

"I'm a vampire. What do I have to lose?"

It was rhetorical, but I answered anyway. "Your head. Your heart. Your—" *Soul*, I thought.

"I get it. But being immortal gets repetitive sometimes."

"Believe me, you don't have to explain."

He gave me an odd look. I couldn't quite figure it out. Maybe it was acknowledgment. I wanted to ask what was so repetitive, but that was too personal and, selfishly, he might ask the same. Not a question I wanted to answer out loud. It was something I breathed and ate, but not something to profess to a stranger. I could, however, offer simple information.

"My name's Ell."

"Okay. Would you like a beer, Ell?"

That was unexpected, though not unthinkable considering we were, in fact, in a bar. Should I drink? I had to meet Gabriel soon. Normally, we met the first Monday of every month to schedule the prospects. For some reason, he had been adamant at the last minute that we meet tonight, a Saturday. And when I'd agreed to the early meeting, I hadn't known I would have any clashing plans.

I sat there, watching Seth wait for my answer. He didn't

make a face or tell me to hurry up and make an easy decision. He was undoubtedly a stranger, but his company almost felt peaceful, like maybe this was how it felt to have a friend. What the hell? One drink wouldn't hurt.

Convincing myself that I had made a wise decision, I said, "Just one."

His expression was pure relief. He had really been worried I would say no. "Thanks." His smile was something else.

"For what?" I inquired.

"For taking a chance on me."

And with that, he flagged Danny over, who brought two beers faster than I could seal a deal with the devil. Danny didn't serve me that often. I never bothered him, and he never bothered me. So, I knew it would be a treat to have my patronage, with added company.

"Thanks, Danny."

He winked before walking back to the other end of the long mahogany bar. Great.

We sat in silence for quite a while. Again, it was tranquil rather than painful.

I was almost done with my beer when Seth said, "Thanks, again. I figured you'd bolt faster than you did yesterday."

"Well, you outlasted everyone else. Guess that wins you an hour, so make it good."

"I didn't know we had a time limit. Danny, two more! I'm on a time limit over here!"

"I don't need another one."

"What's one more?"

"I don't drink much."

"For a girl who spends all her extracurricular time in a bar, that lie reeks."

"I hang out more than other people," I corrected, "but not to drink."

Danny placed the new bottles in front of us.

"Yeah, you just hang out for the company." He chuckled, but he was closer to the truth than he knew.

"I'll pay this time."

"No, I accosted you."

"As long as you don't take it as an I.O.U."

"Done."

We shook hands. It was still early in the evening. I half expected his hand to feel like ice but it was warm, like the residual heat from a heater that had been turned off recently.

The first beer went down quick. The second took longer. We didn't talk about much. No childhood traumas or lost dreams. Instead, we watched the basketball game, offhandedly commented on other patrons, shared stupid jokes, and spent more time in silence. But it was all very reassuring that not everything ended in disappointment.

Before I knew it, we were six beers and two shots of tequila each in debt, and I was two hours late to meet Gabriel.

"Crap!" I stumbled as I slid off the stool. "Our meeting!" My head felt detached from my body, and my shoes seemed to have anvils in them. A few drunken episodes littered my past, but this time I could swear my entire blood supply had been replaced with alcohol. This is why modernation was invented.

Modernation...

*Moderation.*

Crap, I was drunk!

Seth stood next to me. He was a bit wobbly, too. Good. I didn't want to seem like a lightweight.

"Rushing off to another date, are you?" His speech was slurred.

"I'm sure he's long gone."

I had never skipped a meeting before, and could only imagine Gabriel crying in a dark corner somewhere... Yeah, right. Whatever he was up to, I had no intention of finding out. "I'll just text him." I looked at the time again. "And then turn my phone off."

After leaving a horribly misspelled message to Gabriel, Seth and I swayed toward the door, but it was like walking in a funhouse. Hell, we were the goofy mirrors. I bumped into his side a few times.

Seth held his arm out and drew every word with extra effort. "I think this will go much better if we combine forces."

After a long moment of comprehension, I realized he wanted me to hold onto his arm. After another minute of wobbly consideration, I took it. What choice did I have? Arm in arm, we stumbled onto the sidewalk. In our haze, I quietly noted how strong his arm was. It felt more than comfy in my hand. It felt right.

By the time I figured out why we were teetering on the curb, a cab pulled up.

"I know you planned on walking, but get real. I don't think we could make it to that puddle on the other side of the street. Anyway, I'm gonna have to eat again or I'll have an unquenchable thirst tomorrow. Liquor always magnifies my blood thirst."

Well, the guy was smarter than I expected. About the cab. The vamp thing was his deal. I had already started worrying about my own drunken aftermath. Being somewhat superhuman meant my body would metabolize alcohol almost as fast as a vampire's. That didn't mean it was a cure-all for hangovers.

It was only a five-minute drive to my house. As the cab slowed, I started to fumble through various pockets for the little loop with the lone key attached.

A bit of awe touched Seth's voice as he casually remarked, "I'm glad you didn't drive your car. I don't like watching people break expensive toys."

"I don't own a car," I mumbled before looking up to see the quintessential sexy, black sports car parked in my driveway. It had more flair than the Batmobile.

Visually sweeping the entry points, I saw the blinds askew in the living room. In a window that I *never* touched.

"Keep driving!" I commanded.

Someone was in my house.

# Chapter Eight

The adrenaline was extremely sobering as I processed the only explanation and fought away the paralysis of fear. Seth kept his mouth shut, knowing full well that his questions couldn't be answered within earshot of the cabbie. We rode another ten minutes before getting out in a back alley of the business section of town. It was practically deserted, which was perfect for the conversation about to take place.

The cab was parked a good distance from us when Seth asked, "So, how's your evening so far?"

"Well, I think there was a last-minute meeting to ransack my house. That'll teach a girl that drinking and ignoring associates aren't always the best career moves."

"I definitely don't miss being human."

The alley was dank, poorly lit, and every word seemed to soak into the brick walls around us. In the wake of Seth's attempt at comedy, I could hear my own breathing intermingle with his. Yes, vampires breathe. If they acted completely dead, they might as well lie down and accept it, right? Anyway, it was soothing.

Sometimes you find yourself in the oddest moments of suspension, when time is a foreign concept and you never think the moment will end. I was there.

Shutting my eyes, I focused on Seth. After a good minute or two, I found the concentration had cleared the fog from my head. And I couldn't have been closer to Seth if I jumped into his arms. Knowing someone was close by could actually be more comforting than touching. Maybe it's the equivalent of knowing your parents are in the next room to save your ass if an ax murderer springs forth from the dirty clothes hamper.

And right now, there was no hiding how serious the situation was.

"What's really going on, Ell?" he asked, all joking aside.

"A fallible business plan."

"Are you sure it's work-related? Piss any friends off lately?"

"There's no one else." I took a long breath before continuing my admission. "I don't have friends."

"Family?"

I shook my head and crossed my arms.

Seth tried hard to stifle the personal questions that were, no doubt, right behind his thin yet alluring lips. "Business then."

I'm glad he didn't question my family relations. That topic was in danger of becoming taboo.

I was almost positive I knew what was about to go down. Gabriel hadn't tried to hide his suspicions. Now my home had been violated and I was left with a virtual stranger who I didn't know whether I could even trust. I wanted to. But after years of keeping this secret, I was reluctant to give in to my desire in case my heart was tainting my gut feeling. Did I trust Seth enough to share a painful part of my life with him? Or was I just looking for someone half-decent to blab to so I didn't go insane?

Everything in me screamed to trust him.

It might be good for him to know. One, it would be nice if *someone* knew in case my body needed to be identified. And two, I wanted to find out whether Seth could handle my life before I got used to his company. If I didn't take the chance to trust him, how would I ever know?

And this was the test to put all other tests to shame.

Sparing a glance to make sure the cabbie was still reading his paper, I blurted, "Look, I've got to be honest. I made a decision a long time ago, and the repercussions are about to wreak a major shit storm on my life."

"How so?"

It was nice to see that he had a serious side to balance the comedian.

"I experience things that past Cyphers didn't. It's hard to give the souls back once I read them, and when I do, it causes me a lot of pain. Physical as well as metaphysical."

"So you're different. Not every Cypher is the same. Flukes happen."

I looked him in the eyes. He was so ignorant, in such a blissful way. This man was optimistic. I could use a little of that. Too bad I had to kill his theory.

"It's not a fluke, Seth. I wish it was."

It was his turn to look me in the eyes. I think I saw concern. For me? I didn't want him to worry. It seemed almost obscene when I thought about how selfish it was to wrap him up in this escapade. Then again, we had already started the dance. If I walked away now, he might follow. And his ignorance might get him killed, which would leave me torn up inside.

Who was I kidding? The part of my brain harboring the secret had already made up its mind. *Carpe diem.*

Hands on hips, I scanned the alley for the hundredth time before forcing myself to meet those gorgeous hazel orbs. "I'm not the original chosen Cypher."

He sounded more than a little leery. "What do you mean? You were, what, runner-up?"

"No. There was a kind of last-minute executive decision."

It was his turn to fold his arms and look paranoid.

Suddenly, I was overwhelmed with relief, fear, and a sense of dread from finally saying it out loud. Somewhere in my unconscious, though, I knew the day I had to say it out loud—confess—would be the end of it all.

I tried not to cry. In fact, I did a damn fine job of not crying, but my voice wouldn't fully cooperate. It was as even as the ocean during a storm. I was about to talk openly about something that had never been discussed with anyone or even muttered to myself in the lonely darkness, for fear it would echo into the wrong ears.

I restrained my voice as I whispered, "I couldn't let her do it."

"Who?"

"My sister." The air rattled through my chest. Inhaling, I clarified, "Twin sister."

Seth jumped backward before I finished my confession. He looked completely dumbfounded. "What?" It was as if his legs had built-in springs instead of bones. And it was amazing how a smile made him look so young, but a scowl aged him by ten years. Neat trick for a vampire.

We both looked to find the cab driver still reading.

Seth was not happy. "You're telling me you switched places? The Members wouldn't have agreed to that. They had to know, right? How could you get away with something like that? And if this is true"—he leaned in, voice dropping—"if what you're telling me is absolutely true, do you know what would happen if my kind found out? Jesus, it would start a riot. Every soul that you've"—he flung his hands around—"*whatevered* would be under inspection! Hundreds, right? How could you do something like this? How could you fool *everyone*?" He gulped air before falling silent.

I didn't understand whether he was protesting because he thought I was a sham or awestruck because I'd gotten away with it. With something that had never been done before. I hoped it was the latter. Because if a dime-store thief was angry, I was in it deep with the real bad guys.

I didn't know how to reply, so I said, "Apparently, we didn't fool everyone," and shrugged.

Seth picked up on how I was feeling because he inhaled and calmly unlatched his fingernails from his forearms. "You're not the Cypher."

Words I wished I could live by. After hearing someone say it, though, the tears and natty voice dissolved. I *was* the Cypher, damn it. I didn't do this for my sister and me to have it all simply disintegrate. If we were found out, her life would be ruined. Better yet, the likelihood that we would both die horribly would increase by a hundred percent.

"I *am* the Cypher." There was strength in my voice. No, pride—until I uttered, "Just not the first choice." Steadily, I continued. "But what I've been doing has been very, very real. I just have to suffer a few karmic kinks. Gabriel's right. My body doesn't accept my soul's absence like a Cypher's normally would. Seth, if this becomes known, then I did it all for nothing." My eyes glassed with unshed tears. "By trying to spare my sister this life, my weakness might get her killed."

"And you."

"Yes."

"Why do it at all? Why take her place?"

"Because she couldn't do it."

"So? There are always candidates."

I shook my head. "Sometimes, the Members are lucky enough to have a handful to choose from. This time they weren't. She was it."

He leaned closer, almost daring me, though equally as riveted by the tale. "Then how could you take her place?"

"We weren't sure it could be done. We talked about the possibility of failure a lot before the ceremony. Neither of us was sure my soul would even leave. When it came time, well, we had to try. There was no other way. We switched places a week before the ceremony. Even our parents had no idea. And the ceremony went as planned for the Members, other than a 'mystical interference.'"

"Which was?"

"My sister was present for the ceremony. We used each other for strength. I took everything I knew of myself and pushed my soul out, away from my body. I tried to reject it, but that one string hung on. Unbreakable. I could feel my heart lunging for it with every rabid beat, wrapping around it, squeezing it closer. And as the Members said the final words, my sister's soul had been listening. It left. Just like that. She didn't have time to grab it back. It was gone. In that instant, I broke that one string and flung my soul into her...

"The Members didn't realize what had happened. They simply thought, since we're twins, that must have caused the interference. Old wives' tales about twins with conjoined souls, I guess. Anyway, they bought it. It was done. So here I am...hiding in an alley." I finished the glorious declaration with a loud sigh.

"Your sister has your soul?"

"Yeah. It's not an exact fit, but close enough."

"Why did you do it? I mean, I understand the relationship, but how could you do it?"

"She was my best friend."

"Was? I'm sorry if I'm asking a bunch of idiot questions, but this... There's too much to process."

"It's okay. Answering your question, yes and no. She's the

only best friend I've ever had, and no, we're not anymore. It's fun to keep kid secrets. Adult secrets, on the other hand, tend to tear you apart. And lately, I don't know what's going on."

"Ell, they can't find out." He whispered as if the world were listening.

"My real name's Myranda."

That one admission made everything I'd said sink to his gut like the weight of the *Titanic*. "Even your names?"

"I became her and she became me. The Members knew who they wanted—they just don't know who they got."

"Your name is Myranda," he repeated thoughtfully.

"Not anymore. Call me Ell."

"Sorry. So, how can you get out of this? Do you have a plan?"

"I can't go home. My sister might be in danger, and our only way out might rock the entire underworld." Cringing, I added, "But I think I know someone who can help."

"I'll go with you."

"No." I didn't mean to sound rude, but Seth was not part of this equation. "I don't think he'd take kindly to both of us showing up at his home unannounced." I blushed before admitting, "And I like you. I don't want to see anything happen to you."

"Wow, two confessions in one abandoned alley. I'm starting to perfect this picking-up-girls thing, and it only took fifty years." He grinned but continued to fiddle with the drawstrings of his black cotton hoodie.

"You look good for your age."

"I was twenty-five when I was turned. Better than Botox."

"Well, don't look so happy. I'm trouble for an old man like you."

"Trouble's like blood. A little does a body good. Too much might get someone killed."

"Very perceptive. But remember, that 'someone' could be you."

"You'd better like me more than that. Here."

Our hands brushed as he handed me a scrap of a napkin. The way my heart fluttered from the infinitesimal encounter didn't go unnoticed by either of us. Seth looked as pleased as a person could get without actually smiling. I just managed to make the stepping of my feet from side to side look more awkward while the balled-up napkin shifted in my hand.

I unfolded my palm to look at the wayward thing. "Gee, thanks."

Seth had already started to walk away. Without breaking stride or turning around, he shouted over his shoulder, "My number. I think you're gonna need it."

I wanted to say something back, but he began whistling a tune. It sounded as though he started in the middle, something already playing in his head before he released it. I watched him walk down the street until he disappeared around the corner, leaving me alone to hop into the cab.

I reluctantly pushed the little piece of paper with the scribbled phone number into my jacket pocket. Just in case, right?

I did want something from Seth. Nothing I could pinpoint, but something. Anything felt better than nothing. For the first time, my routine had been interrupted. I hadn't spent the evening soaked in self-pity. It was spent talking and laughing and trusting. I felt some relief from myself, but it was short-lived.

Reality swept the hair out of my eyes to see the total picture. This really was happening. My secret—*our* secret—

was out, and the monsters were coming for us. I hoped there was a shred of mercy left in the Members' dusty, ancient remains. I crossed my fingers that it wouldn't come to that. I wished under my breath that the Members were ignorant to our deception, could stay so for eternity, and that this whole mess could be shoved under the sofa of the world, even if that meant cramming it in with my own bare hands.

The thing that sucked the most, as it turned out, was that I could only think of one person with enough pull, short of the Members, to help us.

Would he?

# Chapter Nine

Gabriel lived in a quiet human neighborhood twenty minutes from the business district. Looking out the cab window, I decided I would throw myself on his mercy, no matter how disturbing that sounded, and employ his help to find and protect my sister. Oh, and if need be, help convince the Members to trust me as the Cypher.

Even though I deceived them to get the job.

Finding myself in an up-and-coming neighborhood, I took in the striking three-story residence. It was a bold alabaster colonial home with large front pillars stretching from porch to roof. Not one of the largest homes in the neighborhood, but impressive. It was freshly renovated. The foundation looked old, but the siding and shutters couldn't date more than a year or two. The windows were so clean the panes would have been invisible if not for the reflection of trees and the occasional passing car.

I had been here once before, briefly, but not inside. Gabriel had needed something on our way to read a prospect with special circumstances. Prison does have a tendency to make people come to you.

The backyard was equally as impressive. Walking through the gate, I was met by a hoard of perky bushes and petite, colorful plants. I felt like I was on a tour of the governor's house. It was so private, I wondered whether Gabriel would ever know I was there. Okay, stupid thought. He was a vampire. But I suspected he was the only bloodsucker in this district.

Strangely, I found my thoughts straying to Seth. Should I have accepted his help instead of seeking Gabriel's? Seth was, unofficially, my only friend. There was definitely chemistry, and it went beyond the physical. I wanted to call, but what would I say? Something like "the bird flies at midnight" seemed appropriate considering I was mixed up in a secret-agent wannabe lifestyle all of a sudden. But code phrases are meant for partners or good guy/bad guy teams, not for uninvolved bystanders.

Tempted to turn and run straight to Seth's unabashed smile, I visualized my feet grounded by invisible roots. I was doing a smart thing. I could give up Seth's company to keep him out of the impending bomb blast. He didn't need the trouble, and I didn't need to be reminded that I had a friend for a day. It would be a good thought later, cherished even, once I could think about it without feeling as though I had missed out on something worth having. Maybe that time would come when I could call it a good memory to warm me through lonely hours.

Mustering my courage in one large breath, I marched up the stone steps, crossed the wide patio, and banged on the back door, listening for footsteps that never came. I paused. What if Gabriel had been in my house? What if this whole night had been an ambush? No, I had to believe that the entire world wasn't one super-sized kick to the crotch.

I needed to forget about Seth and focus on the very near-catastrophic future. If Gabriel was my culprit, I would find out when he didn't open the door.

But he did.

The *swoosh* of the door fanned his cologne straight up my nostrils, momentarily stunning me.

I gagged. "Well, that puts the hell into hello."

Gabriel wore a gray button-up shirt with hard lines and breast pockets that came across as a touch militant, although the rolls of his sleeves hung casually below his elbows. His slacks were dark, possibly the sable pair he frequently wore. It was hard to tell because his frame was backlit by a weak foyer lamp. And though his hair was successfully groomed, his bare feet left the overall look incomplete.

"What?" He looked confused by my repulsion.

"Really?" Staring at a blank face, I choked, "Your cologne is..."

"Expensive," he retorted. "But you're not here to admire my taste."

Recovering from the stench, I met his intense glare. "Yeah, I just dropped in for a cup of sugar."

"It's extremely late to have the biggest smart-ass I know standing on my doorstep. Why am I blessed with such company?"

He failed to mention the non-meeting, which meant he was probably uber pissed. And his tone hinted that what I was about to say would not come as a surprise.

The rest of my sassy zings vanished, quickly replaced by anxiety. As serious as I'd ever been, I said, "We need to talk."

He outstretched an arm, resting his hand on the door-frame beside my left cheek. Encroaching on my space, he asked in a hushed voice, "Would this talk involve a confession?"

My eyes widened.

"You think so little of me, but I seem to know much more than you think." He almost smiled, but there was a touch of sadness to it. Or maybe it was weariness. "Come in."

"No." I backed down the steps to stand on the patio tiles. "Outside is fine."

He shrugged and shut the door, following my lead. This was where I started to ramble.

"My sister was the chosen Cypher, not me. And it's definitely safe to presume, at this point, that you already know that, right?"

He crooked his neck in what I could only describe as a predatory movement. His vampire nature was amplified when he was angry. And boy was he angry.

"Correct," he practically hissed between clenched teeth.

This was where it took all of my backbone to ask, "Do the Members know?"

Without reserve, he nodded his head in one brusque motion. "They know and they are very overwrought."

They knew!

I flinched when he demanded, "Why come to me? Why now?"

"Help me protect my sister. Take me to see the Members and explain that nothing has changed. I can do the job. In the process, you'll earn big points for being the one to bring me in."

"The approval of the Members is not enough. You would owe me."

My legs suddenly felt weak. Not trusting them to hold more than a blade of grass, I sat on one of Gabriel's wicker loungers on the edge of the patio, gasping for a deep breath that never reached the bottom of my lungs.

He loomed, inhaling the air, charged with my erratic emotions.

Forcing myself to meet his merciless emerald eyes as if they had the power to burn me to dust right where I sat, I confessed, "If I can't make this right for my sister, the anguish would split my chest open every day and devour my heart...assuming I'm still alive." I shut my eyes and counted a full minute before looking to the sky. "I will owe whatever it takes."

Dead air followed, lingering before he turned his attention on me. I think this was the longest silence ever between us. Neither knew what to say, neither willing to give away more information the other might not already know.

Gabriel withdrew and sat on the second to last patio step. His legs were so long they scrunched close to his chest. I hadn't realized how tightly bound the tension had grown until he relaxed, dissipating the unease.

"Why didn't you meet me earlier?" He almost sounded like a man with a bad case of broken pride.

I knew better.

"I was piss drunk," I declared without hesitation.

His eyebrows rose. "That explains the text. Is this a new hobby?" He was trying to remain calm.

"Maybe. Since I have poor interpersonal skills and my reputation sucks anyway, why not just get drunk and sleep around?"

"This is not a time for jokes."

"You look a little flustered, Gabriel. Do you want to eat before we finish our conversation?"

His extra-chalky complexion was a sign that he hadn't eaten this evening. Also, Gabriel was notorious for being a grouch when he skipped a meal.

"Not unless you're offering."

Vampires can eat regular food. Their organs digest, if prompted by an average human diet. However, it didn't replace blood nutrition. Eating food is more for show because, even though their bodies absorb the nutrients, it just isn't enough. Altering substances, such as drugs or alcohol, work on vamps, too, though not as long as they do on humans. More traditional vamps don't waste time drinking or eating at all. They know what they want and don't like the idea of straying from the known. Blood leaves them strong to defend themselves. Human foods don't get the job done, so why change a good thing?

I had the impression Gabriel was a traditionalist.

"Are you offering, Peaches?"

"Not to you."

"Then I'll refrain until we're finished." He changed the subject. "What prompted such a late visit?" Obviously, it wasn't too late to go fishing.

Honesty seemed the best policy. "A break-in."

He spoke slowly. "You were there when it happened?"

"No. Luckily, someone's vanity was parked in my driveway, and they were too careless to move the blinds back into place."

Wow, without having eaten recently, Gabriel's complexion still managed to change about ten shades of red. He wasn't yelling, even though I could tell he really wanted to.

"Why are *you* so angry? I'm the one who should be livid." Watching the rage ignite in his pupils, I shook my head from side to side. He provoked my own temper. "You're not going to help, are you? I knew better than to ask anything from you."

"Just because I don't have the reputation as a nice guy doesn't mean I am incapable of such things."

"You're capable of a lot of things, Gabriel. Right now, you're just making me nervous."

"I would be nervous, too, if I were you."

"And you mean what by that?"

A violent tremor erupted from his shoulders. "This

could have been so simple!" His voice rose as he stood, but he quickly lowered it when he realized his echo had escaped into normal human society. He stalked closer, gritting his teeth instead.

Not an improvement, but sometimes you have to focus on baby steps.

"What are you talking about?"

"I had planned to abduct you first to keep you out of harm's way. But you were too busy on a bender, which could have gotten you killed."

I went very still. "Why would you abduct me?"

"For your own good."

We locked eyes, and I wondered whether my little visit was a dreadful idea. I had never trusted Gabriel, but I thought I could utilize his skills and status to my advantage. Sadly, it looked as though they were going to be used against me.

With vampire speed, Gabriel was suddenly on my side of the yard. He paced in front of my lounger before abruptly sitting in the middle of it, forcing me to scoot toward the backrest. I didn't want to be that close, especially after his proclamation.

He looked as if he had somehow failed. "I should have confronted you at your home, but I didn't have the authorization to interfere directly."

"I don't know exactly what's going on, but if abduction doesn't count as direct interference, I'm not sure I want to play this game."

He smiled, but it wasn't friendly. "You started the game."

"You know what? I know I came here for help, but I think I can handle it on my own. Nothing a Hallmark card and tasteful arrangement of blood bags can't resolve." The statement was solid, but the part of me that was completely squishy, fragile human was screaming in my head, *"Get out! You're not safe here!"*

Gabriel glared like he wasn't enjoying the conversation as much as I was. But his teeth were still gritted when he talked, so I was doing something right.

Sounding absolutely put out, he said, "It's too late for that."

"You have no faith in me."

"Of course I do," he scolded. "I have faith that you will annihilate everything in your life until your only reality is a wasteland of your own making. For years, I've stood by while you receded into something far worse than invisible. You have youth, life, and power, yet you take these priceless gifts and turn them to ash. Every decision you make lowers you farther into a snake pit. Only, now you seem to know exactly which snake pit you wish to crawl into."

He grimaced before continuing. "This entire mess, from that first moment of deceit, was a personal effort to deconstruct everything truthful about yourself. Now you want to salvage something? The Members have your sister. I can't help her."

My heart stopped.

"You've missed your opportunity to confess and beg forgiveness. The orders for your trial have been issued. You are to be brought to them for judgment. I'll take you myself to ensure you are not given the chance to destroy your redemption because, whether preordained or self-proclaimed, I believe that you are the Cypher."

He brought such heat, and all I offered in return was a blank stare. I watched as he scrutinized me, waiting for a reaction. He probably thought I was going to yell, deny, reject. *Something.* I don't think he expected me to sit there as still as the dead, staring into his eyes. Maybe I didn't, either.

I sure as shit didn't foresee being micro-analyzed and judged by Gabriel. I had no idea he'd even been paying that much attention.

Shouldn't I have been doing something? Couldn't. I wanted to.

I was numb, exposed, like a rock in a garden where nothing else was expected. I was a rock. There was nothing left for me to do. I didn't need to be ornamental or form a barrier. I was a rock in Gabriel's backyard, and he didn't expect it.

His overly passionate views on my life, sprinkled on top of the overpowering doom of being found out by the Members, had given me a brain-freeze.

The timeout left me oddly calm enough to ask, "Is my sister safe, or was she trying to send a message with her lousy letters?"

Screaming would have been nice, but I was just a rock.

"What letters?" His frustration turned to curiosity. He was definitely interested, but there was another emotion I was unable to place. I figured he, of all people, would be having a lot more fun with my dilemma.

More to myself, I muttered, "I didn't even read them all. No wonder they were so wrong." She was under duress when she wrote them, and I didn't have a clue. I had been so angry with her for revoking her friendship without stopping to think there could be other reasons making her act so unusual. She was in trouble, and I hadn't pieced it together soon enough to save us from what was about to happen. At the very least, we might be slaughtered. At most, they would make us pray to be slaughtered.

Gabriel had been talking, but I think my hard shell was making it difficult to hear.

"What was the question?" I asked.

"Why didn't you read them all?"

The small envelope appeared in my hand. I pulled it out of my jacket without realizing I had done so and tossed it in front of him, between us. "Would you, if every single one was like that?"

The letter looked small in his hand. The air grew chillier as I waited. The chill, however, was seeping from my bones, not the atmosphere.

He slid the letter back into the envelope and set it between us once more. Gabriel was very serious when he answered, "No, I would not."

I spit out, "Yeah, right. You probably wrote it."

"Why do you say that?" He was very curious.

"Because you guys have done something with her, and I've been too selfish to realize it."

"Selfish?"

"I thought she didn't want to write because— Never mind. I was wrong and it's none of your damn business."

"Think what you want, Peaches, but cheer up. I'm taking you to see her."

I wanted to see Ellenore, but I figured out I made an error in judgment with Gabriel.

"Why don't you draw a map and I'll just mosey on over on my own terms to say hello?"

"It doesn't work that way."

"Because they're gonna kill us, right?"

He remained calm. "That's not what I said."

I stood. The only problems with a fast getaway were the two stone walls on either side, and Gabriel practically in front of me. I was trapped, and no human could outrun a vamp. Given no better choice, however, I would try.

"Well, I thought about it for, like, half a second and I'm not going with you. You'll have to kill me right here if that's your plan." Stupid! Taunting and goading are never likable qualities. Maybe he should have killed me if I was ignorant enough to blurt out death wishes.

"If you don't go with me now, you won't see your sister, and They will come for you again." He remained in the leisurely position he'd assumed so many minutes before, unconcerned that I had stood up, but there was weight to his words.

Was it fear?

Goose bumps sprinkled my arms as I pondered whom he was referring to. Hoping beyond hope he wouldn't say the name I was thinking, I asked, "Who was in my house?"

At least he had the grace to look away. "You already know the answer."

"The Mass."

Known as They and Them, the Mass are the bogymen of the dead, the living, and anything in between. The Mass are the most feared vampires, twisted beyond human perception. They have a very narrow purpose. Sent on behalf of the Members to collect or kill, to cause inscrutable pain and unfathomable deaths. The Mass would act as bounty hunters to bring someone in, but they preferred the kill. It was literally why they existed. Worse yet, they thrived on it.

The fear of knowing they were in my house was very fresh, and the prospect of being hunted again was gloomy, but everything down to my marrow told me not to go with Gabriel. His admission proved he was untrustworthy, like all the other power-hungry vampires.

"I'll go to the Members myself."

"You have no idea how much trouble you're in."

"Better than you know, Gabriel."

"Then do not agitate the situation. Stop fighting me." I was experiencing a new level of concern from Gabriel as he continued, "I want to be on your side, but don't underestimate me. I'll do what I have to do, even if I don't agree with it."

"Oh, go cry it to your mama. I've got my own conflicts." There I was, being amiable again. Darn, that's why I attracted all the boys.

I needed to get off Gabriel's patio in one piece. Flattery was useless. I might not outrun him, but he couldn't stop me from screaming for help. Every neighbor in a three-block radius would hear me. And I'm guessing in such an upscale neighborhood, people might not run from their homes with pitchforks or pointy flatware, but they could press nine-one-one on speed dial quicker than Gabriel could dispose of my body.

Before I overthought it further, I darted forward, almost passing Gabriel, almost free, before he lunged sideways from the chair, snagging me with little effort. An arm clamped around my waist and pressed my body to his, as a hand cradled that space between the front of my neck and the bottom of my chin. He used the opportunity to force my head up so I could see his face looming above mine, effectively leaving the back of my head pushed against his chest.

My heart thumped like a trapped rabbit. Entertaining the idea of trusting Gabriel had been a major mistake. Of course he would side with the vampires. It's what he was, right down to his compromised soul.

I had a front-row seat to watch the change sweep his features. Eyes transformed into exploding emeralds nestled in the middle of a deep forest ring. Brilliant as much as they were terrifying. I fought back a shiver as his teeth extended.

Anticipating the kill?

In a grave, feral tone, he warned, "They *will* come for you again." I think the emphasis on "will" was supposed to scare me.

"So?"

"Feigning apathy is useless." He inhaled a deep breath, running his chin along the length of my jaw, before coming to rest at my ear. "I can smell your fear."

I shoved the fear spiking my adrenaline as deep down as possible, refusing to give in to his bullying tactics. Did his vampire instincts wish to empty every last bit of blood in my body like a human Slurpee? Gross but yes. Did Gabriel—my coworker of four years and the man who once used a spot-remover pen on his overpriced slacks—plan to kill me? Most nights.

Still...I never took kindly to bullies.

"Is it protocol to be that sloppy on a job?" I goaded, feeling ballsy. "If so, it'll give the Mass away again."

"The Members sent a trusted human—"

"A stupid human who parked in my driveway."

"A human to act as reason. Next time, the Mass will travel alone. They are swift and silent, but death at their hand is not."

He had a point, and I wasn't referring to either of his teeth. The Mass had no rules of engagement, no tether to a conscience. Left to themselves, they delighted in carnage. Even under the control of the Members, they weren't one hundred percent tame or controllable.

"You'll take me to her?" It was hard to talk with my neck craned backward, but I managed.

"Stop fighting me." His voice carried a primal rawness as he whispered in my ear, making me wonder whether part of him would be disappointed not to rip my throat out and discard it as a lawn ornament.

"Okay," I conceded.

Gabriel let go.

I lunged from the patio, making an exhausting dash through the backyard. This time, however, I was ready to stick to Plan B if necessary: scream as loud as possible until my throat collapsed.

He slammed into my back, propelling us through the grass. I landed on my stomach and he took the opportunity to twist my arm behind my back. I began to scream, the air building excitedly in my lungs, when I felt a sharp pain in my arm. Like a moron, I quit screaming. He ruined what could have been a glorious "I'm in trouble, rescue me" scream yet again.

"What was that?"

"Don't worry. I just cured you."

"Of what?"

"You are the most unpleasant person I have ever met. You tricked me twice. I have no idea why I let you. I thought you were smarter than this, but I prepared a little something in case you weren't. The only way you could ever be manageable is if you're unconscious. I've just cured you of your unpleasant demeanor."

I wanted to ask what he was talking about, but he dropped something next to my head. The moonlight outlined a syringe. Oh! I was about to scream again but found my energy tapped as a warm feeling traveled the length of my body, as though I were being tucked in for bed with the warmest blanket from the inside out.

"Damn."

"I asked you not to fight." His voice was too close.

He refused to trust me long enough to release my arm. Even like this. I no longer felt like a rock. A pile of dirt was more like it.

"It was more like a statement. You could have just as easily said, 'I like green beans.'"

He sighed. "What are you doing?"

"Making small talk to buy time to figure out a better plan. I'm not that clever under pressure."

"Your humor is lacking, and your blood is stirring my hunger." More to himself, he added, "This could have been so simple."

We were close enough that I could smell the light scents of sage and spearmint. Gabriel's scent. The real one, beneath the artificial death bomb he called cologne. Every once in a while, I smelled the residual aromas in my house after he had left for the night with a prospect. In retrospect, it was borderline shocking to realize that it had brought a smile to my lips on more than one occasion. Something as simple as a little sage and spearmint had ripped me free of my perma-state of depression. *Temporarily*. A well-earned breath before the next undertow dragged me to the bottom of a cold, lonely ocean I couldn't escape. That's why I had come to Gabriel for help.

That's why part of me trusted him.

Gabriel released my arm and stood, as though he could not create space fast enough.

I rolled onto my back, much more sluggish than I expected. My limbs were weighted anvils, and I struggled to hold open my heavy eyelids.

"Get up."

"Five more minutes, Grandpa."

Gabriel balked, briskly pulling me to my feet.

Vampires, always so helpful. The Good Samaritans of the underworld. Yeah, right. To be optimistic, though, his eyes had turned human again and there were no foreboding fangs in sight.

My feet wobbled and my vision was rapidly diminishing. Everything took on a waffled appearance. Gabriel's left arm ran across my back until his hand gripped my side, guiding me forward. We were on our way back to the patio. What else could I do? I'd lost the battle. Struggling was no use. On a positive note, I would see my sister soon to solve this mess...or die tragically.

Probably both. *Shit.*

Glaring in his direction, I warned, "You better not cop a feel."

"Don't worry. My *mama* taught me better than that." He said "mama" like the whitest Northerner you could ever meet. I would have chuckled if there had been energy to spare. In fact, walking back to the patio took forever. How far had I run? Halfway there, I knew I wouldn't make it.

"What was that?"

"Tranquilizer."

A desensitized feeling traveled quickly through my system, forcing me to wonder whether a body could sleep while the mind remained awake. Either the thought was fleeting or my question was about to be answered because I could feel my brain shutting down.

"It works fast."

"Your heightened adrenaline is responsible, of which I'm quite thankful for."

The subtle attention of his strength was oddly soothing. I never would have expected to find such peace in Gabriel's arms. Granted, I was drugged and he was just doing his job. No fairy-tale ending here, folks.

Almost inaudible, I mumbled, "Tranquilizer... That's cheating."

"When you're involved, it's purely a necessity."

My body sagged against his as I lost the battle with my

eyelids. I grasped at his shirt with the last of my energy, trying to remind myself that I could break a nose or bust a cheekbone open if I face-planted onto the concrete. Of course it would heal fast due to my Cypher status, but it would still hurt like hell and be uncomfortable.

When my knees buckled, I yelped.

The burden of my weight instantly floated away in Gabriel's arms. His muscles shifted effortlessly beneath layers of material and skin as he cradled me against his cool chest. The moment almost felt perfect. If I weren't being abducted. If I hadn't lied. If Gabriel cared.

*If anyone cared.*

I listened to the growing silence as static snared my mind and body. As I mentally stepped aside, surrendering all power. Maybe I was more pleasant to be around when I was unconscious. I heard plenty of complaints about my attitude during my waking hours. Never once had anyone complained while I was unconscious.

Did that even make sense?

And then I was unconscious. No complaints.

The most alarming aspect of the evening, as it turned out, wasn't the sedative, but waking up handcuffed to a very rigid armchair.

# Chapter Ten

Disembodied voices argued somewhere as I quietly slid my wrists around, testing the tautness of the cuffs. They were less forgiving than an anaconda. My vision was slightly blurry from sleep and most of the room was sunk in darkness. I found myself hoping the cuffs were the most uninviting aspect of the space.

The door was slightly ajar, leaving an emaciated stream of light to fall short of touching my legs. I couldn't see who was in the other room. What were they saying? The chair creaked when I leaned sideways, trying to peek through the crack. I cursed Gabriel under my breath as I almost tipped over. It was no coincidence that he walked in shortly after.

He shut the door, rendering me blind. Not given time to listen for footsteps, I felt his hand on my shoulder before it slid down to the handcuffs.

When he spoke, it came low and humorless. Gabriel was always serious, but never as professional and removed as he was unlatching the cuffs. Didn't he just share a dysfunctional fight with me? And cheated, I would like to add.

"Listen to me. And that doesn't mean talk back or make jokes."

I wasn't in a jazzy mood, anyway. This was it. I was about to meet the very angry vampires. And the moment before your death was rarely a joking matter. "Okay," I said, voice strained.

Gabriel dropped to his knees to unwind the freakishly long chain on the cuffs. He was close. Too close. I felt the muscles in his waist against the insides of my thighs. I could even smell the hint of sage and spearmint wound in his dark locks. Those damning smells that had inadvertently led me straight to the monster's door.

Danger smelled like sage and spearmint, and I would never allow myself to forget it.

"When we leave this room, walk beside me. Do not speak unless asked a question. And under no circumstance try to escape."

"Okay."

He leaned in close enough that his lips almost touched my cheek. "Do not speak unless asked a question."

I almost said okay again but realized through the tickle of his breath that he was testing me. My lips remained shut. I passed.

"Stand up."

I stood, unashamed of being scared.

Gabriel moved to my right and fastened his long fingers around my arm above the elbow. We moved unnaturally smoothly through the room thanks to vampire sight, but my footsteps hesitated as he opened the door to a room brightly lit by numerous oil lamps. A dining room minus furniture. There was a large, elaborate candle chandelier in the middle of the ceiling, along with gas lamps in each corner fashioned to look semi-modern.

The illuminated room may have been pretty if not for the five vampires standing smack-dab in the middle. The Members of the Allegiance were made up of two women and three men. I recognized them immediately because I'd had the displeasure of meeting them four years ago, and the fortune of communicating through messengers ever since.

The brunette woman dressed in a conservative pantsuit, hair cut so short it barely held enough weight to lay flat. She could have passed as an executive. The second woman was quite a contrast. She had long, ashen-blonde hair that hung freely down her back. Her dress was of an older style, the waist so high it cinched under her breasts. The royal-purple/wine color draped her entire body. She was the quintessential maiden who needed rescuing, though I'm sure it was often the good knights who found themselves in a predicament.

The men were more uniformed. The two younger-looking men wore sweaters: one indigo and one in maize. Their hair was brown, but one vampire had slightly more feminine facial features: thinner nose, fuller lips, less prominent jawline. The third man was shorter by a few inches, maybe five six, and very portly. He wore a button-up bronze business shirt with overcast brown slacks. Other than the blonde woman, they looked as progressive as you could expect for ancient vampires who had lived far longer than any human mind could comprehend.

As my eyes strayed from the Members, I started noticing the not-so-pretty chains encompassing the room. The walls were silver, so the chains almost blended in. A little understated, if you asked me. I might have gone with a more daring motif, but some people like to conform. Go figure.

The portly man stepped away from the remaining four to approach me. The others were still, unblinking. They stared with icy indifference.

I reminded myself not to panic.

His voice was deep, carrying through the small room. I remembered it from the ceremony. "You are being charged with a very serious crime. If, in fact, you are Myranda Clyne and not Ellenore Clyne, you will suffer due repercussions. What do you have to say in your defense?"

I was still scared, but oddly, I felt as though I had done

nothing wrong. I knew I had, but part of my brain just didn't think so. "I'm the Cypher. My birth name means nothing."

"You are not denying our charge?"

"What's the charge?"

"You are being accused of impersonating the Cypher."

"I don't see anyone besides me in the room when I'm reading souls. I guess that means that I'm the Cypher."

Gabriel tightened his grip around my arm. Oh yeah, I should have been watching my manners.

"Then you shall be tested. We know of your affliction, your unique, painful reaction. We are concerned of false readings and the looming possibility of keeping a soul, resulting in the loss of our Cypher. It has been deemed that what you experience is abnormal and poses a potential global threat. We must investigate, if not for the safety of all parties involved, then to quench our own hesitations."

I was a menace to vampire society? Was that what he was saying? What a crock. I did the job that needed doing, and they were still bitching!

"Gabriel, escort her to the room."

Grim. I mean, I hadn't seen the room yet, but anything referred to as "the room" probably had nothing but bad, bad things inside. And I was positive it would be less fashionable than the eat-in dungeon.

We walked into an open hallway, Gabriel clasped to my arm like a set of bangles. The others were no longer visible, though I could hear their soft mumbling.

Gabriel tried to lead me down the hall but, coincidentally, my feet planted firm enough to make his job more difficult. "I'm not going with you. This is gonna be bad."

He stopped walking, moved closer, and spoke low. "I did not ask your opinion."

"Let go of my arm."

He moved to stand directly in front of me, unwilling to surrender his grip. What was I going to do, run back to the Fab Five?

He bent down until our foreheads almost touched, breath heavy. "Stop arguing. This is not the time."

Don't worry, it wasn't as romantic as it sounds. His voice was harsh, and I did have impending doom looming over me.

"When is the time? When I'm dead? Don't think I'll feel very chatty at that point."

"If you stop fighting and cooperate, you will not die."

"They don't plan to kill me?"

"You will live, at least for tonight, unless you act like the absolute stubborn ass you truly are. Act appropriate. Stop ruining their fun."

He had me there. I was surrounded. I could fight, but I hadn't forgotten about my sister. If I went along with everything, there was a very real possibility that I would see her soon.

As we started walking again, I mumbled, "You're the ass."

I glanced around as we entered the kitchen. There were many expensive decorations, but nothing personalized like the dining room. Nothing jumped out that said the house belonged to an individual, psychopath or otherwise. Did it belong to one of the Members? Before I had time to conclude either way, Gabriel directed me to a wooden door. The basement door. I wanted to protest, having watched many horror movies that ended dreadfully for people in basements. But the door had closed and we were at the bottom of the staircase before I had a chance to finish the thought.

The basement was kind of dark, except for one large candle in the far corner. For a candle larger than my head, it offered poor lighting. The darkness ate away at each flicker.

What upset me most, however, was the blindfolded, gagged body tied to a chair in the middle of the damp room. She was alive, at least. The blindfold was so large it obstructed the majority of her face. The material was more like a huge bandana folded improperly, leaving her unrecognizable.

Gabriel turned to me. "This is your test, Peaches."

"What, her?"

"Perform your Cypher duties. I'll watch, the Members will listen, and you can try to prove us wrong. If you are truly Ellenore—"

"I never claimed to be Ellenore. Get it right. I claimed to be the Cypher."

The corners of his mouth twitched. "Prove it," he dared.

I walked over to the woman while Gabriel made himself cozy on a wooden crate. I pretended this was a normal reading. That's right, just like being at home...if it had spontaneously turned into a thirteenth-century oubliette.

At least it seemed appropriate to talk to the woman as I normally would. Let her know what was happening. "Hi. Please don't panic. I'm the Cypher. I'm just going to borrow your soul for a few minutes and then tuck it right back in that cozy flesh pocket called your chest. You won't feel a thing, and no one is going to kill either of us." Under my breath, I added, "I hope."

Yeah, that would comfort me, too, if I were in her place. I sounded like a loon. It definitely threw me off to know Gabriel was watching, waiting to report. But what else could I do?

*Do what you know.*

The whole show only took five minutes. It would have

been less, but the poor woman was highly stressed, what with being restrained in a basement by the Members and all. When I returned her soul, a vampire flunky came in and removed the woman. I told Gabriel what the woman's soul released, which was nothing spectacular, unless the Members had a hankering to purchase one of the two hundred plus paintings she had created in homage to her guinea pigs.

So many guinea pigs...

This was the point where Gabriel normally left. He didn't. Could I leave instead?

"Happy now?"

Gabriel looked solemn. "No, but the test isn't over."

As if on cue, the pain hit. It started in that hollow space in my chest and spread like a poison. I lacked the privacy to make it seem less agonizing. But I tried to put on somewhat of a normal show by refusing to drop to my knees or roll up into a sad little ball and cry. I didn't let my brain or heart explode. I just leaned against the wall, pretending it hurt less than stubbing a toe, breathing quick and shallow.

"Impressive. Next."

What else was there to do? I didn't feel like playing Bingo. I stood straighter and tried to clear my head, honing my inner strength. "I am the Cypher," I said, more for my own benefit.

Gabriel smiled. "That's what I want to hear."

"Bring it, bitchsack."

His brow lifted as he called in the vamp with another bound individual.

# Chapter Eleven

Miserably, my test was not to pass one or two readings. It was to pass *many*.

They went on for quite a while. I couldn't recall a specific time—minutes, hours, days—because every morsel of self-control was directed at not letting my mind or body splinter to pieces.

It was with the eleventh person that I really started to second-guess whether I could go on. My mind kept wandering, making it hard to focus. And my professional morals were all but gone. Every "next" person seemed to be increasingly more scared. I didn't know what was happening before they were brought in, but I swore they'd been tampered with. It was irregular to have so many freaking scared people, one after another, even under the grim circumstances.

All I had discovered were a series of non-consequential possibilities: Latter-day Saints disciple, Nintendo DX champion, wine aficionado, stalker, overeater, air guitar enthusiast, etc...

As assuring as I wanted to be with them, I really just needed to get through it. I found myself saying, "I'm the Cypher. Don't panic. Holy God, for all things shiny and soft, don't panic and this can be over in a minute or less."

Stifled laughter filled the void behind me.

I turned, challenging Gabriel's smirk with a scowl. He stopped laughing. Why did I look back? Every damned time! Though, as bad as I felt, I couldn't let his laughter slide.

"I'm sure you tell all your dates the same thing."

He smiled.

How annoying.

"Still lively? We underestimated your abilities."

"That seems to be a theme in my life."

I faced the man and breathed slowly a few times to block Gabriel out. Staring absently at the black material covering most of his face, my hand rested over that tender spot on his chest. I thought this one would be harder than the last, judging by their climaxing anxiety.

Unlike my prediction, the vampire was unusually calm. I could feel residual anxiety, but nothing like the others. It was easy to get a grip on his soul, smooth like honey. As I started to pull it in, I had a sense of familiarity. Had they been giving me previously read souls? No. If so, I would have felt it before, like watching a rerun.

I would have remembered the guinea pigs.

No. The others were strangers. This soul was different. Not because of its fearlessness, but because of its warmth, like a home I never knew I had.

As I rolled his soul into that hollow space next to my heart, images and intimate emotions saturated my being. Devastating conflict and sadness were at the forefront. A choice would be made. A heart would break. A power as fierce as an eclipse would consume him.

Standing with my mouth unhinged, I wanted to cry out to anyone who would listen and take pity. There had to be a savior, deity, or overwhelming presence that could absolve me, someone or something that could make Seth forgive me this sin of trespassing on his soul.

I threw it back into his chest and leaped backward. "Get him out!"

"Disappointed?"

There was an edge to Gabriel's voice. A tone I had never heard before.

I stepped closer to Seth's waking form only to whisper, "I am so sorry," before storming over to Gabriel and screaming, "Get him out!"

He nodded and the vamp took Seth away. I watched my only friend stumble silently into the darkness.

"What did you learn?"

"What does it matter? That wasn't the point, was it?"

The problem was, I had learned something, but nothing I would share.

My stomach was twisting in on itself. After the third reading, every muscle had been growing increasingly tighter, and now it was uncontrollable, as if they were shrinking around my bones, crushing them to powder. Was I losing circulation? I worried that nothing but dust would be left when they were done with me.

"You're right. He was your personal party favor. How do you feel?"

I was still breathing.

"Dandy." But my eyes cradled unshed tears, ruining the tough girl illusion.

Screw giving a good show. I had to sit against the wall. I never saw people back to back like this. My body just couldn't take it anymore, and my mind was in worse shape. I was truly unable to think straight. Emotions ran through the top layer of my skin like acid and my heart exploding would be a welcome vacation.

"Just one more. This one's the whole party."

It was hard to pay attention to Gabriel. I wasn't even sure what he had said. It wouldn't register past the white noise permeating my skull, spilling out my ears.

The same vamp brought in another person. He restrained her in the chair before leaving.

"One more, Peaches, then it'll be over."

I felt like a twinge of empathy—or remorse—had escaped Gabriel's emotional tomb. Or maybe my ability to distinguish authenticity from bullshit had crashed.

As hard as it was, I stood and walked to the woman in the chair. "I'm the Cypher, blah, blah, blah. Stay calm." Yeah, my morals were out the window.

I laid my hand on the woman's chest, searching for that coveted life force, ready to play my metaphysical flute as if it were a snake in the thrall of my charms. To my surprise, it practically collapsed my rib cage.

I flew backward, smashing into the ground, flat on my back. That was definitely a first.

Sensations radiated through my heart as if it had finally been doused with water after a hundred-year drought. A burst of sunshine ran through my body, calling attention to just how cold I had been minutes before. No, how cold I had been for four years.

"No!" My voice choked the room.

My own soul wiggled down inside my chest, spreading to fill every bit of emptiness. I wouldn't have been more shocked if I had heard a click. My soul was back. *Mine*. This couldn't be happening. They gave me my sister to read! I had to get rid of it before it took hold again. It was hard enough the first time to reject. And after the evening I'd had, I wasn't sure I had the strength to do it again if I waited much longer.

Before I could extract it, all sorts of things flooded through me. It was almost as though I were reading my own soul. I didn't want to know what she was capable of doing with it. That was too much. I prayed to be released from this pulverizing spectacle.

I threw my soul back into Ellenore, knocking her over in the chair as I ran for the stairs. Gabriel cut me off, hauling me to the earthen floor, but I wasn't trying to get out of the basement. It was my skin I wished to flee.

I pushed away from Gabriel again, kicking and wiggling. Losing my soul a second time sent a resonating chill throughout my being, like jumping from a desert into an icy ocean. And the thought of someone touching me, *wanting* to touch me, for any reason, made me fight harder.

Gabriel got a well-deserved kick in the gut when I fell and couldn't aim for his head. I scrambled to get up. He came from behind and wrapped his arms around the core of my body as I flailed, and lifted me off the ground. I started screaming, wordless, guttural.

The fury pulsing through my empty chest was heart-wrenching. Literally. That hollow space had turned to metal spikes, piercing soft tissue from the inside out. It was pissed that I wouldn't let it be used, that I couldn't let it have what it wanted most in this world. At that moment, it was punishing me for every soul it had held and every soul it was forced to give back.

It wanted nothing more than to see me dead.

Dying would be good. It would release me from the pain I felt day after day, from the judgment that empty space loomed over my head minute by minute. And I understood its anger. I wanted to give it what it desired. Was it asking too much from my heart to stop, to give up, to move on?

Nausea coursed through my world while invisible

fingernails raked at my organs, and nerves were being carved out one by one with dull knives. I continued to fight. Gabriel squeezed tighter. Even his vampire strength had trouble controlling the rage and sorrow. Time passed slowly as we grappled—Gabriel never letting go for fear I would kill us all, I supposed. Or possibly, he feared I had the power to drag every one of them into hell with me.

Suddenly, without warning, my legs went limp, the excess energy drained like a stopper pulled from a tub. We slid together to the ground. When I crumpled with my knees shoved to my chest, his chest at my back, he was forced to extend his legs to either side of my body.

Clearly stunned, he motioned to the other vampire. With one tiny gesture, my sister was gone, carried away into an unknown house full of bad intentions.

Gabriel gathered my withered frame closer to his chest, arms firmly wrapped across mine. His hold turned into more of an incredibly long bear hug than a subduing method.

He was so close, I could feel the scalding warmth of his body at my back. I didn't think he was that warm from feeding because he hadn't eaten yet. The more plausible answer: I was inhumanly cold.

We slowly started rocking back and forth. Not much, but enough to notice. It was Gabriel's doing, and considering he had a death grip around me, I was forced to follow suit.

He was too shaken to hide his concern. As the rocking subsided, he asked, "What just happened?"

I wanted to speak, but a sobbing moan escaped in place of words. That reactivated the rocking.

I hurt so completely. The physical pain was horrendous, but the sadness was a disaster all its own. I had never felt quite like this, not even when I first gave my sister her life back. I was paralyzed with anguish and horror. Yes, horror was the word. My aura was horrified at what I had done. To feel the first moment of bliss in so many years, and then feel it ripped away.

Out.

The physical discomfort was nothing compared to the metaphysical consequences. And after a few minutes, they blended to create a monster trapped within my simple flesh-and-bone casing. My eyes locked excruciatingly tight as I held my breath. A world of static space consumed me.

When that held breath wasn't released, Gabriel shook me just enough to startle the life back into me. He'd been talking, and I'd been oblivious. Space was funny like that.

"What?" I relaxed enough to take a deep breath. Well, it wasn't too deep because Gabriel was still strapped to my back tighter than a baby koala.

Like a whisper from the grave, he asked, "What just happened here?"

"My soul."

Gabriel spun me to face him. We were still sitting on the ground. My left leg crumpled against his chest as my right sprawled out under his left. If I hadn't been distracted with such a magnitude of sorrow, I might have commented on how well he was handling his fear of dirt because, let me just say, the basement was the epitome of grunge.

"Your soul is gone. This isn't a revelation."

My voice was barely there, but I knew Gabriel could hear it. "I know. I gave it back. *Again.*"

"Gave it to who?"

"Ellenore."

"That was your soul?"

He was asking so many questions, I could have sworn he really had no inkling of what just took place. Apparently, he didn't know as much about my arrangement as either of us had suspected.

My voice was very flat. Airless. "It was mine. Gone again."

Anger twisted his expression faster than a lightning bolt. This test had gotten tiresome long before I was forced to relive the hardest moment of my life. Then again, it was almost the easiest moment. I knew what I had to do and did it willingly. It was the pain that was hard. Arduous.

"I gave it back." Through a growing tightness in my throat, I strained to say, "Again." And with a sudden surge of energy, I started yelling. Breaking from Gabriel's arms, I leaned upward on my knees, yelling at the Members through the basement ceiling that separated us. All of my anger channeled toward the five undead bodies upstairs. "I wrenched it out and gave it back again, you bastards! My soul belongs to her because I gave it to her. Because I am the Cypher! What else do you want from me? How else can I prove it if you don't care? I can't make you understand what you refuse to see!"

In one quick motion, Gabriel was gone, fleeing the room.

I was soulless and alone once again—in a dirty, strange basement, to boot. Maybe they would leave me to die. I didn't care. I collapsed to the cold floor, waiting for the pain to recede, though I was doubtful it would ever truly be gone.

After some time passed, a sense of calm flushed the most daring pains far away and I was able to relax enough to close my eyes.

I had never figured myself to be a nap person, but in one evening I was waking up for the second time. This time, I was lying on a light-brown couch. I could see through the doorway that I'd passed this room when we walked to the kitchen earlier. With my head positioned at the end of the sofa, I could see right into the dining room. It had furniture now. And it seemed likely the chair I woke up in the first time belonged to the matching dining suite. In fact, it looked like the table was being prepped for dinner.

My head hurt. My body hurt. My heart mourned.

I could go for some grub.

# Chapter Twelve

Gabriel walked in through a back entrance. "Feeling better?"

He was trying to be friendly now? He helped snare me into the current mess and hadn't even bothered to find out the entire truth of it. I didn't understand him. One minute, he was mean; another all business; and another, nicer than sweet tea on a muggy day. But it seemed, no matter which Gabriel showed up, he always managed to ruin whatever I had going for me. Maybe I could hold an intervention to get him out of my life.

"Don't talk." He was being gentle, but there was an eruption waiting just below the surface. His body was stiff when he sat to my left, though the humming tension wasn't directed toward me, for once.

"You didn't know."

Gabriel's eyes flinched. "I had no idea." It was a splinter in his ass to admit anything making him look less than perfect.

"Did the Members?"

"Yes," he hissed.

"Can I see my sister?"

"Soon. Some things need to be addressed first." He reverted to his inner businessman. "When we enter, sit down. Do not stand when she enters the room. Do not talk to her until one of the Members initiates the conversation. When it's time, you can ask anything you wish."

"Are you, like, my chaperone for the evening?" I was

joking until he nodded. "Really? Why? No one else wanted to do it, right?"

He hesitated, staring at something completely captivating on the floor.

"That's okay. I've purposely built a reputation for people to dislike me. Most people hate me, in fact." Well, contrary to how it sounded, I wasn't proud, but I openly recognized that it was the existence I had constructed to live in.

"They don't dislike you."

"Yeah, they do. It's okay."

He kept talking as if I hadn't interrupted. "You're awkward. That makes people nervous. Nervousness can be viewed as weakness. They don't like the way you make them feel about themselves, so your company is unpopular."

"Point taken. I can wait alone. I don't need a babysitter." I sincerely meant that. There's nothing worse than obligatory company.

"I'm fine where I am."

"Gabriel, leave me alone. It's been a shitty night."

"Your awkwardness doesn't bother me, just your demeanor, although that seems to be fading." He paused, tilting his head just enough to be disarming. Gazing from the corners of his emerald eyes, he added, "I think it's a ruse."

Well, miracles do happen. He was capable of being affable, even downright charming, when he tried.

"Are you flirting?" I pretended to fan myself. "Give a girl time to recover before we send out save-the-dates."

"That would be a spectacle."

A thin smile touched my lips. "I don't think we have enough in common."

Gabriel smiled, about to say something, when the curt sound of a chime pulled us back to the now. The dinner bell left our brief walk to the dining room sobering and utterly disheartening.

I sat on the far side of the table. The tablecloth, like the wallpaper and chains, was silver. And again, I noticed the entire room was lit with oil lamps and candles. Actually, the living room had been, too. The entire house was missing electricity, presumably. I would have expected the Members to be a little more progressive.

Everyone began filing into the humble-sized room. Gabriel sat to my right. I was positioned at one of the corners, so one of the female Members sat at the head of the table to my left. She was the vampire dressed elegantly, though a little overdone for such a setting. The other Members took their seats, with the heavyset vampire at the head of the other end of the table. Lastly, my sister entered and sat at the very opposite corner I was placed. My heart leaped. Could you blame it? She was my only real link to the world.

She looked like me—terminally young. When we thought up this whole sham, it never occurred to either of us that she wouldn't age like a normal human, either. But her soul was gone, tricking her body into thinking it was the Cypher. No one should have realized it, however, because everyone's been staring at me the last four years, not her. Maybe that's why we were here. Maybe we could discount it as one of those twin things to the Members.

Then again, maybe we were totally screwed.

Her dress was lilac, with delicate ruffles. I was never one for dresses, but my jeans and thrift-store blouse, as pretty as they were, made me feel out of place. And my hair was a mess. It always amused me to see how short and clean-cut Ellenore kept hers. I was the tomboy with long, flowing hair while she was the "proper" sister with a short bob. I guess stereotypes are meant to be broken.

Everyone was dressed up and no one had thought to tell me before my abduction that it might be a good idea to change. It also didn't help my self-esteem that Ellenore hadn't looked at me one time since she had entered the room.

Once the happy party settled down, dinner was brought out. The first course was soup. I hated course meals. Just throw it all on the table and fight over it like everyone else. The vampires didn't really care, anyway. They had forever to sit here and play with their food...which might turn out to be me.

The clanking of Ellenore's silverware was the only noise. Mine stayed wrapped in the silver sheath. My appetite had suddenly fled.

The portly bloodsucker broke the silence. "I think we have a lot to discuss. Let's not waste time. Myranda?"

My sister looked up as I stared back, not reacting to my own name. I was no longer accustomed to answering to it. She looked nervous and unsure. Well, I probably did, too.

"Myranda?" He was talking to me.

"Call me Ell."

"If that is what you would prefer. How do you plead now?"

"I never plead, but I'm still the Cypher, if that's what you're asking."

My sister sat up and spoke to the man. Her voice was a little hushed, but I could still hear quite fine. "And that's the way it should stay. I thought that's what we were securing." She spoke as though she were the only enlightened being in the room.

What was going on? And I just couldn't let the use of "we" escape my mind. "Securing what?"

She turned to acknowledge me. Finally. But there was something cruel in her eyes. It had but one translation: devilish satisfaction. A look I never expected to see from her.

My face went blank, voice numb. "Answer me, Ellenore. What are you securing?"

"Your soul."

# Chapter Thirteen

My mind told me she hadn't just said that out loud, that my breaking heart was wrong. My sister sold me out? She didn't believe I gave her my soul for keepsies?

*Twice!*

The emotion was thick in my voice. "Ellenore, what have you done?" I sounded weaker than I meant to.

Grinning, her hesitation diminished before me. "I'm simply securing your place as the Cypher, as we agreed."

"Tell me you didn't do this. Did you tell them?"

"I didn't seek them out, if that's what you think."

"Then how do they know?"

When I stood, Gabriel grasped my wrist, making more of a gesture than an order that I should sit back down. Our eyes locked. He let go when he realized there was a better chance of me pulling a million dollars out of my ass.

My sister spoke. God, I wanted it to be something good, but how many miracles could happen in forty-eight hours?

"My husband and I were at a business gathering," she said, though she stared past me, confronting the memory. "A woman greeted me halfway through the evening and knew. With one handshake, she knew my soul belonged to someone else. This woman is a human council associate to the Members."

"She told the Members?"

"Yes."

"Why isn't she here?"

The vampire sitting to my left spoke for the first time. Her overly feminized voice was piercing. "We thanked her for her hospitality and asked that it be approached discreetly. No one was to be present tonight unless necessary. Her presence was unnecessary."

"So she ratted us out as a good career move? Nice."

My sister was a mixture of disappointment and anger. "You don't get it. Because she discovered this, I don't have to lie anymore. I don't have to live in fear. The Members have been more understanding than I ever thought possible. They can help me."

"With what?" It was my turn to grit my teeth. I was still standing, trying to hold back the urge to lunge over the table. But whom would I attack first: one of the Members or this flesh-and-blood stranger?

The large man spoke again. "If you would sit down, Ellenore can explain."

"I'm not sitting down, but she better explain right now."

Ellenore held her chin high. "I want a soul."

"You have one."

"One of my very own."

As fuming as I was, it killed me to hear her say that. I understood better than anyone. Her body would never ache for a soul as mine did, but she aspired for a normal life. Her mind was telling her she needed a permanent soul. She had a better chance at happiness than I ever would.

And as much as she wanted it, her soul was truly gone. It flew away to wait until her death before returning. Only when a Cypher dies can the soul return. It must, to accompany the Cypher to the afterworld, whatever that entails. Because I wasn't the actual chosen one, my soul would most likely stay in her body if I died. In theory, anyway.

But we had talked about this the night of the ceremony.

She promised to release it no matter what if I died, because my biggest fear was to be lost, half whole, and unable to make it to my final afterlife destination. She promised because, even if she had to live out the rest of her life soulless, hers would come back eventually. We agreed it was unfair for her to have two and leave me with none, in a limbo of sorts. My sister wanted what I wanted: to be whole. But the lives presented to us didn't give us that luxury.

My words were subdued, sympathetic even. "Your soul is gone. I know you want to have a normal life with your husband, but we both have to do the best we can, with what our lives are meant to be."

"Actually, I don't. There is an answer to my problem."

Why couldn't she just accept it? At least she could enjoy the pleasures of life. There were so many normal things she could do that were out of my grasp. She had a husband, something I would probably never find, and she could have children. How could I ever raise a child in my environment? It would be possible, but not acceptable.

I had to make her understand. "You're right. There is an answer: accept your life and live it instead of mourning it."

"Like you, dear sister?"

"I deserve sarcasm. I've given up. I have. But you just got married and bought a new house. Don't let him watch you turn into a ghost. I don't have to worry about breaking someone's heart. You've accepted that responsibility. Don't ignore it and throw away every happy thing in your life."

"I'm not. In fact, that's why I'm here. I am securing a future for myself and my husband."

"How?"

"The friend of the Members spoke of a ceremony, one that will finalize what we started. It's an old ritual that hasn't been performed in many centuries, I've been told. But there are some who know it very well. It will bind your soul to me, trick it into thinking it belongs to me. I will have a soul that cannot be removed by anyone because it will recognize me as its own. No one can have it. Not even you." Her voice was toxic when she added, "Especially you."

There was so much distance between us, more than a table and a few chairs. It was a distance she yearned for. She was done with me. Her promise to leave me whole in death had just witnessed its own demise. My sister was knowingly —no, *willingly*—leaving me to an uncertain life after death and the foreknowledge to live with.

So this was what true loneliness felt like.

The treachery of the situation was unmistakable in my voice. "I gave you my soul and all you can do is turn my life into a nightmare. The basement was an accident. If I had known it was you, I never would have... I didn't do it on purpose. I was set up."

"I didn't know that was supposed to happen, either." She glared at the Members, one by one. Ellenore never did know when to hold her temper. "That was not part of the deal! She could have kept it and then all of our efforts would be ruined. My life could have been lost completely for your curiosity." Now she stood.

The Members only stared with that undead attentiveness that was extremely creepy.

My temper had come undone, the hurt pouring into each word. "But I didn't keep it, did I? Not once in all my misery did I think to take it back. Not once! Because you're my sister! You were my best friend!" My voice cracked under the betrayal. "I would never give something so precious away and not mean every damn bit of it. I've been living this life because I accepted the responsibility. So you better start thinking about your responsibility to me. All you have to do is live with my soul." Tears pressed against the back of my eyes. "Does it mean so little to you?"

"That's what I can't live with!" she exploded. "Talking to you. Writing to you. It's all a reminder. Always the martyr, aren't you? You took my place, but you always remind me that my happiness is due to your suffering. What kind of person does that make me?"

In response, my voice sounded low and animalistic. It was dead, even though I meant my message to be sincere. "I took the job you couldn't. There's no shame in that for either of us. I've suffered, but I never meant for it to haunt you because I did it out of love, not martyrdom. And up until this twisted evening, it was a choice I never doubted. I'm still willing to be the Cypher, to be Ell, because that was our pact before hatred and fear tainted you.

"And just to let you know, even if you force me into this ceremony, my soul will never belong to you. My will is stronger than yours, and my soul will find me. Even if I have to rise from my deathbed to rip it out of your heartless chest myself, I will have it back. I'm not asking for it now, but I will claim it when the time comes."

Ellenore was outraged. Good. I didn't want to be the only party pooper. "You will never have it! It's mine, and the Members know that. That's why they are helping me and not you. Maybe I don't have what it takes to be the Cypher, but my new friends have what it takes to make you stay the Cypher, and that is good enough for me. The ceremony will work. There's nothing you can do now but accept what your life is."

"And what's that?"

She leaned over the table, both hands gripping the cloth so tightly the blood drained from her fingertips. "Eternal servitude." There was nothing recognizable in her voice.

The bowl of soup flew across the room, barely missing my sister's head, before I could even finish the thought that throwing it might be a bad idea. Lucky for her, one of the Members jerked her out of the way, damn it. She stumbled from the woman's force and fell to the ground. Quickly, she jumped up, eyes wild. Well, well. She looked a little shaken after all, but it didn't matter. My patience was short and my forgiveness all used up. No more chances for sis.

My mouth started to move, then my brain caught up. "Remember when we were eight and you threw the bracelet Dad gave me in the road and let the school bus run over it to see if it would break? I loved that bracelet. It was the only thing I owned that was priceless, precious."

She sounded a bit leery. "I remember."

Yes, she did indeed.

"So I smashed your jewelry box and ripped the heads off all your favorite dolls. All because you wanted to experiment with something that wasn't yours."

"We were only eight. So what?"

I didn't have to see a reflection to know I looked like the devil about to drag the entire house into a raging, eternal hellfire. My voice was steady, even casual, when I replied, "This is so much worse."

Gabriel was looking at his soup, probably calculating the odds of this evening ending any other way than screwed. In one move, I pushed him backward, grabbed the tall floor lamp closest to me, and spilled its liquid over the tabletop. Fluid spewed across the linen and food. Faster than one human blink, a trail of fire rose behind it. The entire table turned into a pyre.

The vampires were gone. I hadn't seen them leave. Nothing scares away a pack of vamps like a large, uncontained flame.

Ellenore hadn't had time to react yet, so I took the opportunity to dive under the table and grab her ankles. She screamed, kicking at me as her body hit the wood floor like a rag doll. I had to let go when I realized I was still under the inferno. She screamed again and ran for the hallway. Scooting out from under the heat, I cut her off at the front door.

"I will burn us both alive before you get my soul for keeps."

"You're crazy!" she yelled, eyes wide in disbelief. With that lovely sentiment, she ran upstairs. Horror movie rule number two: never run upstairs, because the monster always follows.

And I was right behind her.

# Chapter Fourteen

Along my path, I made sure to tip over every live flame. I meant what I told her—my breaking point had been her blatant, cruel display of disloyalty. I meant to kill us both. To reclaim my soul and be done with the whole dysfunction called life.

When I reached the top hallway, I saw the hem of Ellenore's dress swish into the room on my left. Ominous crackling sounds filled the house as the first floor was being reduced to kindling. That reminded me—I hadn't set anything on fire in at least five seconds. The nearest wall-mounted oil lantern was promptly thrown onto the stairway. The carpet liner started to scorch and burn where the oil landed.

We were trapped upstairs. When I tried to open the door to her hiding place, it was locked. "I know you're in there!"

A frantic, muffled voice traveled through the heavy cherry door. "Leave me alone!"

"It's too late for that. All you had to do was leave me alone." My voice was hoarse from yelling. "I could have let us both live like that. But not like this!"

There was sobbing. She had no right to cry. That was forfeited when she damned me to a soulless purgatory, and yet she tried the last straw: pity.

"I didn't mean it, any of it. I was doing it out of fear of you and the Members. Being strong was never me. I love you. You're my sister, Myranda! Don't do this." She sounded hysterical.

"Trying to make up? Mom and Dad would be so proud. If only I had a way to commemorate this sweet, sweet moment." Did my voice even belong to me anymore?

I picked up a small, marble statue of Venus from a side table. It was a foot tall and weighed a ton. My weight shifted as I readied myself to break the door down with it. Before I could finish the first swing, something broke through the window at my back and rammed right into me. I landed on the floor and the statue followed, barely missing my head.

Gabriel's eyes bled to bottomless green halos as he hoisted me off the ground by my arms. I was hoping this wouldn't become a routine. Getting battered by him every five minutes was growing tiresome. Especially when he was ruining my fun yet again.

"Let go of me!"

His fists clenched tighter around my biceps. He swiveled us around, using my body as a shield against the heat of the flames. Our faces were barely a foot apart.

"We need to leave."

"Let go," I snarled.

He loosened his grip but dared not let go. "The entire first floor is on fire! We are leaving!"

I tried to push past him to the locked door, to shrug him off, but that didn't work so well with vampires. Any other time, his strength would have been impressive. Right now, it was extremely annoying. I glared at him with glassy, vacuous eyes. He must have been looking at what was left of me, minus the sanity.

I couldn't stand down.

"I'm not leaving."

"I can't stay much longer, and I refuse to leave without you." The heat was getting to him.

"Why? You helped make this possible. All of you! Isn't

this what everyone wanted? To see my life shatter in reality as it has day after day after day in my heart? You should be happy. I've finally found the perfect therapy."

He released my arms. My body was drawn to the door like a magnet. Flames engulfed the staircase. I could feel the heat across my skin like playful fingertips.

"Unlock this door, Ellenore!" I beat at it with open palms.

Suddenly, the heat at my back was replaced with something much cooler. Gabriel's chest grazed my back; his left hand landed on top of mine, pushing it flat against the door.

"I like green beans," he whispered.

It caught me so off guard that I glanced up, questioning his stern expression. "What?" I was too stunned to retract my hand from his. And he was too strong, even if I tried.

He tightened his hold. "I like green beans."

Gabriel had the look of someone hoping the other person would get the not-so-subtle hint. It was code. Only allies used codes. *Gabriel was offering to be my ally, my partner?* The night was getting too strange.

As real as the situation had begun, it quickly turned into a surreal nightmare, like waking from a bad dream where you didn't know you were asleep. Gabriel's words stirred my sanity. I found myself really standing in front of a room, trapping my sister, with a burning house about to eat us alive. My rage had been unleashed so totally that I hadn't grasped the actual concept of what I was doing. I was moments away from killing my sister, myself, and Gabriel. I swear, for a second, I only remembered throwing the soup.

*What was I doing?*

Gabriel stepped closer to the wall, away from the flames. "Leaving any time soon, Peaches?"

"Yes, please."

"Hail Mother Mary, you even said please. Let's go."

I refused to budge. "We can't leave Ellenore."

"You were just about to kill her," he snapped, utterly annoyed.

I couldn't help but look insulted. "I changed my mind."

He rolled his eyes. "You were probably one of those kids who begged for a bunny on Easter and then 'set it free' when the guilt of caging it every day grew too great. Those bunnies get eaten."

"That's horrible. I would never hurt a bunny!"

"Aren't you?" His attention fell to the locked door muffling my sister's sobs.

"No! I'm letting her go."

"Exactly. You think you're doing her a favor."

Gabriel's foot speared the door faster than a stake through the heart. The wood buckled under the force, swinging open, half-hinged. Ellenore was crouched in the corner, wide-eyed and shaken. *Just like a bunny.*

He snatched her up and disappeared faster than my human eyes could track. I held my breath as the world shrunk to the choking, thick smoke billowing up the stairwell and the menacing sound of my destruction hard at work.

I was alone. Again. Not a promising trend. However, I probably deserved it this time.

I was still standing in the doorway, mouth agape, when Gabriel reappeared. "Miss me?"

My head bobbed up and down.

"You thought I left, didn't you?"

"Yeah."

And then we were gone.

Gabriel's chosen method of travel, flying, was unsettling, to say the least, but it saved us from the flames. It was more like gliding than actual flying. Flying was something Superman did. By that standard, we were not flying.

I had no clue where we were going. It was far enough away that I had time to ponder one major blunder: did I burn a stranger's house down with innocent people inside? Was Seth still inside? If so, nothing would be left to save now. Vampires were very, very allergic to fire. I could only hope he was alive.

And what happened to my sister? Where did Gabriel take her? Damn it all! Gabriel had questions to answer when we landed.

# Chapter Fifteen

We stepped down into an expansive, overgrown field, seemingly the backyard of a quaint farmhouse that had seen better days. The siding was old. White paint flaked away with every revolution of the Earth. A skinny porch ran the length of the backside, only interrupted by a door flanked by two windows and a porch swing. I could see a dirt driveway wrapping from the front to the side of the building. Other than a similar residence twenty yards away that looked abandoned, there was nothing but desolate farmland and trees. Utter seclusion.

Without speaking, my vampire companion entered the petite house and turned on the kitchen light. The house may have looked old, but at least it had modern conveniences. In the back of my mind, I was hoping there wasn't an outhouse lurking somewhere in the endless field. There had to be some law that indoor plumbing went hand-in-hand with electricity. Fingers crossed.

Following Gabriel inside, I studied the narrow, tidy kitchen. The bathroom was on the right, and a large open doorway exposed the bedroom off from the living area. There was a door in the living room that seemed to go nowhere, something out of the ordinary. Upon further inspection, it literally opened up to the side of the house. No steps.

Gabriel was still in the kitchen on his phone, so I took it upon myself to peek inside the bedroom. Two windows were boarded up from the inside. I could see black material tucked on the other side, between the boards and the windowpanes, so no sunlight could creep in. There were two twin beds, one against the windows and the second one on the opposite wall.

The closet practically exploded with clothes. Dresses, pants, blouses, shirts, sweatshirts, men's, women's. All there. It was definitely bizarre. Who lived here?

I wandered back to the living room, sitting on an outdated floral contraption. It was a foldout bed. I could just tell. The clock on the side table reminded me that dawn wasn't far. I needed to get information out of Gabriel before he went to sleep for the day.

As soon as he hung up, I closed the distance between us, asking questions. "Okay, spill the green beans. Why are the Members and my sister conspiring against me? Why are you on their side one minute and mine the next? Where did you take my sister? Was Seth in the house when it burned down? And whose house is this?" I stopped to take a breath.

"Out of questions already?"

"This is serious. I almost killed my sister and committed suicide tonight. Answer me, damn you!"

Again, Gabriel was in my face. Actually, because he was taller, I glared up into his. Looking away to ignore his macho display would have been smarter, but I couldn't. If I did, I might never learn what was happening to my life. It was so simple a few days ago: live in a depressed existence, hope my sister didn't hate me, and work. Quite mundane. Now, I hated my sister, my existence was threateningly spontaneous, and I didn't know whether I had a job anymore. Complete anarchy! There was no room for weakness.

"Answer me!"

"Sit down." His patience was teetering.

"Get out of my face and speak."

I knocked him backward with a thud. I was only able to do such a thing because he didn't protest, meaning he let me shove him, which only annoyed me further.

"I want to help, but I can't do that until you cease yelling. I don't want you to burn this house down, too."

"Why would you care?"

"Because it's mine."

I scoffed, "You live in the stuffy McMansion that reeks of self-importance."

"If it *reeked* of anything, it would be human greed—something that blends into mundane society very well."

Of course, in his line of work and with the lack of a pulse, blending in was of the utmost importance. Too bad he failed on every front. Those eyes, alone, told a story far older than his appearance. There was no hiding such a collective of mistrust and intelligence beyond his eternal youth.

I wondered how his cheekbones and the outer curve of his eyes would be affected by a real smile. One that bubbled from his soul. Organic rather than manufactured.

Straightening his back under such scrutiny, he asked, "Why are you looking at me like that?"

*Shit.*

"Just wondering which serial killer you resemble the most."

Well, now he was scowling. The complete opposite of a smile. No surprise there. Gabriel suffered from a terminal case of resting bitch face.

Shaking off the discomfort of his death stare, I quipped, "Okay, Ted Bundy, tell me more about your not creepy at all summer home that probably has no dead bodies shoved in the closet or cut up in the freezer."

"This home belonged to my parents...from when I was

mortal." Gabriel glanced around the room wistfully. An undercurrent of sadness swept his features, making me feel like a complete jerk.

"I'm sorry," I muttered. "It's awfully small for a family home." I pointed to the door that had opened into nothing. "Was it larger?"

He nodded. "That used to lead to the master bedroom. *Their* bedroom. I didn't come back for a long time. When I did, termite and weather damage had collapsed it to the ground. It was disposed of."

"So, this is a keepsake of sorts?"

"I guess."

"Aren't vampires supposed to sever their human ties?"

Gabriel looked worn out. "I did as I was told, for the most part. I changed my name, forgot about relatives, near and far, and shifted funds. When the time came, I couldn't let this go. It's a safe house now—the closest thing to forgotten—which is the best I could do."

"I appreciate the share, but why are we here? I need to make sure my home is still in one piece."

"Until the Members make a decision, this is your home. It's safer this way."

He had done it. He totally threw my mind off the important questions.

"Stop trying to change the topic."

Gabriel was good at that.

"You changed the topic," he blame-shifted.

"I did not."

Okay, I had, but it was too late to admit it without sucking up my pride. Instead, I approached him, trying to seem remotely dangerous.

Using vamp speed, he kicked my legs out from under me. My back slammed into the floor and I was left staring up at him. After a long, awkward pause, he kneeled over my splayed body.

"You're no bully, so stop trying."

"Well, you're doing a great job of it."

"I'm tired and extremely hungry. If you want your questions answered, sit on the couch like a good human and I'll tell you what I know. If you insist on keeping this attitude, I'll go out for a bite and leave you here with nothing but silence." Pointing to the oldest—and heaviest—television I'd ever seen, he added, "There's no cable."

*Bastard!* That was cruel and unusual punishment.

It's tough trying to be a badass. There's a lot more to it than just being angry, so I gave it up. "I'll sit if you stop pushing me around."

He sighed. "I wanted to eat."

I sat on the foldout couch along the wall. "Too bad, Green Bean. Where did you take my sister?"

He sat on the other end of the sofa. "She's safe. Her Member-appointed bodyguard took her home."

"She has a bodyguard?"

"He sat in the other room while we tried to talk at dinner."

"He wasn't very helpful."

Gabriel shrugged. "He's very young, and you were very scary. The fire was too much for him. There was no reason for both of us to risk death."

"Why don't I have a bodyguard?"

He sighed again. "I'm your bodyguard."

"They don't like you very much," I said matter-of-factly.

"Not very."

"Why?"

"That's not a question you have permission to ask."

I sank into the couch, leaning sideways, sinking into an

oversized pillow. "Noted. Was Seth or any of the other prospects in the house?"

"No. They were removed immediately once their purpose had been served. You will see Seth again."

A weight in my heart lifted to hear that I hadn't burned my only friend alive out of blind rage.

"I just wanted to know if he was okay. I'm not looking for a reunion. Had enough of those lately." I was uncomfortable talking to Gabriel about Seth, so I quickly changed the subject. "What's this ceremony my sister is so obsessed with?"

Gabriel squirmed, glancing toward the kitchen. I think he was stalling. After what seemed like a lifetime, he shook his head. "You know as much as I do. I had no clue she had your soul. I was told..." He cleared his throat. "I was told that it was in our best interest to make sure you had no plans of desertion, that steps may be taken involving your sister to maintain your appointment as the Cypher. The Members also thought it necessary to make sure that, while not first chosen, your skills are accurate and true."

"They wanted to know if I was making everything up."

"Had you, they would have known eventually when nothing accurate happened. But time, even to immortals, is precious. They had to be sure."

"Understandable. I hadn't read those people before, though, so how do they know I'm still not making stuff up?"

"They were read by the previous Cypher."

"I passed the test. They know I'm not a fraud. Not where the important stuff is concerned, anyway. Why are they helping my sister?"

His eyes wandered again. "I don't know."

The vampire was lying. He knew something he was

unwilling to share. No freebies in my future, but I was desperate and tired of fighting.

"You haven't eaten all night. If you tell me what you're hiding, I'll be a willing meal. No throat punches. No awkward anniversary gifts in a year."

He met my proposition with a skeptical eye.

"Scout's honor." Unable to remember if they used a hand signal, I threw up the peace sign.

"If you're the product of any troop, the state of our mortal youth is tragic." Even as he spoke, Gabriel was quietly mulling over my proposition. His attention had shifted to my neck.

I could almost feel the icy tingle of his gaze, as though it had manifested into a transparent weight caressing the bend of my neck.

Was it too late to renegotiate?

*Yes.* This was the only offer I knew he would consider.

"I wouldn't normally conduct business like this."

I smiled knowingly. "But you're starving."

"And you should know anything that might help you figure out what you're up against."

"Accept it, Gabriel. Drinking my blood wouldn't be the worst part of your night."

He tilted his head like he always did when he was deep in thought, like he did right before he agreed to something. I knew he'd say yes before he closed the distance between us. It's funny to know someone so well just by being around him so often, even when he's not someone I would consider myself to know at all.

Until recently, we never spent time together outside of unpleasant greetings, but I saw him almost nightly. Before his dinner and sometimes after, if it was late. I knew when he was having a good or bad night just by his greeting.

Unconsciously, I picked up the cues for when he was happy, sad, or just going through the motions. I knew this weird, ornery son of a bitch sitting in front of me better than anyone else.

Somewhere deep inside, it made me happy to know that I still paid attention. I still cared to notice the world around me. Then again, it was sad to note I was the one who never gave anything back. It was me who had given up. I had said as much to my sister earlier, but it hadn't sunk in. The words weren't backed by real emotion then. They were now.

Gabriel looked skeptical. "Do you really want to do this? I can miss one meal."

There was my chance to back out, but Gabriel wasn't the problem. He never had been. It was time I gave something back. This was a start. He'd saved me from killing my sister and myself, and had unknowingly kept me company for four years when no one else could or would. I could give him this, my blood. Screw the deal. I wanted to know what my sister was up to, but it could wait until tomorrow.

My brain ached.

"Gabriel, just do it."

"I won't take much."

"I trust you."

He expertly absorbed his surprise and lifted the crook of my arm to his mouth. I saw a flash of fangs. A second ago, they were normal human teeth. Now, they were the teeth of a predator. Long, exact, and deadly. They could pierce my skin and drain everything I was in less than two minutes, and I wouldn't care at all because I would be dead.

The sound of his teeth puncturing my soft flesh caused a shiver up my spine. The noise was barely audible but unmistakable. Luckily, my donation wasn't excruciating. It was like getting a bunch of shots at once rather than having an oversized, life-sucking leech dangling from my arm.

This was the first time in years I'd shared blood with someone. The last vampire to take a bite had dumped me soon after he discovered my occupation. Said something about how I was the equivalent to a spy and that he could never love something like me. Not someone—*something*. This, coming from a supernatural being who was technically undead. There was nothing to do but watch him walk away. He wasn't my first love, just my first and last real boyfriend after becoming the Cypher.

Keeping to myself eliminated those pesky, inevitable good-byes.

Once my memory stopped wandering, I realized that Gabriel was on top of me. His chest rested against mine as his hand gripped my arm to his mouth like the Last Supper. Those dangerous green orbs were barely visible under heavy eyelids, drowned in blood lust.

We were in quite a compromising situation, and he wasn't the sole guilty party. It should have felt wrong intertwining my legs with his, enjoying the power struggle of our give and take. As I wrestled for dominance, trying to push right through our clothes in the hopes of feeling skin against skin, I trapped one of his preternaturally strong legs between mine. The action challenged Gabriel's predatory instincts, causing him to snake his legs around mine, binding me closer in the process, as he drank my blood at an increasingly furious tempo.

To make matters worse, my hand crept up his shirt, rubbing his bare back as though I were trying to start a fire. His muscles responded to my touch, dancing under my fingertips, and my breath hitched. He might have the fangs, but I felt pretty damned powerful.

We were swept away by pure adrenaline and pleasure. I couldn't remember the last time I'd closed my eyes and just let the moment ransack my judgment. God, I'm surprised we didn't burst into flames.

Fortunately, we paused long enough to remember who we were.

Gabriel retracted his teeth and, avoiding eye contact, stared at my arm. "This is highly inappropriate." His shirt was still disheveled.

"In all fifty states," I mused.

After licking leftover blood from my puncture wounds with his tongue, he made me bend my arm. "Hold it like that to slow the bleeding as it heals." And then he practically catapulted himself into the kitchen, pacing in an ununiform pattern. Assassinating the last personal boundary between us, he said, "I underestimated you."

I narrowed my eyes. "How so?"

"We can sense emotions. Vampires, I mean."

Full of distrust, I quipped, "I didn't think you meant poodles."

Gabriel became very serious. "Tonight, I saw past your familiar exterior into someone I've never met before. Your eyes were haunted by everything you've been denied. I never thought you were capable of such devastation."

Sitting up and shaking off the last self-conscious molecule, I spat, "Yeah, well, sometimes you don't know what you're capable of until someone else starts making the important decisions for you. It was wrong to burn the house down. I know it was wrong, but while I was doing it, it felt very right, like it was the only answer."

He nodded. "I know. I tasted that truth in your blood."

"What does self-ruin taste like? Let me guess. Chicken?"

Choosing his words wisely, Gabriel's brow creased. "Bitter, as if two perfectly appetizing things on their own have merged, leaving a strange aftertaste. Or the way it might feel to have something precious stolen, such as the promise of a new day. The same way I would describe the last moment I saw my mother."

A light glow grew stronger through the curtains, illuminating old memories.

"A new day is breaking, Gabriel. This one is promising a fight. Go to bed."

"We made a deal."

"It can wait. My head is full."

He nodded. "Pick out some clothes to sleep in before I turn in for the day. They're clean."

And just like that, we were back to being business associates.

Our conversations were a series of flipped switches. At any given moment, it could flip from an argument to friendly banter, from laughing to screaming, from complete suspicion to a truce teetering on a balance beam and, apparently, from making out to psychoanalysis. That was us. It would probably always be this way. This hard. But with each flip, there was a spark. And I was left wondering whether it was static electricity or the lightning bolt of destiny.

We walked toward the bedroom. He stopped in the doorway as I proceeded, forcing me to brush past him as I entered the room. I looked in the closet that ran along the same wall as the door. Quickly flipping through the choices, I settled on a black T-shirt with white and brown band lyrics and a pair of red cotton pajama bottoms.

I changed in front of the closet because Gabriel didn't have a view from where he stood. What to do with my old, smoky clothes? I balled them up and carried them out of the room, clearing Gabriel in the doorway by only two inches.

"You couldn't find something more interesting to wear, Peaches?"

That was the Gabriel I was used to, and it actually helped stabilize my world a little. I turned to face him with a sly grin. "Not for you, Green Bean."

As he lowered his head and laughed, dark hair swooped to cloak his face. When the laughter died, he held his head up and used both hands to push the wild mane out of his face. His hands remained locked together between the back of his head and the door jamb. I saw his youth in that action, an inkling of what he must have been like as a human.

He turned slightly in my direction. "There's a washer and dryer beside the pantry in the kitchen. Push the curtain aside."

"Thanks."

"No one knows where to find us. It's a good idea to lock the doors, just to be safe."

"Okay."

"Good day."

"See you tomorrow—um, tonight."

He retired to the bedroom and shut the door. It had been unspoken that I would sleep on the foldout couch. I don't think either of us disagreed.

Finding the washer, I dumped my clothes in and pushed the buttons.

As tired as my bones felt, my mind wasn't ready to settle down. Before I could stop myself, I walked back to the bedroom door, cracked it open an inch, and rested my ear against the opening. "Gabriel?"

"Yes?"

"Why do you call me Peaches?"

"Because you are the most sarcastic, pessimistic, distrustful, self-tortured, bitchiest person I've ever met."

"You should write greeting cards." I was almost sorry I asked, but thankfully he kept talking.

"And...because deep down, you're none of those things."

"Why are you being so nice to me all of a sudden?"

"Someone has to be."

I could hear the humor in his tone and suddenly wished I had vampiric eyesight to see in the dark, just in case he was smiling. Seriously, what would that look like?

Instead of sneaking a hopeless glance, I snorted. "We'll see how far that gets us."

I shut the door on his laughter and walked out the back door. A porch swing hung from the ceiling to the left. It wasn't the most comfortable seat, but it would do.

The sunrise was beautiful, stretching cotton candy hues through the sky as if it were a tentacled jellyfish. Soon, the rays caressed my face, slowly drying the streaks of tears. Yes, I'd had a minor breakdown. It was stupid to cry when nothing could be done about it, but sometimes the tears fall when you least expect them. I tried to be quiet because the swing was right in front of the bedroom windows. Didn't need Gabriel overhearing. A few loud sniffles escaped, but I could easily blame them on the dewy, crisp morning air.

So my sister had turned out to be the enemy I feared most. The would-be thief of any dreams I dared harbor. My heart throbbed in repulsion to the veracity of it. Fresh tears smeared my cheeks as I came to terms with the entire catastrophe. I needed to explain to the Members that my intentions were pure, no matter how skewed their origins.

The ceremony could never take place.

I sat there until the late hours of the morning, swinging back and forth, watching the grass blow in the slight breeze, taking in the colors of the wildflowers. The setting was peaceful and my brain was effectively lulled. Better than any therapy I knew.

When my eyes fought to stay open, I went inside, locked the door as Gabriel had requested, threw the clothes in the dryer, and crawled under the sheets of the squeaky foldout bed. I didn't even remember falling asleep.

# Chapter Sixteen

I slept right through the day. A blanket of darkness had fallen outside as I rustled into consciousness, presumably woken by Gabriel's footsteps in the kitchen. He was talking on the phone in a hushed voice, pacing back and forth. He must have just gotten up because he was still wearing checkered men's pajama bottoms and a white cotton T-shirt. I appreciated this version of Gabriel. It was disarming and more than welcoming. Particularly after our heated, late-night episode.

His words cut short. The cell phone was discarded on the countertop in a blunt, clearly irritated motion. He propped himself against the sink, one hand on each side, lightly gripping the metal, eyes closed.

Glancing at the microwave clock, I realized that I'd slept for roughly twelve hours. Nice to know my scattered life hadn't interfered with a good day's rest. Jeez.

Gabriel turned his head and offered an exasperated expression.

"Who was on the phone?"

"Ben. Seth is home."

"Good."

"I have to meet with the Members tonight. I'll let you know how much trouble you're in."

"Acceptance is the first step."

"I doubt they'll let you work through a twelve-step program to make what you did last night okay."

I laughed as I walked into the kitchen and pulled my

jeans out of the dryer. Inappropriate laughter is quite a stress reliever. Still grinning, I put the jeans on right there in the kitchen. The sleep shirt was long enough to obstruct a compromising view. It's funny how you can do something like that in front of a stranger, but when it's someone intimate, self-consciousness takes over and everyone runs for cover.

Gabriel definitely looked amused. I doubted he would change in my company. Not because he thought of me intimately. He was just uptight. If ever someone needed guinea pig art in their life, it was Gabriel.

I glanced around the room, bare of personality. The dark windows suddenly felt oppressive. The old walls looked imposing. What was outside, beyond the nothingness of grassy fields and empty space?

Anxiety wormed into my chest, making my heart lurch.

"I'm going with you."

There was no hesitation when he flatly stated, "No."

"Why?"

"It isn't safe."

"Will my sister be there?"

It took him a little longer to say yes.

"Then I'm going. You're my appointed bodyguard, not my representative."

"You burned a house down last night." He was dry, humorless.

"Probably not the entire house, right? You know what they say. If the foundation is good, anything can be rebuilt."

"I don't think they care about minor details. You were reckless and overly abrasive. I feel it necessary to also mention scary and insane."

"Yeah, but in a hands-on, working-through-my-issues

kind of way." If he didn't want to joke, I could. His mood wasn't law.

"This is not a light issue."

"How can the Members be so squeamish? They were out of there before the flames hit the table-cloth."

"They are debaters, not fighters. That's not a bad quality. Be thankful they covet peaceful negotiation. They can take your life without ever touching you if they wish it so."

That comment lit a fire I hadn't thought was ready to burn. All of the hostility from the night before rose up and spewed out. "Then why didn't they? It would have ended everything. They could find a new Cypher, my sister could go back to her Martha Stewart life without worrying that I might pop in for a cup of tea and a soul, and you could go back to your life instead of playing the babysitter from Hell! So why didn't they?"

Frustration drove me stomping onto the porch like a complete three-year-old.

Gabriel matched my pace until he was directly in front of me, blocking the steps to the overgrown field.

"That's what you wanted. Whether you said it out loud or did it unconsciously, you didn't plan to leave that house. By their hands or yours, you wanted to die."

It's odd how a few words can wash away pretenses like a bikini in a wave pool. What a mood-killer.

I had acted like a madwoman, but I took it to be rage, an uncontrollable outpour of sorts. The truth of his words shocked me. Unconsciously, I'd hoped the Members would dig my grave before I dug Ellenore's. And they failed. That's why I was so furious. I'd braced myself for death and they didn't follow through, so I had made a new plan. All without really knowing what it was, what I was doing.

Gabriel broke my concentration. "You can't even argue."

It was my turn to sigh. "No."

"You're not the only one with lost dreams. Stop allowing your job to dictate your life. That's your problem. That's why you have a death wish. Stop overthinking the simple things."

"I don't. I usually don't think about them at all."

"Start!"

"Who the hell are you to tell me what to do with my life?"

His human eyes transformed into the glistening green orbs I was becoming accustomed to. They had taken on a whole new dimension. They were so mesmerizing that I didn't immediately react to his protruding fangs. Vamps don't really have the capability to hypnotize people with their eyes. They wish! But they do have the ability to calm their victims. I think it has something to do with pheromones, but I'd never thought about it enough to ask. Maybe I should have, although I wasn't feeling very calm when my brain registered that Gabriel had just changed, and I was certain it wasn't for a reason I would like.

He crept toward me, closing in until I felt his waning body heat. Note that it was heat obtained from my blood. Clenching my jaw, I tilted my head up as he tilted his down, coming face-to-face. He was up to something, and I didn't feel like budging an inch.

I spoke before I allowed myself to fully process my growing fear. He definitely had the potential to be dangerous, but I couldn't stop myself from saying, "You look awfully pretty tonight."

He snarled. It reverberated deep in his chest.

"That's the problem," I quipped, though I didn't feel like joking. Nervous habit. "All the dead guys have attitudes."

I received a rumbling growl in response.

"Do you want to die?"

"Stop it." I shoved him, though he never budged. "Stop trying to change me."

He mirrored my movements as I side-stepped to get away. "Think of it as therapy."

Blocked as I side-stepped him yet again, I balled my hands into fists, demanding, "What do you want, Gabriel?"

"If you want to die, I can drain you right now. Or, if you prefer a little pain, I'll rip your heart out of your chest." He pointed to a lone tree. "I'll bury it under that tree. The rest of you can rot where you drop."

"Your attitude stinks today! You need a hobby that doesn't involve homicide."

Every muscle in his body relaxed as he closed the remaining space between us. I swallowed the dry lump in my throat.

"Fight, and I'll take you with me."

I mocked him with laughter. In retaliation, he used his vampire speed to twist an arm behind my back, incidentally smashing my face into the hard lines of his chest.

"You're already losing."

"I wasn't trying," I contested, spitting the material of his shirt out of my mouth as I spoke.

He wrenched my other arm behind my back, making a show of how easily he held my wrists in one hand. Leaning in, he whispered, "Time is running out, Peaches."

"For your balls!" I warned. "What's this supposed to prove?"

"If you really don't care about your life, you won't mind missing it."

"You want to kill me?" My heart stung as though it had fallen off a shelf and hit every organ on the way down. I tried to look calm, but my breathing was short and defensive.

"I want you to make up your mind. Stop talking. Fight or die. It's your decision."

He was serious, which ticked me off. It was one thing if I chose to let someone kill me. It was completely different if I was being bullied into it.

"I can't win a fight against you. This is ridiculous."

"Then die out here in the middle of deserted farmland for no reason. Meaningless."

"You're judging me on the basis that you think you know me. You don't know who I am. You didn't even know I loaned out my soul until last night."

His breath grazed my throat. "Show me who you are."

Tensing, I hauled back and swung my knee into his crotch. Gabriel's hand slid from my wrists as he swallowed a groan from the depths of his gut. I never got a chance to cock my leg a second time before he knocked me off the side of the porch. I met the ground with a thud, gasping for air. My arms tingled and my elbows rang with pain. Hitting your funny bone, especially two at once, is never, ever a laughing matter.

I couldn't get up immediately. My lungs struggled for air and my body had to return to three-dimensional form. Once my lungs stopped stinging, I was able to flip over and push up onto my hands and knees.

Gabriel stalked down the stairs. "A dirty hit for a dirty hit."

"That was dirty, all right."

"Threatened?"

"Bite me!"

Oh, not something you say to a vampire.

He savagely grabbed my arm above the elbow and jolted

me off the ground. "A part of me is destroyed each time I hurt you, but I'll do what it takes."

"For what?" He had officially pissed me off.

"To see signs of life!" He released my arm as though it were something slimy and despicable.

Gabriel wasn't allowed to bully me, especially after he had made it clear that, on some level, he cared for me, and after all the nice things I'd thought about him.

Before he had a chance to shove me again, I gave him a good, hardy punch in the face. All of my weight leaned into it. He still didn't fall but that was okay. I could tell it stung. Vampires were hard to kill, but they're just as easy to hurt as anyone else. *Almost.* I punched him again on the same cheek. Without recuperating, he pushed me with such force that I landed ten feet away.

"Assbag," I murmured with what air I had left to form words.

My eyes focused on the grass. It stuck to my hands and face as I slowly stood. When I could hear him walking up behind me, I leaped, spinning to meet him.

Gabriel tried to knock me off my feet again but I swerved, punching his beautifully formed mouth. Blood showered my knuckles. It was a little of his and a lot of mine.

I knew he wasn't using a hundred percent of his strength. It was clear that killing or maiming was not his intention. Gabriel was right. The whole show was quite therapeutic, but we weren't done. I might not feel the same in, say, a minute.

"More than I expected, Peaches. Care to actually impress me now?"

"You son of a bitch!" I swung toward his head but he ducked, catching my hand in his. I kicked his foot out from under him and used my free hand to make contact with his jaw. It was Gabriel's turn to spend some time on the ground. But it's a known fact that vampires don't lie down quietly. He snatched my foot in his steel grip. In a blink, I was on the ground and we were rolling in a heap of flailing arms and legs.

Gabriel was right. I only wanted to die before because I hadn't been living to begin with. I wanted to prove that I wasn't a pushover. I wanted to speak to the Members myself. I wanted to secure my future. It was my right as much as Ellenore's to make sure I got what I could out of life.

As the world spun and the sky was rightly at my back, I straddled Gabriel and cupped my hand over his chest. Without thinking, I used my metaphysical link to call his soul out of hiding. It swirled into that empty space in my chest, filling it with emotions and a future that wasn't mine.

Uh-oh.

# Chapter Seventeen

It was too late to take back the blunder once I registered what I'd done. I heaved his soul into his chest and promptly leapt from his still form, running full speed for the house. There were no footsteps to warn me of his proximity. Vampires wake from that unanimated state much faster than humans.

His eyes and teeth were human again as he confronted me. "Did you read my soul?"

"No!" I tried to act normal, as if everything wasn't turned upside down. Even as I marched away, trying to grasp at what I'd seen from his soul, it seemed to be slipping away. This had never happened. I wanted to list what I'd freshly gleaned from Gabriel's soul, to burn it to memory, but it dissipated faster than smoke on the wind. And then it was gone.

He blocked my way into the house. I'd never met a pushier man. This time, however, was validated because I was lying and he knew it.

I tried to push past him as I thought of something to say, but each frantic attempt was thwarted.

"You took it."

"I didn't mean to. I wasn't thinking."

"Why did you take it?" He closed in.

"Because I had to."

"Why?"

I stopped fidgeting and raised my chin, suddenly unashamed. "To win."

"To win what?" Gabriel crossed his arms.

"The right to take my life back."

He smiled. A true smile that reshaped his cheeks and lifted his eyes, just as I'd imagined. A first in my company.

"That's what I wanted to hear." He released a breath and relaxed.

I hid my relief that he wasn't mad, extending an olive branch. "It doesn't matter anyway. It's gone."

"What is?"

My voice was shaky. "I had it in here." I grasped at my chest. "There was so much noise. It was loud, and hard to breathe." Meeting his eyes, swearing I saw what could only be Gabriel's version of fear, I shook my head.

He looked shocked. His nostrils flared as he braced himself for what I might say next.

"It disappeared," I confessed. "I chased it in my mind but there's nothing left. No one's soul has ever done that. I can't remember anything."

The thought crossed my mind that it had happened because I wasn't the real Cypher. But I knew in my used-up, nomadic soul that I was wrong.

This time, when Gabriel smiled, the muscles in my chest constricted until my chest ached. This smile was the mask. The pretender.

"I was taken to a Cypher years ago. I know enough for both of us."

The look in his eyes was bare. I didn't know how to interpret it, so I didn't try.

My heart thumped. "I'm going with you tonight."

"That was the deal."

Grudgingly, I noted, "You didn't use your full strength."

"You could have killed me when I was suspended. You won."

He walked into the kitchen with its dim bulb.

Our relationship was so weird. One minute, we kicked and screamed. The next, we hung out like it was casual Friday. Only, I had won. Did I feel like a winner? Kind of. In a fair fight, though, Gabriel would win every time. And my life? How much could I take back? What did I want to take back?

Gabriel wet a dishtowel and handed it to me before dampening one for himself. "Let's clean ourselves up and cross our fingers that this is the last bloodshed for the evening."

I could see the beginnings of a black eye stretching all the way to Gabriel's left cheekbone. Also, his lip was swelling at quite a pace. It would all heal before night's end, but it was strange to see him in such a vulnerable state.

Before laughing at the total absurdity of us, I caught my own reflection in the window. I had a bloom resembling a rug burn on the side of my face. In fact, we both had grass stains embedded in our skin, along with tons of minuscule scratches. My elbows were skinned. My knuckles were cracked and bleeding. I would suffer achy muscles and bruises for a day or two. At least I'd put a dent in the vampire.

We stared at our reflections, taking inventory, when Gabriel startled me. "Now we both look pretty," he exclaimed, his proximity so oppressive that it drove me a step back. We couldn't afford a scene like the night before. Neither of us would recover our dignity.

He'd been right, though. There is something to be said about fighting to work out your problems to find out what you really want. To find out where your will is. Don't get me wrong. Never again would be too soon. But sometimes an extreme act is called for when dealing with extreme situations. A soul-swiping sister and a mad band of vampires was definitely an extreme situation. Maybe my life needed to be classified as an extreme sport. Nah, it wasn't that dangerous. *Yet.*

Gabriel mentioned the Members were thinkers, not doers, but they were also ancient. How much could I really trust them?

Gabriel took a shower first. He had been using a dish-cloth to wipe away the smudges. Watching a neat freak use a toothbrush to clean a castle is beyond pitiful. Plus, the pain from taking his soul consumed me, and I wanted to deal with it alone. At least the night before had been so extreme, the regular pain wasn't bothering me as much as usual. I just thought, *It'll pass.*

I occupied myself by looking through the closet. Dresses were out. No reason—just because. Shorts were very informal, and my legs would look really pale against all the rosy cuts and scratches. Funny, I was worried about looking too pale next to a bunch of vampires.

There was a nice blouse in the back of the closet that seemed right for the occasion. Reckless blue and purple flowers popped against a wheat backdrop. It buttoned up the front and felt soft. And the best part was that I could wear it with my own jeans and boots. I snagged the blouse and ran for the shower when Gabriel emerged.

I spent the better half of an hour standing under the water, feeling the hot beads baptize my skin. It had really been stupid to pull Gabriel's soul when I knew what would happen.

Once finished, I found Gabriel sprawled across the length of the couch, hands resting under his head, eyes closed. He wore a snug burgundy button-up with the darkest boot-cut jeans, minus shoes. At rest, his sex appeal idled on "hot damn." I couldn't help but gawk.

His eyes sprang open, body unaffected. "Should I be flattered?"

He'd known we'd be staying here and didn't grab a change of clothes for me.

"I was just thinking how nice you look in *your* clothes." I kicked his foot dangling from the couch. "Why didn't you pack mine, Ass?"

He sat up, leaning against one of the oversized pillows. "It seemed too personal. Choosing someone's clothes is very intimate."

"But tossing me to hell and back, drugging me, and kidnapping me isn't?"

"Not really. You don't like the clothes?" He leaned to the side of the couch to view my entire outfit, eyes traveling from my shoes to my face. "You don't like the blouse?"

"Yes, but it's not mine."

"I'm giving it to you. Everything else is yours. The shoes. The pants. The attitude."

Was he trying to say I looked bad?

Without blinking, he anticipated my reaction. "I think you look very nice, except...you're still green, too."

It was awful. The grass was literally embedded under my skin. Most of it had come off, but there was a green sheen that refused to wash down the drain. And in some spots, like my elbows and the cuts on my face, it blatantly reminded me that no one should resemble a Chia Pet.

"I couldn't scrub it off." My voice sounded defeated.

He sat all the way up and glanced at his hands with disdain. "It looks like I beat up the Jolly Green Giant. Everything is green."

"Your lip is a little green, too. It clashes with your black eye." I laughed.

"You find that funny? You're much more radioactive-looking than I am."

It was a fact I'd been trying to ignore.

"Are we ready to leave?"

"Yes." He sounded relieved. There was a slight pause as he slid on a pair of aged black Diesel boots. "I owe you information. It's important. Your sister's husband is Nicholas Grant."

"The Nicholas Grant I met? *The* Nicholas Grant?"

"Yes."

I wanted to act shocked, which I was, but after the dips and turns in my life recently, was it really that unbelievable?

I shrugged. "Figures."

And then we left to meet the Members for another glorious evening.

Hopefully the party favors wouldn't kill us.

# Chapter Eighteen

We drove instead of flew. It was a definite improvement. The drive was at least an hour and a half. I had no idea whether it was because it was farther out of town or because we'd started farther away. None of the roads looked familiar.

As we pulled up to the end of a long driveway, a tall, skinny house sprouted from the earth. It may have been light green, though it was hard to tell in the shadows. Great —there was a ninety-nine percent chance our skin matched the house. I was really starting to dislike green.

Gabriel parked the car and turned the engine off. After unbuckling his seat belt, he turned to face me. "When we go in, do not talk. Do not make sudden movements that could seem threatening. And, most importantly, do not touch anything flammable."

"But that's, like, everything," I said, not meaning to sound so whiny.

"Exactly. Although I expect fire safety standards to be pristine, try to be non-threatening."

A little too forcefully, I said, "I am non-threatening."

He let out a scoff that abruptly ended when he exited the vehicle.

I followed, releasing my own grumbles under my breath.

An elderly maid with silver hair and bleach-white skin answered the door and flagged us toward a modern sitting room. The house was completely electrical. No candles or torches to be found.

The Members stood to greet us. Their actions were choked as they glimpsed our beaten appearances.

I quickly noted the fireplace was barren of anything flammable, and I could have sworn it had been recently dampened. Where was the trust?

The vampires looked the same as the night before. Well, different clothes, same stiffness. Alarmed, the larger man stepped forward. "What has happened? Have you been attacked?"

Before thinking, I answered, "No. The house is so nice, we're green with envy."

*I* thought it was funny.

Gabriel almost melted from embarrassment. His voice was as presentable as his face. "It was a learning experience."

"What kind of learning experience?" the vampire demanded.

"A hands-on method."

I couldn't help but jump in and explain. Every time you see someone struggling in a conversation, it's just irritating if you can't jump in and fix it. "More like communing with nature. Go green!" I'm sure my point would not have been lost if Gabriel hadn't kept tripping over it.

"A therapeutic exercise of sorts."

"Like a game." After I said *game*, he gave me a death glare.

"Not a game. A conduit to express her emotions."

I had to step in again because, come on, it was fun to watch Gabriel squirm. "Like being a tree with shallow roots during a windy hurricane." Okay, maybe my tree analogy wasn't working, but it was amusing...to me. "Or channeling the plight of a squirrel during a nut shortage."

Gabriel gave me that sweet shut-the-hell-up look again, but the vamp in front of us didn't look like he was buying any of it. He was rather disgusted, actually, like finding a wet, dirty dog on your five-hundred-dollar rug next to a really big pile of crap.

"You're both green! Can you explain this or not?"

Wasn't he listening? I didn't even give Gabriel a chance to answer. "Sometimes that's what happens when you experiment with nature. It has a tendency to throw up all over you and then it just won't come off, no matter how expensive your soap is."

The look on Gabriel's face conveyed that he was unmistakably disgruntled and quite uncomfortable. He took a step forward, blocking my view of the other Members.

The inquisitor spoke with an authoritative air. "What is this? You are her acting bodyguard. This behavior is unacceptable and crude."

Gabriel matched his tone, speaking the way people do when they want to appear discreet but don't really care. "She needed to work out some frustration before the meeting, which she refused to miss. I thought it would be better if she didn't arrive angry. I used my active judgment and thought it the best choice."

The Member pondered Gabriel's response. He may have even experienced a flashback to the night before, because his attitude dramatically shifted from outrage to understanding. "Very well. I trust your motive. Miss Clyne, would you please make yourself comfortable by taking a seat?"

"Sure."

Was the man insane? All of that explaining, and Gabriel wins him over with one semi-honest statement that makes him look like a scholar, while I came across as the crazy one.

I sat as far away from the fireplace as possible. The chair was stiff, matching the rest of the motif. Gabriel remained standing, though he hovered around my position. The head

Member sat in front of me, surrounded by the rest of the happy entourage.

It was a stupid policy that the Members couldn't share their names. I hated not knowing his name. I could always rename him, at least in my head. Bob sounded good. His name would forever after be Bob.

"I apologize for what was most likely a long drive. After last night's circumstances, however, we found many of our human council members to be rather unaccommodating with the use of their homes."

My chance to make amends presented itself. "I'm sorry about last night. You can tell your council associate that I will pay for all the damages and for the costs of a rental home while the house is being...rebuilt."

It absolutely sounded psychotic when I had to say it out loud. I burned a woman's house down. A stranger's house! But she'd helped rat me out, so how bad did I really want to feel?

"Thank you. I am sure she will appreciate your gesture. Moving forward, I would like to grant you a chance to speak freely about this situation you and your sister have created."

"I didn't create a situation. I fixed a problem before it got worse. My sister is the one creating a mess. And there's something that's been bothering me. Do you think things have gotten so out of hand that you had to use last-resort tactics?"

"How do you mean?"

"Does the dirty business of the Mass in my home ring any bells?" I was throwing every punch I had because I was tired of taking a backseat in my life.

"Admittedly, it was poor judgment. The stability of the situation was unsure. Had we known Gabriel was up to the task, the intrusion never would have taken place."

"Did you ask him?"

"He had already offered to act as your bodyguard. It seemed inappropriate to ask such an undertaking of him. However, he rose to action in the wake of their failure. I applaud his resourcefulness."

"He *offered* to play bodyguard?" I stared, dumbstruck, at Gabriel. He had *offered*? It wasn't the right time to ask why, so I shut my mouth.

Gabriel stepped closer and addressed me quite formally. "I took a chance when they failed. The Mass has a tendency to be senselessly brutal. I thought they might cause you serious harm if given another chance. If that had happened, the negotiation would have suffered and we would not have the answers the Members seek."

He was such an ass-kisser.

An incredibly attractive, perceptive ass-kisser.

Turning my attention back to Bob, I asked, "Did any of you think to send an invitation or make a phone call to get me here? An email or text would have been acceptable, too."

The room was silent. The vampires exchanged glances of discomfort.

Bob spoke again. "I am afraid we did not consider those options."

"Well, next time, please do." And just to drive my point home, I added, "It could save a house."

"We certainly will keep that in mind. Is there anything more?"

I shifted, teetering on the edge of the rigid chair. A pillow fort would have been better—preferably with s'mores. "Why did you send my sister's husband to see me?"

"Our first test. We thought you would know exactly who he is."

"I did. I do. He'll be a very important man."

"You could learn those particulars yet fail to discover his personal details, such as who he is married to? That is what heightened our concerns as to your abilities to act as the true Cypher."

"I search the bigger picture. I don't probe their personal lives. Sometimes I catch a random glimpse by accident, but do you realize how many twisted things I would subject myself to if I purposely focused on intimate details?"

"Understood."

"I would hope so. Can I see my sister tonight?"

"Possibly, if temperaments remain controlled."

"That's a yes, because my temper was left smeared across the lawn."

He fought an odd expression, wishing to smile but thinking it a bit too un-Member like, perhaps. How hoity-toity of him.

He motioned to one of the women. "I think we have come to an understanding. The true Ellenore may enter."

The tall woman left the room without hesitation. A moment later, she, Ellenore, and Ellenore's bodyguard entered the quaint sitting room. My sister wore a moderately fashionable orange and pink dress, fitted without being tight. It trailed to mid-calf. Ellenore was always such a girl.

I didn't fail to notice that she sat on the other side of the room, close to the Members. Her vamp bodyguard stood behind her.

Our mediator spoke yet again.

Was Bob capable of zipping it? I didn't think so.

"Ellenore, would you like to address your sister? We are allowing open conversation this evening."

Her eyes roamed over my cuts and scrapes with distaste. She settled on glaring at me and spoke in a bitter tone. "If your intentions are so pure, why won't you agree to the ceremony? Why are you doing this?"

"Because we have our own agreement. If I go along with the ceremony, it breaks our deal. I want my soul when I die. Which, if you stop to think about it, will probably be long after you're already dead and don't need it anymore. It's not fair for you to have two and me to have none. Those were *your* words. Why is it so different now?"

"Because you're not my sister anymore. You're the Cypher."

That stung. Heat flushed my face, but it wasn't anger. It was the heat right before tears scald your cheeks. Everyone in the room tensed, waiting. I was sure Gabriel and the vampire standing behind the shell of my sister were trying to decide when to intervene.

It made sense to refrain from belligerence. I was just plain sad.

"Why can't I be both, Ellenore?"

"It's no longer possible."

"Why?" My voice rose an octave. No yelling. Yet.

Even Bob, a bad, bad vampire, looked on with curious eyes, as though my sister was quite possibly the only monster in the room. When he caught me looking, the indifference returned.

"You're not part of the human world anymore, Myranda. Not really. But I still have a chance, and I'm not going to let you take that from me."

"Oh, I must have been mistaken when I traded futures with you. I thought I was giving you a chance to live like a normal human. I didn't realize that trading fates—working at *your* job every. Damned. Night—would cramp *your* style. I'm damn sorry about that. I should have stopped to really consider *your* feelings."

"Don't taunt me. I know what you gave up. But you didn't really give it up, did you? You're not willing to give it to me. It's just a loaner. Well, I'm not satisfied with our deal anymore."

I reminded myself to control my temper as I snapped, "Tough. I already said I'll carry on as the Cypher, but you can't get everything you want. And that's a completely, utterly human fact. How does it feel to get 'human' answers?"

"You bitch!"

The Members became restless as my sister's temper flared.

"I'm the bitch?"

"Worse. I will have a soul. The Members already promised me yours. You don't really have a say in it, anyway. This whole 'negotiation' means nothing. It was just a means to get you here."

Once Ellenore stood, Gabriel moved to my side. Her poor bodyguard leaned over the couch, ready to detain her if the occasion called for it. He did seem young, especially for a fanger.

My sister glowered. "Your soul is already mine, Myranda. And that's all that matters, isn't it? What you may be is important, but who you are isn't."

I had fibbed a little to the Members about Nick. I hadn't realized he was my sister's husband, but I had picked up on a lot of hurt and personal turmoil someone would cause him. I was betting it was my sister, and I blurted it all out.

"Do you know how Nick's soul felt about you? It was scared. It loathed you. It felt like you stain everything you touch and refused to address you by name. It also felt relieved at the thought of being free of you. That's your future, with or without a soul. So you'd better think if you're really doing this for the right reasons. If it's for Nick, don't bother. If it's just out of selfishness, you've already lost him, and it won't change what you've become. You don't need my soul to be heartless."

"You think you're the only one with a secret to wield? Powerful Myranda, trying to exact revenge. Throwing around your status, only to realize that you're just a wingless bug in the sights of a bird. If you even knew that Mom and Dad don't—" Ellenore choked on her words. She looked positively stricken. "Never mind."

She had almost spilled her secret in the heat of anger, but it was enough to set me off. I needed to know whether Mom and Dad were okay. They don't think *what*? Did they even know that we switched places? I figured they had come to that conclusion long ago. We were adept at switching places for a few hours. A handful of days, at most. A lifetime act was beyond my sister's ego and, apparently, my acting skills.

I willed her to tell me.

I willed myself not to beg.

# Chapter Nineteen

Ellenore just stood there. It was almost as if she'd done it on purpose, giving me just enough to worry about. But I knew it was by accident because she had a big mouth when her temper was hot. Whatever the motive, it worked. I was too curious to let it go. But proudly, I didn't beg. *I boiled.*

"Tell me."

"No!"

I jumped out of my seat and stood across from her. Gabriel and Ellenore's bodyguard were immediately by our sides. The Members merely sat and observed their little lab rats.

"Tell me!" My voice shook as I tried to control myself.

Her tone matched mine. "No!"

I crossed the imaginary line in the middle of the room. Gabriel placed his hand in front of me, respectfully making me take back that step. He was right. I was trying to be non-threatening, but it was so hard, given the shrew in front of me. I took a moment to inhale and exhale a few times.

"I'm calm. I'm at peace. I just want to know what she's hiding about my parents."

Ellenore claimed a step toward us. Her bodyguard was floundering. He didn't know whether to grab her, shield her, or save himself. She took one more step before he loosely rested his hand around her arm. A fly could have done a better job.

"You don't need to know anything about *my* parents, Myranda."

I was reaching my limit again, fast. It would have been worth all the money in the world to shake her by the collar of that stupid dress.

Gabriel rested his hand on my shoulder and started mumbling oh-so quietly, "I like green beans. I like green beans. I like green beans." I didn't think Ellenore could hear it, but nothing gets by the satellites on the Members, who were, most likely, confused.

As stupid as it was, it worked. If I could control my temper, it left a good impression on the Members. I wasn't on the best terms with them after the night before, as you could imagine.

Ellenore smiled, thinking she'd defeated my calm. "I know you want to hit me. Do it. Just do it and get it over with." She braced herself, looking as pitiful as she was able to in front of the Members.

"I'm fine." I wasn't, but I was catching on to her games. If I kept talking in a soothing manner, she would lose at her own game. "I just want to know if anything has happened to Mom and Dad. I'm worried."

"I already told you that's none of your business. Are you going to go mad again? Feel like burning anything?"

My body started to shake noticeably. I tried to get it to loosen up, to let each muscle relax, but every time one did, the rest would ball up.

"I'm fine. Let's try this question a different way." Through gritted teeth, I asked, "How are *your* parents?"

Bob intervened. "Her question is not unreasonable. She shows restraint and patience. Does this not warrant courtesy?"

Ellenore's face crinkled to a pout as she listened to Bob's

wise words. For once, his big mouth was helpful. Ellenore felt compelled to offer some answer, though she made it clear that Bob's interference was unappreciated. "My parents have nothing to do with you, Myranda." She smiled sweetly when she added, "By choice. But they are in good health. In fact, I spend a lot of time with them when they visit every month."

She was trying to provoke me into another fit of rage. That was exactly her game. She was trying to prove to the Members that my actions were unstable, that my word couldn't be trusted. She just didn't realize that I could win.

With a few lies of my own, maybe I could win at her game. If she attacked me first, I could beat the hell out of her and it would be justifiable self-defense.

"You're wrong, Ellenore."

"They do so visit. We go out to dinner and have long talks."

"No. You're wrong that they've had nothing to do with me. I've played stupid long enough. You'll find out sooner or later, so I might as well tell you."

"Tell me what?"

"I've been talking to Mom and Dad." A complete lie, but I was sure she was buying it.

"No, you haven't!"

"Not for a long time. But after your letters dwindled and you didn't put anything in them except a bunch of filler, I got worried. I called them to make sure everything was okay. We didn't think it was the best idea for you to know, so we didn't tell you. I talk to them quite often, in fact."

"Liar!"

"Really? How does it feel to be the one left out?"

"You're full of lies!"

"Why do you think you know anything about my life? It's

not like you're my friend, or my sister, as you've proclaimed to everyone here. You don't know how I spend my time."

"You haven't talked to them!"

I was winning. My voice remained soft and earnest. If the Cypher gig didn't work out, maybe I could go into theatre. I had her.

"Yes, I have. I'm sorry you had to find out this way, but it doesn't change anything."

"If you had, you would have realized that they think you don't want to talk to them because that's what I told them before the ceremony. And they would have yelled at me or would have been mad at me for lying, and they're not!"

There it was, her little secret laid bare. All this time, I thought our parents had abandoned me. We'd all been under the thumb of her lie. It didn't feel too good to be a winner when my prize was an awful fact: my sister was a ruthless stranger. Never an easy thing to register.

She had the look of a deer in headlights. Gave her secret away because she couldn't control her own temper when, the whole time, she was counting on mine to seal our fates.

The air hissed through her teeth. "You tricked me!"

I couldn't bring myself to yell. My words came out flat. "No, Ellenore, you're just not very good at keeping secrets. I wish you were, though. I don't think I can look at you much longer."

"Don't ever judge me! You think you're so much better but you're nothing."

"I never claimed to be...until now, because I would never have done these things to you. Never."

The Members looked on with resignation.

I was going numb again. My heart had just been run over by a heavy, yellow bus and I couldn't fix the damage. My body stopped shaking. The muscles were comatose.

She ranted, "You don't know what you would do if you were me."

"I have to believe I wouldn't have done this. I wouldn't —*couldn't*—live with my own conscience if I did anything like you're doing now. I just couldn't."

"But you could kill me! You could burn us both alive!"

My voice remained low and unemotional. "I was reacting out of anger. You planned all this. Premeditated. I'm not making excuses for what I was thinking last night, but I hadn't planned any of it. You knew what you were doing here, and I can't forgive that. I'm sorry I almost killed us, and you don't have to believe me, but I can't forgive you for this. Do you really understand what that means?"

"Enlighten me."

"You may look like me. You may keep a place in my memories. You may think you know how I'll react. But you were right: you're not my sister. You're not the same person I knew." Unable to stop, tears slid down my cheeks. My voice never regained any form of emotion as I wiped the tears with the back of my hand. "You're not my sister, Ellenore."

She was shrill and angry, but I could hear the disbelief breaking through. "You can't disown me! I disowned you first!"

"Whatever."

"Not whatever! You can't tell me you're not my sister when I already told you the same thing!"

"Are you really that petty?"

"Yes! I mean, no. But I don't believe you."

"Believe it."

"No! It wasn't supposed to be like this." She turned to the Members and ranted, "Why are you letting this happen? It's not supposed to be like this. Can't you see that she's irrational?"

It was my turn to push her over the teetering edge. "*My* parents will be so disappointed in you."

That did it. An open palm swung toward me. Ellenore's bodyguard grabbed her mid-swing while Gabriel pulled me backward, out of reach. I just went with the flow, not ducking Ellenore, not fighting Gabriel.

I turned my attention to the Members. "Are you happy? This is what you wanted, isn't it?"

Bob looked perplexed. "What do you mean?"

"This." I motioned to Ellenore and myself but didn't lose my thoughts. "It just floors me that you're all so old, yet you haven't learned a damned thing. Gabriel said you were debaters, not fighters. News flash: this isn't debating. You're tampering. You didn't make Ellenore do this, but you gave her the chance. Handed it to her and bought front-row tickets, so you're no better than any of us. No more innocent, no less guilty. But you're in it, just the same."

Gabriel leaned over to whisper something in my ear but I put my hand up, blocking his intervention. He reluctantly backed off.

"I'll say this one more time, so you'd better listen." I took one of the deepest breaths of my life and let everything go. "I don't want my soul back right now, even though I don't know the implications of getting it back from the depths of such treachery. I'll take the chance because I stand by my word. But if you make me go through with the ceremony, if you think my word isn't good enough, then I will kill every one of you. I won't have to hunt you, because if we do this, you never had a chance." I made eye contact with each of the Members. "I don't care who you are. You're all just grownup children trying to find something to experiment with, and I'm done playing."

I grew venomous. "I gave something willingly out of love

that you all mourn for every waking minute. That you yearn for with every beat of your crusty hearts. I've committed my life and my soul to your futures, and you're all so trifling. The hole in my chest feels like the Grand Canyon, but my heart will keep beating because it's stronger than the pain. I don't have anything else to give." I brought myself to look into Ellenore's blazing eyes one last time and spoke in a strangled voice. "If you had asked for a heart instead of a soul four years ago, I probably would have given you that, too."

Bob spoke, although his words held no true conviction. "I don't doubt that, Myranda. However, I feel your threats are out of place."

"Do you? Well, I've finally gotten the chance to see just how much my life means to everyone, Bob. Apparently, it doesn't amount to much, so excuse me if I'm a little forlorn. Excuse me if I'm a little put the fuck out! But I've been asked to live with a lot of crap, so I think you can wade in it for just a minute. Can you understand any of this? What I gave wasn't good enough? Well, I don't have anything left to give that I'm willing to part with. Debate that, assholes."

I gave the remains of my sister one last glance and stormed outside to Gabriel's car. He followed a few minutes later, discovering me huddled in the passenger seat of the black BMW. I wasn't crying. I wanted to, but the pain was so deep and so loud that it paralyzed me. There was a very large chance that I'd just sealed my death warrant, but it was at the bottom of my discrepancy list. You know, a list of everything that was going wrong in my life.

The only thing on my mind was my sister.

My word wasn't good enough. My life wasn't good enough. My soul wasn't good enough.

Some days are a crapshoot.

Gabriel got in and turned the key in the ignition, searching for words but failing.

Was he trying to think of something comforting or a gentle way to tell me what an idiot I was for threatening a group of vampires? I guess he gave up because he put the car in drive and we zoomed off into the night. We made twenty miles before he broke the silence.

"I think that went well."

# Chapter Twenty

As much as I tried, my voice just couldn't sound lively. It was still flat from the yellow bus. Lifeless. "It went better than I expected. The Members are incredibly sweet. I think I'll invite them over for brunch one sunny afternoon."

"Is there an invitation for me? If so, I'll be busy that day."

"You're not on the guest list."

He exhaled. "Other than the hand-delivered death threats to the eldest vampires on the planet, I'd say you fared well against your sister."

"I don't agree." I closed my eyes before requesting, "If you really want my trust, you have to stop treating me like someone who can't make up my own mind. You have to trust me, so no more abductions and crazy fights. Okay? If something's wrong, come to me and we'll figure out the answer together. But these deceptions, as well-intended as they may be, have to stop."

It took awhile for him to react. It was worth the wait. A "sort of" apology from Gabriel Vertiline was a small miracle.

"I've spent years trying to kill the last trace of human residue in my heart. It's a curse far more dangerous than fangs, and I've had little use for it. I cannot be vampire and human. The conflict between heart and bloodlust is too great."

I studied the contours of his profile. The way his features warred to conceal all traces of emotion as he uttered, "But I'll try. For you."

"Why are you helping me?"

"Your sister's no prize. You were the lesser evil."

"Stop jerking me around. I have a right to know. I need to hear you say it."

"You are the most interesting Cypher I've met. I forgive the cranky-bitch part because you've been dealt the scourge no one wants. I was told your sister was the original and there was a strong chance you'd make her take your place if you were unable to salvage any part of living. So I agreed to help secure your status...without asking what that entailed. What they ask of you is unforgivable."

"Then why not tell them?"

"Believe me, I did. But I had already taken an oath to fulfill my duties. I could only voice my objections. My only option was to help you in subtle ways. I'm serious when I speak of the Mass. They would harm you as soon as look at you. Having the Mass unleashed can be life-threatening, even for a simple detaining order. It was careless of the Members to call on them."

"But you did know I'd have to read Seth and my sister."

"Yes," he hissed. "I was unaware that Ellenore has your soul. Did you read it?"

"No."

"Seth's?"

"Yes. When I realized it was him, it was too late."

"You can talk about it."

"No, I really can't."

He waited a full minute before speaking again. "Learn anything interesting?"

"I'm not sharing."

"I apologize."

Stretching my legs, I asked, "So what happens now?"

"The Members will discuss and decide tomorrow evening what their final ruling will be."

"I look forward to their decision." The sarcasm was thick.

"You don't think much of them, and I don't blame you. They haven't made a good impression during this investigation. However, they're very capable of making sensible decisions."

There was nothing left to say. I just wanted to listen to the car hum over the asphalt. Thankfully, Gabriel felt the same way. It wasn't a comfortable silence but it would do, given my mood.

The densely forested landscape arrested my troubled thoughts as a dream catcher might snare nightmares, vaporizing them. Only one got through: a memory of my mother.

*I sat in the window seat in our living room, with a book resting in my hands. Dad was working overtime and Ellenore was with friends. It was a rare occasion to be alone with Mom. She walked in, wearing a melon summer dress that made her wavy brown hair even more striking. Her skin glowed under the mid-afternoon rays pouring through the windowpanes. The combination made her look like a fairy godmother.*

*Before she said anything, she smiled. It was her personal smile, reserved only for me. Trying to explain it would be like trying to explain the complexity of the* Mona Lisa's *to someone who's never seen it. Mom's smile had a certain power over me. It coerced me into obedience from the time I was old enough to make my own decisions, or thought I was. And it sheltered me from the fallout of any regrets that my choices—or lack of—may have stirred up. It made everything better than okay.*

*I moved my legs to make room for her to sit down. A white envelope jingled ever so slightly in her hand.*

*Mom smiled even larger. Ellenore and I had a silent joke that we could tell Mom's mood by the number of teeth showing. No teeth signaled run for the hills. Most showing conveyed that her excitement was uncontainable.*

*I could see all of them.*

*"You graduate this year."*

*I shut the book with an, "Uh-huh," knowing conversations starting in this manner meant I was supposed to pay attention.*

*"Your dad and I are extremely proud. Graduating early is a huge deal. This is the beginning of anything you girls want in life."*

*"Mom." I sighed like the whiny teenager I was. "I know."*

*She waved away my grumpy attitude. "Let me say this, Myranda. We know Ellenore applied to a lot of colleges. A lot!" She paused to chuckle before continuing. "And that isn't what you want. We understand that. It warms our hearts to know that you don't want to run across the country to get away from us. And your dad is ecstatic that you'll be working at the shop. But we also don't want you to pass up new opportunities just because you might be hesitant to try new things."*

*"You mean 'scared' to try new things. It's okay. I'm not scared."*

*I really wasn't. I was just comfortable living the life I was in. Why was everyone having a difficult time accepting that? I'd planned to work at my dad's shop, learn the trade, and maybe keep the business going, one day, when he retired. Staying in my hometown to build a career and overall life for myself was a priceless idea. Ellenore was the one with gaudy, excessive dreams.*

*"We don't want to push you into anything. I just want you to know that you have options. And it's okay to exchange one for another if you feel it's the right thing to do." Mom gave me that smile again. Genuine love. "Your dad and I got this for you." She tipped the envelope upside down. A circular pendant on a long, silver chain slide into the palm of her hand. Holding it up, she explained, "It's the tree of life."*

*Dainty strands of silver intertwined to create the branches and trunk of a tree inside a loop.*

*"It represents family and growth. One day, if your choices lead you far away, this will be a little piece of us to carry along. You will never be alone." She draped it around my neck, adding, as she clasped it shut, "Don't be afraid to let the world know that you're in it."*

I blinked rapidly as I found myself back in the car with Gabriel. The fresh memory made me want to cry like a lost child, as though I were that naïve girl, once again. I had believed every word she told me. That little tree hung around my neck from the day my mother put it on, to the day I walked out of their house for the very last time, to the many days I spent wishing I wasn't alone. Then, one day, it sat on the top of my dresser. One day turned into many until it was moved out of sight. It's interesting how something so immensely important could turn into the splinter that bleeds your heart dry.

That necklace meant almost as much as the charm bracelet Ellenore had broken in the street. The bracelet had the spell of youthful wonder attached, causing it to forever trump anything for the top-shelf prize in my mind. There had been many times, even as an adult, when I wished I had that bracelet back, only to be met with disappointment.

Coming to terms with the loss of the bracelet and the shame of disregarding the necklace, along with my mother's earnest words, made the little tree that much more important. The need to have it grew beyond overwhelming to downright ferocious.

I wanted to go home. Because the home I yearned for was no longer mine, I had to settle for my actual house. Staying there was out of the question, but Gabriel should have enough decency to let me collect a few precious mementos.

When I brought it up, he said, "No," without hesitation.

I saw that coming. "I'm feeling upset. Do you have a match?"

"No." He was humorless.

"I'm kidding! I just need to get a few things."

"No."

"Why not?" I was getting a little belligerent. "I want my own damn clothes and my own grimy toothbrush and..." My voice lost steam when I confessed, "A necklace my mom gave me. It's the closest thing to having her with me."

He almost looked sympathetic. "It's not a good idea."

"I know I can win this fight with my sister, and I know that if I'm stupid I can just as easily die. I'm not asking for a parade. I'm just asking for the comfort of my own stuff. I want to feel normal for two seconds. Is that so much to ask for? It'll take five minutes, Green Bean."

The car was silent as he relaxed into the seat. He was beginning to crack under my scrutiny. The final nudge: I began singing under my breath. That had the power to break any monster. My singing lacked every component that identified it as actual singing. I was naturally screechy and off-tempo.

He cringed. "Stop singing."

"We can go?"

"Yes." He sighed reluctantly.

"Thank you."

He mumbled something under his breath about crazy women, and then we were speeding down the road in silence. We were close to the city because I could see the lights on the horizon.

"Is my singing really that—"

"Yes."

Didn't have to tell me twice. I had discovered a new weapon. If anyone attacked me, I could hold them off with badly sung limericks. Would that be my superhero power? I'd prefer mind control, but natural talent would have to prevail.

It only took a few minutes before we pulled up in front of my house. Gabriel parked the car on the far side of the street and started to get out.

"What are you doing?"

"I'm going in. Wait here." He held up his hand. "I don't want to hear another tune."

"I can do it myself. Thanks, though."

"You're not going. Stay in the car."

There was that aggressive demeanor again. I didn't think it was warranted for a few personal effects. He was starting to agitate me.

"Well then, I'll tell you what I want. My shirts are in the top left dresser drawer. The handle is loose, so don't break it off with your freakish vamp strength. Take the top two T-shirts. Grab a sweater from the laundry basket. They're clean. Grab some jeans from my closet floor. Oh, actually, they might be in the bottom dresser drawer. Look in the closet first. I'm a little pickier with my underwear. Look in the small dresser by my bed. Don't take the thongs or granny panties... You're not listening."

"You will take what I bring out."

"I might end up with the granny panties. They'll pop out of the waist of my jeans. Do you expect me to meet the Members with my underwear rolled up over the waist of my pants? Really? If that's where you want to take this, I'll go there."

And there was that look he gave so well. I could have

sung again, but I kind of feared he'd toss me out of the car and run me down for cruel and unusual punishment. I didn't sing. But I did point out a fact. "I could have been in and back by now. Don't turn this into something difficult. It's not a Navy SEALs mission."

He sighed for the five hundredth time. "Let me go in first."

"Deal."

Finally, we agreed on something! He turned the car off and we walked up to the front door. I was glad I had my keys. He walked in first, making me wait in the doorway so he could keep a firm eye on me. The streetlight shone through the door, illuminating a path through the dark room.

Once Gabriel cleared the kitchen and living room, I was allowed to come in, but the door had to stay open. He checked every room before I could even walk down the hallway.

I'd only been gone a few days, but it felt weird standing in my own living room. The natural smell—my smell—was more alien than home. The magazines spread across the coffee table that I'd been flipping through seemed so right before. Now, they were messy and abandoned. The skinny sitting chair had turned into an odd choice for a coat rack, with the coat hung on its corner. The overall eclectic décor was mutinous. They had never really matched, but they used to click. Nothing clicked as I stared through the streetlamp's wide, grubby rays spreading over what was supposed to be my space, my haven from everything.

I was a stranger in my own home.

That was the moment my life really felt invaded. Not much has the power to take every aspect of what's yours and turn it against you. Everything has the power to change something, but very few things have the force to get into your head and change the way you perceive everything. It was like having a stranger in my head, using my eyes to see. I didn't feel like me. I wasn't Ell or Myranda, and this wasn't my neighborhood or my house, because a ghost couldn't claim anything. I felt exactly like a ghost fleeing the cold dirt, only to run to the light and find...nothing.

When Gabriel was appeased, he took my place in the living room and I went to pack. He stood guard, acting as a lookout for anything suspicious. I'd decided to be as quick as possible, though the importance of having my own clothes had suddenly become meaningless. But we were there, so I wasn't going to leave without what I threw a tantrum to get.

I grabbed my small black travel bag, ran into the bathroom, and dumped all of my personal stuff in, like my toothbrush, toothpaste, and hairbrush. Then I swiftly hopped back inside the bedroom and poured my wrinkled clothes into the bag. Bras and underwear last.

I couldn't believe Gabriel had been so squeamish around women's underwear. In an attempt to break my sullen mood, I razzed him from my room. "Hey, Gabriel, sure you don't want to frisk my underwear for bombs or tracking devices? I'd hate to hear an, 'I told you so!'"

He didn't respond. Was he being stubborn? Had he walked back to the car?

"Gabriel?"

Okay, his paranoia had rubbed off on me. Along with the feeling that I was in a different universe, my hands broke into a light, nervous sweat. My heart sped. I didn't know whether it was smart to yell again or whether I should jump out a window and stealthily roll into one of the bushes like a commando. On the other hand, if evil sons of bitches had gotten him, they were probably outside and would see me belly-flop into the thorny shrubs. Hell, they probably already heard me if anyone was actually out there.

Screw it. I had to check it out.

It was nerve-racking, inching down the short yet very dark hallway. A turtle passing would have been considered warp speed. No one could blame me for my stunted descent, though. Human nature is to be inquisitive. Learned behavior is to be cautious.

I slowly, stubbornly hugged the wall, sliding around the corner to face the open door. Unplastering my arms from my sides, I focused on Gabriel's form just outside the doorway. He turned to meet my frozen expression of horrible expectations.

The streetlamp shone at his back, casting the front of his body into complete shadows. Everything kind of took on a hazy bluish glow. It never made sense that lights seem white or yellow, but nighttime morphs them into a completely different color.

Gabriel stepped inside to escape the direct blue halo and addressed me very seriously. "Are you ready? Where's your bag?" He paused long enough to step forward a few more feet. Almost tenderly, he asked, "Are you okay?"

I hadn't expected to feel such fear. It was hard to walk down the hallway, not knowing what to expect, but the fear had utterly gripped my senses. My voice strained in an uncharacteristic manner as I muttered, "I was making sure you were still here."

Gabriel's militant form was put to shame by my sudden seriousness.

"I was listening."

Not budging, I noted, "But you didn't answer."

"I wasn't listening to you. I was listening out there." He nodded toward the yard.

"Did you hear something?"

"Maybe. I think it was the neighbors. Just in case, hurry up."

No movement. I stood, body rigid, staring at him, waiting for my muscles to uncoil from around my bones.

He took a step closer and really looked at me.

Had I ever been this frozen with fear? No, not fear. It was relief. My brain simply hadn't passed on the good news to my body yet. Gabriel was there. He hadn't disappeared or fled. There was nothing scary waiting to grab me.

Acknowledging that Gabriel could have been hurt and that I cared enough to risk my own safety was a scary realization. It wasn't driven by lust or love, whatever it was. He was part of my team. My partner.

And I was freaking him out.

"I'm sorry I didn't answer you." He leaned closer. "I'm sorry I scared you."

"It's okay," I whispered.

"Retrieve your bag so we can go home."

I nodded, turning on my heels as my brain followed.

*Home? Where was home?* I knew he meant the farmhouse. I guess he was right, at least for the moment.

The hallway was less threatening walking the other way. I took a few deep breaths, clenching and releasing my hands to relax them.

Where was my forgotten necklace? I raced through my mental files. It was too important to leave in my humble jewelry box. Check. It was too small for large storage. Check. It would be painful to look at often in any of my usual hiding places. Check.

I dropped to the floor and ran my hand under the

dresser until it came out gripping the same white, padded envelope my mother held years ago. After spilling the pendant into my palm, I closed my eyes, appreciating the weight of it. Putting it on again—the familiar snap of the clasp, the cool silver kissing my skin—brought back a piece of my parents that I needed badly.

Now I was ready to leave.

The bag was still on the bed. It was promptly zipped and tossed over my shoulder.

I was looking forward to stretching out on the old foldout couch. It wasn't much, but I couldn't accuse it of being uncomfortable. If we got to the farmhouse soon, I could pass out and Gabriel would still have time to chase down a willing meal before the sun came up.

Walking down the hallway the second time was a hell of a lot less threatening. And this time, I had a plan. Granted, it was only a short-term plan, but it was better than nothing.

My entire body ached, and I wanted to return to the safe bubble of forgotten farmland.

I turned the corner and locked the door on the way out. I realized by the hum of the motor that Gabriel had already started the car. Couldn't he have waited one minute while I locked up so we could flee together? Muttering under my breath, I walked to the car.

The streetlight wasn't on a timer, but it was known for shorts. It sputtered out a few broken rays, a repetitious evening ritual, and shorted out. A quick glance as the light died told me the car was lacking my chauffeur.

Time to panic.

# Chapter Twenty-one

I was left alone with my little duffel bag, waiting for my eyes to focus in the darkness. If only the bag had been large enough to climb into. No, what I really wanted to do was run to the car, jump in, and lock the doors. However, what I wanted to do and what I did were two different things.

I made it to the mailbox before noticing the flattened flowerbed. The colorful flowers were mangled, smeared out of their little wooden bed. It wasn't like that when we arrived. I'd been careless not to notice on my way to the car.

Carefully, I started down the walkway to my house. It was hard to suppress the impulse to run. My hands did crack the nonchalant look I was going for as I fumbled the keys out of my pocket and dropped them. They hit the pavement with a loud thud that seemed to echo through the entire city. That was all it took to set my inner track star free.

I bent over and grabbed the keys as my feet took off as fast as they could go. The key slid right into the lock and I got the door open in record speed. I slammed it shut and locked it back, along with the deadbolt and chain. With my back against the door, I let myself slide to the floor.

Gabriel was gone and I was trapped in my house by something I hadn't seen yet.

I froze on the floor, waiting. For what, I wasn't sure. Daylight. Life. Voices. Pleasure. Laughter. Crying. Pain. Death. Was this how people felt when they sat in that chair in front of me? Were these the scattered emotions animating them in my presence? Was that my mark on the world?

A small noise at the living room window drew my attention. Scraping, like fingernails being run across something slick. It screeched. My breath hitched. Slowly, it traveled across the side of the house. Nearer.

As I fought to breathe through the terror, the unnerving noise stopped at the door my back was glued to. What was it?

Something sharp, promising danger.

A subtle vibration ran over my skin as the noise zigzagged back and forth on the other side of the wood, stopping directly where my heart was. Then, nothing. I listened intently, unable to move a centimeter. I forced a breath when it was necessary, and only then in a shallow succession. Enough to keep from passing out but not enough to call attention.

All of a sudden, a light tapping began, and I flinched, as though darts had struck my heart. It grew louder as the tapping became merciless. I only moved when I expected it to break through the door and pierce my heart.

What was out there?

I hunched over, knees bent, leaving the bag in front of the door, and moved toward the hallway. Before I'd cleared the turn, a shadow caught my eye in the kitchen.

"Gabriel?"

It was too tall. Not Gabriel.

Only a vampire could move with the silence of a ghost, but it wasn't the vamp I was hoping for. Had Gabriel set me up? After everything, did he stab me in the back, too? No. I had to believe in something, and I chose to believe that he cared too much to do such a thing. I needed that thought to not feel so alone.

The man in my kitchen had been sent by someone else. I would have bet my life. In fact, I think I was.

I decided to try to make it to my bedroom, but the hall gave way to another silent, hulking shadow. And to my horror, I remembered leaving the keys in the outside lock as I heard the doorknob turn. As I recalled the deadbolt and chain, the wood of the doorframe crackled. A second later, my high-tech security system was swinging haggardly in the breeze. What was behind door number one? A third shadow man with a very sharp hunting knife: the origin of that horrid sound that would forever haunt my waking hours as well as my nightmares.

I was successfully trapped.

The man in the hallway addressed me, speaking with a deep, inhuman roll of the throat. "Did you think you would get away from us a second time, Cypher? There are no humans with us tonight." His chuckle embodied all that I'd feared as a child.

People sometimes thought that I brought death. The Mass *always* brought death. Humans scared their children into submission with tales of bogymen. Vampires scared their own kind with the Mass. Only, their threats were very real.

I faced the man, limp and sorrowful. "Did the Members send you?"

There was a long pause before he responded. I already knew the answer. "Not this time."

"My sister."

It was strange. His eyes were piercingly blue, so alien, yet oddly familiar. I felt a sense of déjà vu but knew it was totally amiss. Something about him was wrong.

"The Members have judged you."

"I thought they weren't deciding until tomorrow."

"The decision was unanimous. A messenger is waiting at your bodyguard's home. Unfortunately for you, we knew where to find you."

I thought I would yell and fight when death faced me, but I wasn't doing either. My voice was low and methodical. Just sharing sad truths with strangers. "They voted against Ellenore."

He nodded.

"I don't suppose you're here to give me a trophy or a soul?"

"No."

"She always was a poor loser."

When they began to close in, there was some yelling and fighting in me, after all. I lunged for the man in the hall and jumped on him. The other two pulled me off, but not before I swung and randomly hit them a few times. The one who'd been by the door twisted my head back and lifted the knife. I stopped moving the second the chilly blade pushed against my neck.

His eyes glowed blue, too.

The one I attacked stood up. I could see his smile in the pale-indigo halo of the streetlamp that miraculously came back on during the one time I didn't want to see what was in front of me. I swear, they must have had a hidden switch for it somewhere. In the light, the Mass just looked like a bunch of oversized thugs. Well, thugs with tattoos. And fangs.

Don't forget the fangs.

Mr. Hallway, Mr. Kitchen, and Mr. Door were watching. So far, Mr. Hallway was the only one who'd ventured to speak. And overwhelmingly, I'd begun to feel trapped in a bad game of Clue. Before I could explore that thought further, Mr. Hallway invaded my personal space. He was at least six and a half feet, with a statuesque build and dark hair so short it left his scalp exposed. There was a tattoo on his neck, but it looked more like a brand. The ink was a light tan, only a shade darker than his light skin. I leaned in for closer inspection. Two interlocking semi-circles. There was something in the middle where they met, but I couldn't tell what it was. Possibly writing of some sort. I looked at Mr. Kitchen, who was the leanest of them all. He had the same tattoo in a shade of brown, one shade darker than his skin, but it was on his forearm. It was safe to bet the third vamp had a matching bestie tattoo.

The large undead ass spoke. "We were hoping you would fight."

"Why? Gonna give me a cool tattoo like yours?"

"This is the mark of the Mass. You would not be worthy to wear such an honor."

I motioned toward the tattoos. "If those are the riches, I'm honored to be poor."

Without so much as a memo, he backhanded me. His hand was so large, it blanketed the entire right side of my face. The jolt caused the knife's blade to graze my neck a little too close for comfort.

"Take her to the car."

Say what you want, but the quiet monster was no slacker. Clamping down on my arm, he yanked me out the door.

On our way to the car, I took a second to scan for Gabriel. It was as if my lawn had sprouted ninjas. My eyes bugged out when I saw men fighting to my left and right, rolling on the ground, tossing one another like beach balls.

The Mass were unmistakable, wearing complete black. But there were others. Vampires I didn't recognize. A swift count totaled eleven. None of them fit in with the lawn gnome décor the neighbors had. I would have to do something drastic, such as colored lights at Christmas instead of white, to get the neighborhood committee off my back for this.

I was still being tugged through the anarchy, shocked at the sight, when I caught a glimpse of a dark form on the ground. It moved, dragging a nearby member of the Mass to the ground. As they rolled, I realized the form was Gabriel.

I screamed louder than I ever had. "Gabriel!"

He looked up, but as he opened his mouth, two more of the Mass attacked, crushing him.

I screamed, "Get up!" until my voice cracked.

I was in the car so fast that I didn't remember walking the rest of the way there. Probably because I hadn't.

A truck came to a screeching halt on the road as my other two escorts joined us in the car. Trapped in the backseat, I turned, kneeling to look out the back window, unable to see who jumped from the familiar rusty, cherry Ford. The occupants joined the clash with such enthusiasm, I never saw a face, even though I searched wildly until we turned the corner, leaving me with nothing but my new tattooed friends.

# Chapter Twenty-two

The car ride was long. Because the Mass refused to play I Spy and I refused to play Punch Buggy, the only thing left to do was stare out the window. I wasn't worried about Gabriel. The Mass might have taken him by surprise, but he was under the Members' protection. As far as I knew, they didn't want him dead. It would have been nice if the same went for me. Riding farther into nowhere did not bode well with the unsettling feeling growing in my gut.

You would think being the Cypher would have a few perks, like *not* getting killed and dumped in an unmarked grave. But Ellenore was running this show. The Members probably didn't know what was happening. How did Ellenore gain power over the Mass? This was why I didn't play competitive games. Good sportsmanship is a myth. And no one was making me feel like a winner. My victory party was reduced to suffering and pain.

We pulled over on a stretch of road with nothing in sight. Thick clouds packed the sky, forming a barrier between the moon and my dire situation, creating an eerie glow. Visibility was a joke, though I saw enough to be wildly uncomfortable.

The Mass exited the vehicle simultaneously. One of them opened my door.

"Get out."

"As long as you're being so courteous."

But I didn't budge. Jokes weren't making it any easier. It

was the end of the journey. I couldn't get out. Leaving the car suddenly meant death. Maybe I was already dead, even before they broke into my house the first time. But my body was breathing and moving and thinking. In a few minutes, it might not be.

"Get out!" He reached in and pried my fingers from the door as though they were feathers. Vampires are strong like that.

One of the others came around to the driver's side where we were wrestling. I wasn't scared of his knife anymore. If anything, I preferred dying on the side of the road, where someone could discover and identify my body, rather than being abandoned to rot alone, soulless. Well, there was always the possibility that my soul would come back if they killed me. It didn't belong to Ellenore yet.

My muscles tensed during the struggle, but the bully had no trouble hauling me over his shoulder. And so we began our descent into a special type of hell. The woods were thick enough to cover a homicide, growing thicker with each step. The Mass had to make their own path between the claustrophobic trees and blooming sticker bushes.

After thirty minutes of being jostled like a sack of potatoes over a murderer's shoulder, we stopped. I was thoroughly lost from multiple twists and turns.

We were in a small clearing, still in the thick of the woods, but there was a section with a slow-moving stream where the trees receded, offering a good fifty feet of open space. Mr. Kitchen remained on the outskirts with the trees. The other two were not so accommodating once I was tossed to the ground.

"Give me your jacket."

"No."

"Comply or I will take it by force."

The thin smile on his lips curdled my blood.

"Try to take it," I seethed between gritted teeth.

The burliest of them rushed forward, using vampiric speed, and knocked me to the ground. I should have given him the jacket, but it was the principle of the matter. They were going to kill me anyway. Let me keep a scrap of self-respect. A weak shred of dignity.

I leapt to my feet faster than my body wanted to and jumped to the other side of the babbling water.

He stared with bad, bad intentions. To say he was really pissed would have been a major understatement.

You know what? I wasn't too impressed, either. If I wasn't going to live through this, making their job harder would be a going-away present to myself. A pony would have been better.

I grabbed a rock the size of my palm and clutched it tightly. My only weapon, considering I doubted my super-hero discovery would prevail. He sped toward me again. I backpedaled to gain footing on higher ground, but he was too fast. I used all of my body weight and swung to meet him with a rocky punch to the nose, no pun intended. Bones crunched under the rock and the sensation traveled through my hand with a sick shudder.

When he held his face, I rolled across the ground to find the second psycho waiting eagerly for his turn. Unwilling to open that box of treats, I ran back to the nose-bleeder and kicked him in the core of his gut. He motioned for the blade-wielder to back off.

Circling the way a cat teases a mouse, I moved to keep him in view, gripping the rock like a magic charm. Our dance lasted a small eternity.

His voice was husky and rough. "You're not so tough."

"I'm not the one bleeding."

He didn't like that. "You will be."

I saw a blur and then sky. My hand involuntarily opened, allowing the rock to escape. The vampire sat on top of me, swinging his massive arms. Each connection between his fist and my face throbbed, as though someone peeled the skin from my skull one strip at a time. Miserable, choking on my own blood and the rotten stench of him, I raised my arms, shielding what was left of my face. He was undeterred, making ground beef of my arms. Each blow tore at the nerves, reducing them to the last pickings on a chicken wing.

I thought he would beat me to death, but he grew bored of his game and stood. Maybe he wanted me to guess which punch would be the last, the one to knock me from this world.

"Get up."

My body was numb. Every pain receptor had gone offline, shushing my brain while my limbs were none the wiser to their destruction. The pain had vanished and that was the only thing that might get me through this.

I struggled to my feet, gawking at the giant looming dangerously close. He waited patiently. What a gentleman. Before I could straighten my back, he sucker-punched my left cheek, sending me stumbling into a tree. I pressed my face into the crook of my arm. I was drenched. I'd been so nervous, my clothes were lined with sweat. It wasn't until I straightened my arm that I noticed the copper scent in the air. Blood smeared my skin. It looked sickly under the muted moonlight.

Gruffly, I noted, "Nice shot."

"I've been holding back."

The other two stood their ground.

"Did they lose the coin toss?"

"We have our specialties. I enjoy the fight. He enjoys the kill."

"And he enjoys the show. I get it." So that's why the third assailant took the best seat rather than get involved. "I'm glad this worked out so well. I'd hate to think someone felt left out."

"You're not as weak as I anticipated."

"I eat a lot of carbs."

"Good. I love the taste of a fighter."

He began closing the desperate few feet between us.

So my last activity involved being a meal for that thing? Unacceptable.

When that precious gap disappeared, I threw my hands out to stop him. Stupid. My arms became trapped in a grotesque embrace as he embedded his large fangs into the meat where my shoulder and neck met. Teeth ground into flesh, a sound not dissimilar to salt in a grinder. A regular vampire bite wouldn't have been half as malicious.

It was the death grip of a great white shark, pulling and ripping, although this predator wasn't gobbling my flesh by the mouthfuls. Nevertheless, my legs buckled, though we never fell to the ground. The sensors in my brain clicked to panic mode. The numbness dissipated. Every nerve screamed, making me wonder whether the cosmos had forsaken me. I was a giant circuit board of damnation as my body burned from the inside out. I prayed to pass out before the sensation intensified.

So, this was my death? It was lonely. Void. It was like being suspended.

As my brain prepared for permanent retirement, my heart retaliated. What was I doing? I was the Cypher. The Mass had made me feel so helpless, so dead, so nowhere, they made me forget who I was. I was the Cypher, and I had the power to do something, damn it.

My hands moved tightly between our bodies. They slid over his chest to that spot beside his heart.

"Yes. Fight." His words slurped around the blood pouring into his mouth.

Hypnotized by my pain, he failed to notice the strategic placement of my palms. With every bit of strength and concentration, I blocked the pain and coerced his polluted soul into my being. It fought, but not hard enough. The vampire's soul hopped right in, leaving him in a frozen suspension. I could keep him there as long as I hung onto the soul.

His teeth slid from my flesh as he dropped to the ground with a *thud*.

"I was holding back, too," I bragged, breath rattling in my chest.

Instantly, his soul swelled, filling the space in my chest with forbidden information, codes of the Mass, and secrets. I gasped for air.

The Mass were old and their souls had a lot to say, but I didn't expect the uncensored outpouring. I dropped to my knees, hovering over the sleeping man, as footsteps approached from behind. The second vampire wanted me to hear him coming, to build my fear.

A sharp blade slid between my ribs. The vampire, who was no longer at the top of my BFF list, twisted the knife deeper, using it as a skewer to toss me aside. I rolled down a small incline, forced to release the slimy soul in my possession.

The trio stalked my ragged body, offering a terrific view of their muddy shoes. Almost unwilling to recount what I saw next as fact, I witnessed one of the burly vampires pull a seasoned tree right out of the earth and toss it aside like a broken pencil. A grown tree with a six-foot diameter!

The noise echoed through the forest. An ultimate death cry. Proof that the thick roots and robust trunk had enough life to mourn. Such a feat left a gaping, juggernaut of a hole that, unlike the tree, I refused to pity.

Hands grabbed my limp body, shoving me down the newly formed crater. I rolled, unencumbered, settling into the earthly elements below on my stomach. I begged silently for strength to climb out of the pit. Hope was a short-lived beast of burden. They successfully collapsed the sides. I flailed, shielding my swollen face from the dirt and rubble as it careened down upon me.

This was my burial. I was still breathing, but they had called the time of death. Over and out.

Everything carried forward in slow motion. I could feel every grain of dirt, every stone, every earthworm, every particle that used to belong to something bigger. My limbs relaxed between broken, jutting roots as my left half sunk into enough moist earth to wrinkle the skin.

Every muscle spasmed, and my neck throbbed to an ancient tribal beat. This bite would have left a nasty scar. Gabriel's bite would have been gone the next evening. *Would have...* There wasn't room for vanity in death. There wouldn't be a body for a funeral because no one would find me. No one would look or mourn because I hadn't taken the time to love. So who cared about a scar that would never have a chance to heal?

Between the rocks and dirt, I heard them retreat until they no longer existed in my narrowing world.

This was where I should have dug myself out and made a dash to safety, having a great story to tell anyone who would listen. People spend a lot of time telling themselves how they would react in hypothetical situations. Well, my situation wasn't hypothetical. My situation was that I'd been beaten, bitten, stabbed, and buried alive by Hell's Three Stooges. And there was no fight left. I wanted to. My heart was crying out, *Work!* It knew I didn't want to meet death, but every other part of me was INOP, AWOL, unplugged.

My eyes closed...

Just as I awoke, hearing the strange sounds of the forest, something caught my attention: The crunching of leaves. Footsteps! They grew closer at a quickening pace, stopping next to the pile. I strained to hear the voices. Male. The Mass? It didn't matter. I was turned off. My voice didn't work. My limbs were pinned. When hope was all but fleeting, the sliding of rocks and earth jolted my heart.

Little by little, the pressure decreased and fresh air swirled into my nostrils.

A breeze swept the entirety of my stifled, near-lifeless body as hands gently rolled me over. Gabriel and Seth looked relieved.

"You almost scared the life back into us, Peaches." Gabriel lifted his brow, losing the battle to hide his utter gratitude to whatever higher powers had been at work during my miraculous rescue.

As mud and moss were wiped away, their joyful expressions died. I could only imagine the monster they were looking at. The taut skin and lack of basic movement suggested that my face was beyond swollen.

Blood smeared their hands as they grabbed my arms, working in tandem to plant my feet on the ground. It was a painful battle, but I helped as much as I was able.

They had come. Hope had been smothered, but they'd come for me. Not for a funeral or a lifeless body, but for me, breathing and wanting life.

Where had my faith gone?

Seth smiled. He was overjoyed not to find a corpse. Gabriel looked pissed. He'd tried not to let the Mass get to us, but it hadn't been good enough. That's what he was thinking.

*Don't!*

I wanted him to blame me. I had led us right into their trap.

Gabriel's posture relayed that he wasn't ready to share the blame yet, so I didn't press it. There would be a better time to apologize, like when my jaw could move again.

Seth took my left hand in his and placed his right on my elbow. Ever so tenderly, he walked me out of the woods. Gabriel stayed busy clearing a path ahead of us so I didn't risk stumbling.

As we breached the tree line, the oddest realization dawned on me. It was daylight.

How were they in the sun? Under the canopy of trees, they might have been safe from direct rays, but no vampire on Earth survived a sunbath.

My heavy eyelids fluttered, rearing against the mounting pressure of caked, moist dirt. The comforting weight of Seth's arms evaporated into the dream, leaving a tear in its wake.

# Chapter Twenty-three

My dreamy rescue had seemed so real. I felt tears well up and the terror of abandonment set in. I was immobilized in the makeshift tomb and no one was coming to rescue me. No one could dig me out because I was nowhere.

In an unmarked grave, tears burned my skin and blood saturated the surrounding dirt. It's funny how everything in life cycles. My skin was so damp from the moisture, I could imagine the tears being soaked right back into my pores, only to be cried back out into the water to maintain the cycle.

Each time my lungs inhaled and exhaled, a rasp escaped my throat. My arms were cramped from shielding my face. The darkness was claustrophobic. I wanted to feel the sun so badly. And as I wished to be rescued, to bask in the warmth, my will stirred from its grave slumber.

Why was I waiting for someone to save me? I was the former Myranda Clyne—the current Ell Clyne. I was the North American Cypher. I had saved myself from the Mass with my own power. *Well, I postponed my death, and that counted for something.*

I refused to let myself slip away so easily. There was no excuse to passively fade from this world, especially without my soul. Where would I go without a soul?

Slowly, my hands unfolded and started to push. There wasn't much movement at first, but I figured it wasn't a race. I focused on the task at hand, pushing pockets of earth loose. Gradually, I made progress. Sometimes, it took one minute to shift the debris. Sometimes, it took ten. My efforts doubled once I was able to scoot from side to side.

Hours passed before I hoisted myself up and rolled onto my back around mid-day. A light breeze whispered a silent blessing over my broken body. My dream hadn't been a complete lie. The skin on my face tightened and stung under the scrutiny of the air, and my arms were bloody and battered, covered in bruises. The bite pulsing through my neck was untouchable. And blood oozed from my ribs.

At least I still had inner beauty and a sunny disposition.

I pushed the dirt back into the hole in case anyone cared to check, and then I followed the stream. A few minutes into this riveting escapade, I remembered my cell phone in the side pocket of my jeans. Thankfully, it wasn't in my confiscated jacket.

Amusing fact about cell phones: most people buy them for peace of mind in case something bad happens. But people fail to grasp that cell phones are unreliable little pishers.

I stood in a field, two hours from where I'd started, staring at one bar.

*One bar!*

I tried to call Gabriel every twenty minutes, though I wondered whether he would be alive—er, still creating a carbon footprint—to answer. Sometimes, it would ring once or twice before cutting out. I was optimistic that the Mass hadn't killed him. It was daylight, so maybe he was sleeping off the damage from the fight. Hopefully, my signal and his consciousness would collide, sooner rather than later.

While scanning for more bars, I wondered why the Mass had taken my jacket. Was it a memento for Ellenore, to prove the job had been done? But why would she try to kill me? I was pretty sure I had to be present for the ceremony or they would have already done it. If I died first, I might claim my soul in death and she would be left with nothing.

Unless they weren't really trying to kill me.

They'd been detaining me, not killing me—not on purpose, anyway. But they had wanted to kill me. Would have taken pleasure in it. I could feel that. I saw it when I took that disgusting soul.

I had to get far away before they came back to collect my remains.

My vision had blurred hours ago in the woods. Too much blood loss. I called one hour before I would take a permanent dirt nap.

The phone rang, but it cut off before I could answer the call.

*"Crap on a log!"*

Forcing my legs onward, I walked up to an abandoned house, where the phone wavered between four and five bars. When it rang again, I answered immediately with a scratchy, "Hello?"

"Ell?" The voice was very relieved. And very Southern.

"Danny?" Maybe I'd started hallucinating.

"Yeah, darlin'. Where the hell are you?"

"Oh, just taking a stroll through God's country."

"Well, are ya' done yet?"

That brought a smile to my swollen lips. "Sure. I'd hate to overstay my welcome."

Maybe he heard the small lisp, but he asked, "Are you hurt?"

Not wanting to answer his question, I examined the house. It was one story, with broken windows and a bird's nest sticking out of the gutter. The paint flaked in many places, showing older paint. "I'm by a house. It looks... It used to be orange, I think... Pretty." I was trying to make sense as I talked, but it was getting harder.

Danny tried to remain calm as he asked, "Where are you?"

"A house. It looks abandoned."

"Is there a mailbox? Look for the address. It might be on the front of the house."

I could hear Danny talking as the phone dropped to the ground. Didn't want to risk losing the connection. The paint was too seasoned to tell whether it had really been orange or whether it was some deeper color that had faded from sun damage. Vines and random bushes consumed the porch. They partially covered the windows, but it looked as though they'd been torn away from the door. Probably kids using it as a hangout. Which also meant I couldn't be too far from civilization.

My hands ran eagerly across the sides of the door, accosting vines that fought back, wound so tightly into the wood they didn't want to let go. I held my breath in hopes I wouldn't have to walk the long road in search of a mailbox.

My luck was crap. The house didn't have any numbers. Walking past the dirt pile that cradled the phone, I could hear Danny's voice again. It seemed too hard to pick it up, so I yelled, "Mailbox!"

Painfully, I made the trek to the end of the driveway. Contrary to my luck, it was short and led to a street sign and an address on a rusty, busted mailbox that had not been so lucky. Cause of death: baseball bat.

The driveway wasn't as long as the traditional country farmhouse in the middle of Death County, but it took awhile to get back to the phone. The oppression of fatigue made it unbearable to speak full sentences. Wasted too much energy.

"'M back." I sat and leaned against the side of the porch, lounging in the bushes, which felt like the offerings of a five-star hotel.

"Address?"

"Five eighty-three Mitchell Carriage Road, Highway...something East."

"That's not far from our neck of the woods, actually. How bad are you hurt?"

"Could be worse. Could be dead."

A very good rule to live by was to never admit how close to death I'd come when I wasn't totally sure I was still alive.

"I'm leaving right now."

"Won't scamper off." I hung up and let the phone slide to the ground.

Small tears streaked my puffy, deformed face. I did need help. Lots of it. But I couldn't help but wonder how Danny had gotten involved.

More importantly, whose side was he really on?

# Chapter Twenty-four

I woke from a short nap in front of the tattered house as the sun fell, filling the sky with the illusion of fire. I watched, blurry-eyed, as oranges, reds, and blues filled the sky, each blazing color fading sluggishly, dying, only to be reborn tomorrow.

The air was light and moist. Another freakishly warm spring day was ending. I wished it meant a pleasant evening would take its place. It would have been nice to sit on my small patio, relaxing with the knowledge that I was home and safe. But I wasn't.

It didn't help that I was being stared at by two men.

Looking from left to right, I blinked rapidly, settling on the figures now squatting in front of me.

"Danny?"

"You recognize me. That's gotta be a good thing. This is Edmont." He jabbed the air with his thumb in the other man's direction.

Edmont was in his mid-thirties with short, mouse-blond hair. His nice pants were getting mud stains on the knees and his white shirt had seen cleaner days.

"You didn't have to dress for the occasion." My throat felt hoarse.

"You look atrocious," he retorted.

"Really? I feel like Miss America." The sarcasm made him blush.

Danny backhanded Edmont's shoulder. "What the hell is wrong with you? She had a run-in with the Mass and managed to stay in one piece." Looking at me, he added, "You're allowed to look like shit."

"I'm sorry." Edmont was truly ashamed of himself.

"So I'm not winning a crown or Porsche. What about a runner-up sash?" I looked at Danny. "I've always wanted a sash."

He shook his head.

"Fine. Help me up so we can get out of here."

Trying to be gentle, Danny allowed me to grab his arms as leverage and pull myself up. He winced as he scanned the entirety of the damage.

Edmont's hands fiddled over my back. I'd never seen anyone who wasn't a vampire turn that pale so quickly. "You're luckier than I thought," he said, stricken with fear.

"My body doesn't feel lucky."

Walking to the truck, which bore an exact resemblance to the one that pulled up at my house during the fight, Danny chimed in, "It should. It's a good thing the Cypher is tougher than ordinary humans or you would have been burnt toast in the trash hours ago." He motioned for Edmont to squeeze into the tight utility seat behind the cab, leaving me with the spacious passenger seat. "You got some real nasty injuries, but they'll heal faster than you can ever imagine." He handed me a clean car chamois and sounded apologetic. "This's all I got."

"It'll work." I held the cloth to the backside of my ribs to slow the bleeding, as well as to keep the "slaughtered lamb" motif to a minimum on the tan truck upholstery.

Once everyone was belted in and the roar of the engine signaled the end of my immediate ordeal, I was able to ask, "How did you know?"

Staring ahead, he talked into the darkness as he drove. "About what? Your lies, the Mass, that you're alive, or that you could use some help? And a drink." The vocabulary was harsh, but not his intention.

"Uh...yeah." I wanted to be suspicious of Danny—cautious—from the moment he'd conveniently called. But this was the man I had seen daily since I moved to Mission. When I thought of my life, Two Cents was a large part of it. Danny's tender smile as he said hello or good-bye always made me feel like someone cared. Like it would matter in his world if I vanished. Apparently, it really did. I never imagined he'd come looking for me, though.

His voice filled the cab. "I know your life is tumultuous right now, and what I'm going to tell you will likely make you feel worse, but you gotta know, I think of you like a baby sister." Danny took an extra second to scan my reaction in his peripheral vision. "A troublesome one." Through a smile, he continued. "I knew you and Gabriel might need help back at your house because that vamp don't scratch himself without calling it in. I knew to look for you just now because you're too stubborn to die. And I know about the vampires and who you are to them because I work for 'em, too."

I took a deep breath and nodded for him to continue. Every bit of information was pertinent to my life, right now.

Eyes on the road, he confessed, "I'm your guardian. Have been since you came to town and started frequenting my place. The elders knew I had ties with their kind." When I turned inquisitively, he shook his head. "All personal. Nothing concerning you."

"They chose you as my guardian?"

"It seems you chose me—or Two Cents, rather. Package deal."

Edmont leaned forward from the back, interested.

I tried to ignore his head poking between us as I asked, "What exactly is a guardian?"

"The job doesn't come with a set of wings. I just keep an eye out, make sure no one's giving you trouble, and that you stay alive. An easy paycheck 'til the other day."

"You're paid to keep an eye on me for the Members?"

"Yes, but I wouldn't have done it if I hadn't liked you from the get-go. There was no do or die. I had a choice. You seemed like a sweet girl—lonely, but genuine. And you made it abundantly easy to stay out of your way."

"I think I'm okay with this... I think." Was I? I guess I had to be.

His hands loosened on the steering wheel. "Good. I was hoping it wouldn't upset you."

"You kept an eye out for trouble, minded your own business otherwise, and saved me. I can live with that. *Literally*."

"I've always minded my own business...other than that one time."

"What time?"

Men always bitch about how complicated women are. Honestly, they spend plenty of time creating their own hurdles, and I think they enjoy it.

"You've looked really down lately and I knew someone who had, coincidentally, run into you and found you curious." My eyes narrowed, but he ignored it. "So I invited him down to the bar for a proper introduction."

"You set me up with Seth?"

"I nudged you in the same direction. You've been more than just lonely lately. You were drifting. Don't blame you. Anyone can lose their mind spending too much time with Gabriel Vertiline. His company's for shit."

"Why do you think that?"

Danny liked everybody. Or so I thought.

"He was an enforcer for a long time after they turned him. For years, he imposed the will of the Members on unwilling vamps. Entombment, fire, and the sun were his preferred methods. You know him to be a docile right-hand man, but there are certain circles where his name is synonymous with the Mass. Took him awhile to earn respect instead of fear."

"I had no idea."

"The way he wants it, I'm sure."

I shrugged. "I doubt he'd care if I knew."

"Then you are naïve."

Painfully shifting my weight forward, I asked, "Excuse me?"

"It's easy to see you're the switch that lights his bulb."

"Thank you for those beautiful words of wisdom, but I doubt I'm the one who flips his flapjacks. I'm just a girl in his big, bad, immortal world. He doesn't have time for me if it doesn't involve his career. There's no commitment ring on my finger."

Edmont, whom I almost forgot about, interjected, "Vampires have been known to die for mere humans who never returned an ounce of commitment. They do it because that's part of what they are. Humans expect something in return or a guarantee before offering someone their loyalty. Gabriel has made a commitment to you, whether you acknowledge it or not."

Partly shocked by the depth of Edmont's observation, I couldn't help being a little snippy. "Is that all, Yoda, or do you have stock market advice, too?"

"You're just lucky it's Gabriel and not his brother, Gideon."

Danny snapped, "That's enough," harsher than I'd ever heard him speak. Lighter, he noted, "We're here."

"Gabriel has a brother?"

He killed the truck engine. Before hopping out, he

gripped the door handle, thinking. "Eternity changes people. The vampires they become don't necessarily reflect the people they once were. That's all I'm comfortable saying. If you see Gideon, you go the other way, girl. And fast."

He was serious enough that I was compelled to obey with a nod.

"Good. Your ride's here. This is only the second time I didn't mind my own business."

# Chapter Twenty-five

Seth sat on the hood of a white Mazda, wearing a brown shirt with crazy colors splattered across the front, classic blue jeans, and a pair of rugged brown work boots. He sat alone, waiting in the darkness at the end of someone's gravel driveway. I wanted to run over, scoop him up, and cover him in a thousand apologies for what had happened. Instead, Danny helped me down from the cab and I watched the light leave Seth's eyes as I scuffled his way. Once I stood in front of him, Danny walked back to his truck to give us some privacy.

"You're not dead."

"Everyone seems shocked by that." I smirked, though it was painful.

"And you keep getting prettier every time I see you."

I was going to laugh, but he swept me into a bear hug. I settled on closing my eyes, burrowing my head into the notch of his shoulder, and breathing in his scent: that mysterious stream that could only exist in a universe with unicorns and effervescent fairies.

Without moving, I muttered, "Danny is the smartest man I know."

"What?"

"Nothing. Are you okay?" I pulled away as much as his arms would allow. Staring at the ground seemed the safest hideaway from his scrutiny. "From the other night, I mean."

"That? Pish. Occasional abductions and soul-jackings do a body good. Better than drinking vitamin-enriched blood."

Even the smart-assed smile on Seth's face made the whole situation lighter. My line of vision shifted. It felt better to stare at his stubbly face, but I was trying to have a serious conversation. I had to know that he was really okay, that he hadn't been hurt just for knowing me.

"Are you really fine?"

"Well," he said thoughtfully, "I think one of the guards touched me inappropriately the other night." He looked left and right theatrically, adding, "But I may have made the first move." Seth took a step back, looking me over. "How do you feel?"

"So far, the vacation from my life has taken a dark turn."

"You should always read the pamphlets first and hire a good travel agent."

"Next time."

"Next time, I'll plan the trip." There were unsaid things behind his hazel eyes. Unsaid, not indecipherable.

"I'll remember that." The sentence ended abruptly when blood spouted from my side. The rag from Danny was sopped with blood. My shirt stuck to my side like a second layer of damaged skin.

Seth reached for a towel in his car and exchanged it for the bloody rag. Adjusting the new bandage, I couldn't help but notice that, while Seth held the rag as far away from himself as possible, he inhaled deeply when the breeze shifted. He stopped the second our eyes met.

Curiosity struck me. "What does my blood smell like?"

"Wildflowers." He grinned when he realized I wasn't disgusted.

Seth had the ability to lift my heart up, and with it, the weight that usually held it down. I knew I'd enjoyed our time together before the death threats, but I chalked it up to doing something different after so long of everything being the same. But it wasn't just spontaneity—it was specifically Seth.

Clearly, I was going to be that girl, the one who picks up a date at a train wreck, even if I'm the wreck. And all I could do was smile like an idiot.

I fought back tears. The recent events had risen to the surface. The house fire, abduction, beating—which could easily have turned into my murder—my sister's ruthless abandonment, Seth's kidnapping, and so many countless smaller things. Yeah, I didn't need to throw in the smaller things. The tears weren't falling, but they were waiting. Hovering, to be more accurate.

"I'm glad you're okay, Seth, and I'm really glad to see you. More than you realize." I felt like I was jumping out of a cake, smeared in frosting. I broke into a nervous sweat.

"Are you asking me to go steady?"

I caught myself smiling, washing away the pressure of unshed tears. "You're such an ass."

"So that's the attraction, huh? I'll settle for a date."

Danny cleared his throat loudly. Without closing the distance, he said, "We need to get out of here. Finish your conversation in the car. On your way to nowhere, as far as I'm concerned."

"Thanks, Danny." I tried to give him my best bloody smile.

"I'll see you when this blows over." Getting into his truck, he added, "And it will." Edmont got in, too, and they were gone before the roar of the engine died into the night.

"Where are we going? I might need medical attention."

Did I? Cyphers healed fast. I could wait it out a little longer to find out.

"A safe place. A place like no other."

He chivalrously helped me change shirts, but I assured

him I could do the rest myself. After putting on a baby-blue shirt and loose, washed-out jeans, Seth and I got in the car, on our way to a place like no other.

Little did I know, he meant it.

Rolling through the darkness, I asked, "Do the Members know what happened?"

"I heard you and a few others had a drastic misunderstanding in your front yard, in plain view of the public. I'm sure the Members know something went horribly wrong."

"Why don't we just go straight to them and ask for backup?"

I shifted in the gray seat, dooming my body to a wave of pain and nausea. The baby-blue shirt was already absorbing a gross amount of blood from the knife wound. However, it was growing sluggish.

"Would you trust them, right now, to stop what's happening?"

"Maybe."

"Maybe not."

"Agreed. What about Gabriel? Has anyone heard from him?"

I tried not to sound like every bit of will was in overdrive, hoping that he hadn't been scraped off my front lawn into a Ziploc baggie. I tried to act like whatever answer Seth gave would provoke the same nonchalant, "Oh."

"No one's heard from him."

He offered nothing more. I noticed his hands tighten, practically strangling the steering wheel.

Danny's voice echoed through my head, saying, "That vamp doesn't scratch himself without calling it in..."

"We need to find him." The alarm was bare in my voice.

"Would you be this worried if I were missing?" His tone

clearly told me he thought he knew the answer and didn't like it.

I held the towel as I shifted to face him. The blood flow had slowed considerably, though the pain was obscenely present. He winced for me, obviously opposed to the movement.

"Gabriel means something to me. I don't know why, but the bastard gets to me. I can't help it, and I shouldn't have to hide it. I've known Gabriel a lot longer than you."

"Now I know why all the men swoon over you."

"Shut up and listen."

He did.

"I've known him for several years, and it's taken that long to just now break through to the next level. I've known you for a number of hours, but we skipped all the bullshit levels from the moment I saw you."

Trying not to look overly pleased, he pointed out, "You didn't like me when we first met."

"I liked you too much, which is why I didn't like you." He smiled, forcing me to add, "And because you're such a jack-ass, and that never translates well the first time around."

He laughed, but soberly added, "*He* likes you, too. Everyone knows it. That's why they stay away from you."

"Who, men?"

He nodded.

"I just thought it was my natural charm." When I noticed he was serious, I added, "Edmont mentioned that it was some kind of loyalty or infatuation."

Seth appeared more sullen. Or was that defeat? There was a ring of honesty in his tone. "It's not an infatuation."

"Well, it sure as hell isn't love. So why are we talking about this?"

"Because I really like you." He hesitated.

I watched the shadows play across his features, highlighting the stress around his eyes and the short laugh lines flirting with his lips. Suddenly, the tension vanished.

"I don't want anything more to happen between us if you figure out you like him more. I'd rather know now. I'm dead, but my heart and brain still work, and I try not to make the same mistakes twice."

The whisper of a name slipped from my lips. "Malice."

While he had been talking, it jogged emotions from his reading. All I could gather was that name and the feeling that it meant something broken and desolate to Seth. I couldn't remember more but wished I could take back saying it out loud.

His eyes widened. "What did you say?"

My tongue felt dry. I stuttered, "All this! All this is overwhelming."

He released a hellacious sigh. "Tell me about it." Seth leaned back in his seat, turning his attention back to the road.

The tension at the thought of hearing her name evaporated, although I suspected it was buried deep. Never truly gone.

Tell me about it! On top of everything else, I didn't have the guts to tell him I was remembering his personal secrets. I just wasn't sure what to do about it yet, but it would have to wait. There was already too much to think about at the moment, like what to do about Gabriel and Seth, my sister's vendetta, and this whole gnarly mess of lying to the vampires.

Suddenly, I grew tired. If I wasn't so busy saving my world from collapsing, I think staying in bed for fifty years would have been the ticket. The more energy I lost, the more my world was looking less and less meaningful. Was it really worth the fight? I guess I answered that question when I dug out of my grave. But it was becoming harder and harder to care. I felt cold, distant from everything. No, not from Seth. Confused and oddly misplaced, but not distant.

The car hummed as Seth drove. We were content in our silence. I think he wanted to just "be" for a little longer without hearing my answer concerning Gabriel. Truthfully, I didn't have one.

My thoughts looped for an hour until my brain wound in on itself. Every worry plagued my mind, consuming it with numerous possible outcomes. Hideous outcomes.

I leaned my head against the chill of the window and stared up at the stars. *Make a wish.* Could I cheat and cram every bit of hope into one wish? Before I could find out, my weariness revolted and my eyelids refused to open. The pain in my body disintegrated as darkness cradled a dreamless sleep.

I couldn't hear Seth, but his presence stretched over the bounds and divides to comfort me. I let go of everything for a little while as we traveled through the night. We didn't know where we stood with each other, but it was okay. At the moment, we both just wanted to exist in our little bubble and let go of everything else, even if this state of existence was temporary.

# Chapter Twenty-six

"Is she gonna wake up soon? Don't look at me like that. I was just asking." The voice was tiny yet fervent.

"Girl, you best leave her be," said a wizened voice, not by age but experience.

"What happened to her? She's all broken."

"She ain't broken. Just knocked around."

"She's not having a baby, Mama. She's not fat."

"Knocked around, not up. There's a big difference. She's not pregnant—I pray, anyway. She's been beat pretty bad. Worse than I ever seen, but she'll heal."

"Oh."

"Come. Let her rest."

"Mama!"

"Hush. Come now."

I heard little feet stomp a short distance before a door *oomphed* shut. I was awake. At first, I thought it was a dream. When the voices grew faint, I pried my eyes open. The room was dark, but there was a tiny plug-in air freshener that doubled as a nightlight.

The room must have only been ten by twelve. The walls were dark wood paneling, barren of decorations. The floor was a lighter, more battered wood that I could tell had been walked on for many more years than I'd been alive.

The mattress I laid on took up a good amount of space, but there was a cot only a few feet away, which left a bit of walking space through the room. Seth was tucked away, snug as a bug. I hadn't worked up the strength to pull the heavy comforter to the side enough to sit up. It was nice, smelling of fresh summer rain and strawberries. I think my mom used a similar detergent. The smell instantly soothed me. Enough to stay put.

Also, I was scared that too much movement would draw the attention of the little girl and I would be bombarded, which I was not in the mood for.

It seemed we were in good hands. I didn't know these people, but Seth felt comfortable enough to pass out for the day, so it was undoubtedly safe. I didn't venture his way, either. I kept my distance and snuggled back into the comforter.

I must have slept like the true dead. The next time my eyes opened, Seth's cot was empty. It would have been a good idea to tie a bell around his neck to keep track of him. Remembering the strangers earlier didn't make me enthusiastic at the prospect of exploring.

Before I was able to think up a bunch of terrible things that could have happened to Seth, he walked through the large wooden door. Thankfully, he closed it behind him. I heard muffled footsteps looming close to our room, hoping for an invite.

"What time is it?"

"Not quite midnight." He sat on the edge of the bed.

Rubbing the hair out of my face, I asked, "I slept another whole day?"

"Yep."

"Great. Where are we, the place like no other?"

"Yep."

"Have you been up long?"

"An hour and a half."

"Who's outside?"

"Lucy, Paula's daughter. You'll meet her soon."

"I heard them earlier. So, they do this a lot? Harbor wanted vampires and Cyphers?"

"I think you're their first Cypher, but I've been here before. Paula is really nice and Lucy is enthusiastic, but also very cute. She's five and probably smarter than most university professors."

"What makes you think the other vamps don't know we're here?"

"Full of questions tonight, aren't you? Paula doesn't and has never worked for the Members, and the Mass will never come here because she's given them no reason. Pinky swear. Now, do you want to meet Lucy?"

"Why is she up so late?"

"She's been waiting all day to meet you. Paula barely kept her from waking you, like, a thousand times today." He stretched out across the bed and my legs, sinking sideways into the overstuffed comforter. "Are you going to grant her wish?"

"In a little while. Have you heard from Gabriel?"

He was reluctant to tell me that he hadn't.

"Just great."

"Stop freaking out. I'm sure Romeo is licking his wounds."

I didn't want to get right back into the bad vibes with Seth. Not again. "Look, Seth, I like Gabriel, but I think I like you more. Is that good enough, or are you going to act like a foul fart all night?"

Overwhelmed by a cocky grin, Seth scooted closer. "That was the sweetest thing I've heard in a long time."

I pushed his face away with the palm of my hand and

laid my head down on the bed, all eyes for him, of course. His smile was so intoxicating, I couldn't look away if someone had bet me all the good luck on the planet. Sappy? Yes. True? Yes.

He wrapped his arm over my shoulder and gently rested his head on the top of mine, minding not to cause pain to any of the boo-boos. It brought about a sense of peace.

All too soon, Seth shifted, resting on his back. "He'll contact us."

Oh, now he was being nice. There must be a rule somewhere: after cuddling, one must apologize for one's assholery.

"I don't think you know what the hell's going on." I laughed at his mock outrage.

"You didn't have to call me out." He rose, leaning on his forearms, and gave me a dramatic don't-make-me-cry look. "I'm trying my best. What more do you want from me?"

"Don't be so damned whiny and cute." *Did I just say that out loud?*

You know what? I deserved it. Why couldn't I flirt and have a boyfriend if I felt like it? I wanted to experience the better things in life, especially if that included an adorable undead surfer who was winking at me.

He scooted closer. A tingle ran the length of my spine as he traced my knuckles with his fingers. "What are you thinking about so hard?"

"You... And how nice this comforter would look around your naked body."

That took him totally by surprise, and I loved it. Before he had a chance for a rebuttal, I closed the space between us with a kiss.

While I laid dying, the world had narrowed to the size of a needle's point. My life was downsized to a hole in the ground, where I expected everything about me to end. Our kiss was the opposite. Seth's firm touch opened a gateway to possibility. Hope. Acceptance. The feel of his breath caressing my skin as his silky lips sparked purpose within my being was the first real step of my recovery. Because I wasn't merely healing what the Mass had done. I was healing a greater wound. A slow demise that began that first night the Members came for Ellenore.

Wow! Why had I shunned the male species? Okay, we all knew the answer. Just any guy was just that: a rando. Seth was unique.

Regretfully, I didn't have time to explore my feelings before we were interrupted.

"Whoa! What are you guys doing? That's gross!"

We immediately broke our contact and turned to find little Lucy in the doorway with a scrunched expression that made her look as if she'd been sucking on lemons. She was a string-bean of a girl with deep-brown skin. Her face was as round as the sun, with dark, round eyes and cherub lips. All of her Shirley Temple curls were drawn into a clip, allowing them to dance gaily without falling in her eyes.

Seth sat up, but not as fast as I did. Not thinking before moving, my muscles jolted and cramped up. Still bruised and battered. I'd forgotten in my steamy Seth haze.

"So, you're Lucy."

Her grossed-out expression transformed into an amazing smile. "Lucy Abigail Brockhearte. And you're the Cypher."

"I am."

"I know you are. That's what I just said. Why do you look like that?"

I followed her finger down to the bruises on my arms,

and watched her little hand travel back through the air until she was barely grazing my cheek with the tip of her finger.

"My sister and I aren't getting along right now."

"I'm glad I don't have a sister. Why are you mad at each other?"

What could I say? Instead of trying, I raised my eyebrows and shrugged, deciding to change the subject. "No sisters. Do you have any brothers?"

Her little eyes grew large. "One," she whispered.

Seth hopped off the bed and squatted so that he was almost at eye level with Lucy. He smiled and she immediately lit up.

"I want to know what it's like to be the Cypher," she said.

Lucy and Seth turned their gazes on me. Lucy was determined, while Seth actually looked as though it would break his heart to tell her she had to leave.

Reluctantly, I answered, "It's confusing. It makes me feel good when I can help people become who their souls want to be. But it makes me feel bad when those people don't want to be who their souls want them to be."

She contemplated my words before opening her mouth. "Do you get good insurance?"

It was so unexpected, I laughed. "Insurance?"

"Yeah! You should have doctor insurance."

I hesitated. Having a five-year-old call attention to the fact that I looked worse than roadkill had a tendency to make me feel a wee bit self-conscious. "Yeah, I have insurance."

"Oh, good. You'll be fine." She looked relieved.

Seth recaptured her attention and asked, "Can I show her around?"

"No, I want to."

She didn't wait for me to scoot off the bed before

bounding out the door, rounding the corner, yelling, "Come on, lazy bones!"

I dodged the small mirror in the bedroom. Even though everything felt more like me and less distorted, I was still scared to look at my reflection, thinking it would be worse than I remembered. And from Lucy's reaction, I knew I was still an eyesore.

The three of us walked through the long, planked hallway into a small kitchen. It was white and yellow and had everything a kitchen could ever want, down to the chicken-themed eggbeater and manual can opener hanging on hooks next to the handmade potholders. The mess on the counter and the aroma of fresh pumpkin pie made me scan the room for the woman I'd heard earlier.

Seth extended a hand. "Paula's outside." Grabbing my hand in his, we walked outside behind Lucy.

I glanced back to study the exterior of the log cabin. It was small but complex. From the exterior alone, I could tell there were many nooks and crannies. Some were never meant to see the light of day, I suspected. The entire home was surreal under the evening sky, with rampant vines and colorful flowers muted in shadowy hues. The flowers resembled dancing ballerinas. I think they would have been purple in the sun.

Lucy ran past her mother to stand on the edge of a large pond.

Paula yelled, "Don't get too close!" and turned to smile in our direction. "She loves the water."

I smiled back. "Is she a swimmer?"

"No." There was a hardness to her tone as she set the large woven basket down that she'd been working on and walked over to greet me. "I'm Paula. It's real nice to have you here."

She was thin, wearing a loose, faded dress that hung all the way down to her ankles. Her hair was tied in a bun, but the light brown and blonde waves fought back. She had a russet complexion, though it was hard to distinguish whether it was natural or an even tan. As Paula moved closer, I could see the sun's effects around her eyes and brow. She was young and old alike. Her chameleon appearance was stunning.

"Thank you for allowing us to stay here with your family."

"Don't be so formal. Seth's an old friend. We'd like to see him more often." There was no sense of longing or history between them other than friendship, which eased the slight pang of jealousy that had momentarily stirred.

Lucy made a small noise that caught our attention.

Paula gasped when she caught sight of her daughter walking across a freshly fallen tree hovering over the water. She and Seth ran toward the girl.

"Get away from it, baby!" Paula screamed.

Seth was already at the water's edge but did nothing, horrified.

The grip on the bottom of Lucy's shoes gave out from under her. When I blinked, the silhouette of the little girl was replaced by a splash.

Paula screamed, "No!" It was guttural, a wildness not heard since man's first footprint on the world. Only a parent could scream with such feral pain coursing through each breath.

The edge of the pond failed to contain her as she flew past Seth, stopping in the middle of the fallen tree trunk.

"Paula, step back!" Seth yelled. The authority in his voice surprised me.

Not understanding why someone hadn't jumped in after

the little girl, I changed course. I veered from Seth and Paula, swerving left.

Paula reached for Seth, allowing him to wrench her back to shore. They barely had time to register my airborne body as it splashed, disappearing beneath the eerie, dark water.

# Chapter Twenty-seven

I expected to swim blindly through muck, my own panic brimming until we both succumbed to the cold nothingness. I was ready to swim as fast and as deep as I ever had in my life, searching with gut instinct alone for that cute little girl, hopeful that I could return her to her mother's arms.

When I opened my eyes, ready to acclimate to the darkness, I almost lost my breath. Unidentifiable balls of light floated through the dark water, surrounding me like stars. Some were motionless, while others streaked by with such speed they left glowing trails behind. And then something frighteningly new emerged: translucent figures floating ubiquitously. At first, only one or two drifted out of the obscure abyss. Then more came, arms outstretched, stopping short of touching me, though it was clear they possessed no greater wish. Some were whole. Others appeared from the waist up, sometimes missing the left or right side of their bodies.

I didn't understand what was going on. Were they ghosts? Did they wish to harm me? As I swam, it was clear they were following me. Trying to fight back the hysteria growing within, I used their unnatural light to search for Lucy. I swam past them, between them, and through them.

I decided to search outward for Lucy's soul. It was my last option and only hope. Too much time was passing. We would both die very soon without oxygen.

Slowing my arms and legs, I floated limply, giving

every bit of energy to her soul. If she were close in proximity, my power as the Cypher might save her. But I was met by the horror that her soul was one in a tub of thousands. One of the closest diaphanous faces slammed right through me before getting sucked into my chest. My scream tried to cut the water as I pushed the thing back out. As I swam backward, another filled the void. After countless attempts, I stopped the search. Thankfully, I hadn't read any of them and didn't want to without knowing what they were.

Precious seconds passed. My lungs burned and my unhealed body ached. The souls watched, studying every move. Maybe my every thought. Finally, I shoved them in every direction, and they gave way to a concrete figure. I swam to Lucy, tugging her clothes free from the half-forms. They grabbed at her, pulled at her clothes and hair, kneading her flesh with malleable fingers. The shimmering forms were only successful when Lucy's own skin wavered between shimmery and solid. She was being attacked and they were winning.

When I swam to her, I could see her mouth open, frozen with fright. I opened my hand and she filled it with a tight grip. The attack stopped as soon as I pulled her to my chest, as if they were afraid to challenge me for her. But that fueled a frenzy. The balls of light swam more rapidly and dared to come closer. The beings circled us like sharks, waiting for any opportunity to steal Lucy from my arms.

We were twenty feet under, which doesn't sound like much until you're on the bottom looking up. I swam with one hand and held her with the other, making certain not to loosen my grip. In the peculiarity of the mute water, I made a promise not to emerge without her.

I gasped for air as my head broke the surface. It was an

awful noise. Seth and Paula looked up from where they had collapsed beside the pond.

"I have her!" My throat felt restricted, my words rough. Tugging Lucy to the surface, I yelled, "She's okay! We're okay."

They ran over and pulled us from the water's grip. Lucy fell into her mother, crying out, "I'm sorry, Mama," over and over. But Paula didn't look at all angry. I think she was too busy thanking God.

Struggling for a clear breath, I leaned back into Seth's chest and coughed as though someone had dragged nails down the inside of my throat. When I was able to stop choking, I asked, "What's in there?"

"Souls." He spoke into my hair.

"Dead?"

"Some of them."

I tried to stand, but he pulled me back down into his arms.

Frustrated with his answer, I struggled to make sense of it. "That's not an answer."

"This is the River of Souls."

"But it's a pond."

Paula, gripping Lucy with white knuckles, said, "The name refers to the path of the souls, not the body of water. The River of Souls never stops. Some are waiting to be born. Some died, but it wasn't time for 'em yet, so their souls come here. Others were never meant to be part of this world, so they're trapped and angry."

I lowered my voice for Lucy's sake. "They were after her. They wanted to keep her. I could feel it."

Tears welled in Paula's eyes. "I know." She squeezed Lucy so hard into her body, the little girl was in danger of disappearing into the material of her mother's dress.

Seth and I stood. He told Paula to take Lucy inside for some dry clothes. Once they were out of earshot, he confided, "No one's allowed in the water."

"That little girl was about to die." My tone was full of scorn and I refused to hide it. "I'm so sorry I had to, *gasp*, break a rule to save her."

He moved in front of me, blocking my view of the still water. "This water is dangerous. Promise you won't ever go in it again, for any reason. Even if it's me in there, or..." He hesitated. "Gabriel."

"I don't know how you or Paula can reconcile it to yourselves, but I won't ever stand idly by while a child, or anyone else, suffers a death like the one Lucy almost experienced. She was seconds away from death."

His voice was hushed. "Ell...she *is* dead."

"What?" I pulled wet strands of hair out of my face, slicking them into place. "Lucy's fine." I pointed to the house. "She's alive, Seth."

Shaking his head, he exhaled intensely. His explanation was devoid of any true emotion, maybe because it would have slammed his heart with a hammer, otherwise.

"She was a healthy five-year-old until her brother killed her four years ago. Accidentally, of course."

My eyes were glued to him.

"He never had the same morals as humans often do, but he never meant to hurt Lucy on purpose. Paula's husband, Cole, was the caretaker of the River of Souls. She won't speak about it, but I know Cole made a deal with someone —or something—to bring Lucy back about a year after they buried her over there." He pointed to a far-off field, where two headstones rested beneath the stars.

"Who's there?" It sounded like the beginning of a bad joke. I already knew the punchline, but had to ask anyway.

"Paula's husband and fifteen-year-old son. Cole traded his son's life for Lucy's. But he couldn't do that and live with himself so, on the warmest, brightest day that summer, he cooked a huge bacon and egg breakfast for the family. Afterward, he pulled his own boy into the water and sank them both." Taking a moment, he closed his eyes and held them shut tightly before saying, "It's dangerous to even touch the water here, Ell, because it kills everyone. No one is immune." A mixture of relief and pain shaped his features as he took my face between his palms. "Why are you?"

# Chapter Twenty-eight

Seth and Paula practically ran in opposite directions once we went inside. Lucy was effectively cloaked deep in the cabin's interior. And I hadn't dared one step from my room after changing into dry clothes amid a growing buzz of muddled voices.

I was glad Danny reminded Seth to pick up the bag I'd packed, but I felt a little silly sliding on the yellow raglan, three-quarter-sleeved shirt with orange writing that asserted, "When it's good, it's really gouda." Seth had obviously taken the liberty to flip through the side of my closet I hadn't worn in years. Granted, the thin, oversized shirt looked good with my distressed stretch jeans. For the finishing touch, I threw on a charcoal hoodie because my hair was still wet.

I had a few minutes to myself, so I decided to study my injuries in the small vanity mirror. My body was healing amazingly fast. The small cuts and scrapes were no more than subtle discolorations. The knife wound was mending slower on the inside, but I was no longer walking around with a gaping, bloody hole in my body. The nasty vamp bite —the one that would haunt my dreams and stalk my fear— was the slowest to heal. Paula had given me a roll of bandages to cover it. Not because it aided in recovery, but because it was a chilling reminder to them—to me—of what this world was capable of doing in the supernatural shadows.

The chatter abruptly ended. I sat on the bed, waiting...

for anything. And then someone yelled right as the door swung open. Gabriel stood in the doorway with a menacing posture, clearly lacking his stylish attire and normally cool composure. He loomed in brown leather shin-high boots with buckles across the calves. And he wore ripped jeans with no designer label in sight. His shirt looked as though it hadn't seen a washing machine in months. Thankfully, it didn't have an accompanying smell. It was just littered with stains, ruining what used to be a very posh dress shirt.

His movements were different, too. Unlike his usually controlled form, he moved erratically, as if someone had connected him to a car battery. What called the most attention was his face. I was looking at a face I should have recognized, but it made me take a step backward. His expression was alien, his eyes wrong. Something restless lived there, staring at me as if it could eat me or love me. Or be happy doing both.

"Gabriel?"

Seth stepped in behind him. "Not Gabriel." He was unhappy but not panicked.

As soon as I backpedaled another step, the stranger grabbed me, spun me in a circle, and dipped me, pressing my body indecently close to his.

With a little squirming on my part and a slight battle on his, I gained enough distance to look him in the eyes. "Who are you?"

The stranger pulled me to his chest. "Gideon."

"Gabriel's brother?"

He let go, looking quite pleased. "You've heard of me."

"You're twins?"

Distastefully, he countered, "Apparently you haven't heard enough."

Seth groaned. "Am I the only one over the twin thing?" Then he collapsed on the bed.

"Jesus," I muttered.

"You kiss my brother with that mouth?"

Caught off guard, I glanced at Seth before stuttering, "I've never kissed Gabriel."

Gideon stepped closer. "Wanna kiss me? I like it dirty."

"She won't be kissing either of you," Seth asserted.

Paying no attention to him, Gideon seemed much cheerier as he addressed me. "I'm the better-at-everything twin." He winked. "It seems we have something in common. It's fate. Marry me!" He dropped down on one knee, looking quite sincere.

"Um...no."

He stood, unruffled. "Hard to get. Alluring. Say it again."

Was this guy for real? I didn't have to answer like a puppet. "No."

"That drives me crazy. Say it again."

"I'm not falling for that again. Why are you here? Do you know where your brother is?"

"Oh, he's met a horrible fate."

I gasped.

He smirked. "Trapped in a cheap hotel room with dirty, low-thread-count sheets and no room service."

Not amused by his humor, I demanded, "Tell me everything you know."

"Since you're all bothered, I can't say no. You call to me like a siren in the mist."

"Yeah, I hear that a lot." I must have gone insane. Finally, after everything, I was absolutely batty and Gideon was my punishment. "Just tell me."

"He's safe, handcuffed in a dungeon. Don't worry, the dragons don't bite."

Before I replied, my hands landed on Gideon's chest as I shoved him against the nearest wall. I was closer than stupid to a strange, insane vampire. Even though he was the same height as Gabriel, I leaned in so that we stared at each other. I don't think he expected such intensity. It helped that my face was still bruised and slightly swollen, lending to the badass vibe that was, otherwise, an alien concept to my petite, youthful appearance.

I practically growled, "Give me Gabriel's exact location. For your personal safety, answer without jacking around."

Gideon looked as though I was breaking every preconceived expectation he had of the Cypher. His insanity drained faster than a sink, leaving a serious residue. "He's in a cellar. I'm not telling where. Not yet. How do I know? Because it was my idea to put him there."

"If you harm him—"

He waved my threat away with the brush of a hand. "He's fine. Probably having the time of his life, fulfilling a fetish fantasy or catching up on his beauty rest."

Each word compelled me to press harder. My hands hurt and my left arm started to quiver.

Gideon's eyes dropped to let me know that he'd noticed. With a nudge of his wrist, he shifted my shirt collar to see the bandage. The smell of my blood roiled his senses, causing his viridian eyes to erupt. While my heart beat faster than a tribal drum, I noticed that his eyes, in either form, were more on the blue side of viridian than green. Gabriel's eyes were pure emerald. Such an inconsequential difference was, nonetheless, imperative to my heart.

Artfully shifting back to his human gaze, he peered down with his head against the wall, smirk reestablished. "I'll tell you, but only if the others leave the room. However, I'm an animal and I'm sure you would never agree—"

"Everyone out." I didn't need time to think it over or give him the pleasure of trying to scare me again. Well, he was a little scary in that caged-dog kind of way. But there was information to acquire. I didn't waste time.

I couldn't help but notice Seth hadn't budged and Paula hovered in the doorway. Trying to control my temper, which was teetering on the edge of failure, I slowly reiterated, "Everyone who is not a Cypher or clinically insane, please leave."

Gideon raised his left eyebrow, full well knowing that he wasn't the Cypher, but I wasn't asking his crazy ass to leave.

Seth spoke up. "You can't trust him, Ell."

"Maybe not, but I'd appreciate it if you and Paula would give us some space. If he tries to bite, I'll—" Waving my arms, I settled on, "I'll scream louder than a flock of frightened guineas and you can rescue me, okay?"

After thinking it over, he caved. "Okay. We'll be right outside the room."

"Thank you."

They left, shutting the door. I heard Paula walk down the hallway, but I knew Seth stood right outside, just as he'd vowed.

Gideon leaned down and spoke low. "If you're in pain, let go. I don't bite on the first date. *Much.*"

He could have tossed me through a wall with a flick of his eyelash, so it was silly to try physical intimidation on him. I lowered my arms. God, did that feel good!

"Tell me everything you know."

"If I tell you everything, you might not have further use for me."

"If you don't, I don't have any use for you."

"True. I concede. I'll even help rescue him if you pin me to the wall again."

*Gross*. "You need a girlfriend." A twinkle of hope filled his gaze. For good measure, I added, "Not me."

"But you look so gouda in that shirt. It's hard to resist a woman who takes fashion risks."

"I set the bar high for women everywhere."

*I wanted to kill Seth.*

Gideon laughed. It was a lighter version of Gabriel's. Of course, I'd never heard a sincere laugh from Gabriel. Everything about his brother seemed to be more animated and uninhibited.

"I surmise from your humor that you're healing well?"

"Yeah. I never expected it to be this quick, actually."

I was happy but it also freaked me out. This was my proof to everyone that I was the real Cypher. It also made me face the fact that I was different from all of them, vampires and humans. Surviving the River of Souls for unknown reasons only drove it home. My luck concerning both incidents was a badge as well as a cross to bear.

Gideon was fascinated by my reaction. "You're very candid with your expressions, though you keep your true feelings safeguarded. Trust issues. That's hot."

I gave him a kiss-my-ass expression. "Don't go there, Gideon."

"Give me a shard to dream."

"Not gonna happen."

"Fine." He sighed dramatically. "Let's talk business."

He settled down long enough to have a serious talk. Gideon had gotten wrapped up with people who knew my sister and her husband. It just so happened, he was hanging out with them and, apparently, didn't want to be left out of the fun. Not that I would label any of this fun. In his defense, he claimed to know nothing of my sister's dealings with the Mass.

"Why would you leave Gabriel to starve in a cellar?"

"We're brothers. Brothers kid."

"That's not kidding, that's attempted murder."

He shrugged. "I wanted to meet you without him skulking about. Don't worry, his rescue was imminent from the time you groped me. We may even have time to play a round of miniature golf before it's all over."

Ignoring the majority of what he said, I asked, "What's so great about meeting me?"

"You've captivated my brother. I wanted to meet the woman capable of such a deed."

Captivated? No way in hell!

"Think what you want, buddy. You obviously don't have all your dominoes lined up, but whatever."

He leaned his back against the wall, very reminiscent of Gabriel's habit. "Think what *you* want, Cypher. I have no reason to lie."

"I'm not lying, either."

"Not if you believe what you say."

"Maybe you should keep your opinions to yourself."

He didn't like that. I was annoying him. Good.

"Gideon, we need to save Gabriel before my sister lets him play with the Mass again."

"I would never have left him if they were near." He seemed utterly affronted by the implication.

"Well, they're pretty bloody sneaky. If my sister has anything to do with it, he'd have better luck kissing copperheads."

His eyes lit up. "That reminds me! I have a very pleasant surprise for you. I couldn't meet the Cypher without bearing a gift."

Great. Would it be headless chickens or flowers?

He saw my unease. "It will be unforgettable. I promise."

"That's what worries me."

He smiled. "It will be very helpful in our plan. Let's include Seth in the conversation before I unveil your gift."

I agreed because I didn't want to waste time trying to convince Gideon to stay out of it. Actually, he'd proved to be somewhat helpful. But all I could think of was Gabriel's safety.

A strong sense of possession overpowered my senses. I wanted him back in one piece. He would have demanded the same if he were in my position.

Damn, he *had* done the same thing.

Secretly, I admitted that Gabriel and I shared some questionable feelings. However, it wasn't the right time to indulge my psyche. It was enough to acknowledge that our friendship bordered on deeper emotions.

I also needed to come up with a good plan that involved Seth being far away from the cellar. Fifty miles would be too close. I had feelings for Gabriel, but that part of myself that enjoyed long walks and rainy day cuddles carried a majority vote for Seth.

I eyed Gideon decisively. "Let's do this."

"I see why Gabriel likes you. You're spunky."

# Chapter Twenty-nine

After some consideration, Seth and I agreed it was best not to involve Paula. After all, she had a daughter to safeguard, and we didn't want to be responsible for what would happen if the Mass got hold of either of them. Once she agreed—more than relieved, I'd like to add—the three of us came up with a plan. Well, Gideon already had the plan. Seth and I simply nodded as he told us our parts. Thankfully, my wish to keep Seth out of the hot zone would come true.

Gideon and I were going to infiltrate my sister's house, where Gabriel was being held captive. Seth would wait a few miles away with the getaway car, until Gideon signaled.

Oh, and the best part: how were we going to break into the fortress? My present from Gideon was a very pissed off sister stuffed in the trunk of her own vehicle. Gideon had stolen it immediately upon kidnapping her.

Call me old-fashioned, but I was starting to like the crazy, spontaneous son of a bitch.

The worst part of the plan: because I would be walking into the fortress as Ellenore, I had to lop my hair off. Seth had the honors. When he was finished, my hairstyle was sadly reminiscent of Gabriel's. Gideon found it amusing. Even giggled, the bastard. Maybe bad karma had come back to bite me in the ass.

The plan took action immediately. Gideon had the foresight to snag a few of my sister's clothes. I decided on a stretch-satin halter with black detailing that tied around my neck, matching black pants, and dainty black sandals. This was the most expensive outfit I'd ever worn. I've always been a no-frills girl, but damn if I didn't look good at my sister's expense.

Ellenore was stashed in an abandoned house nearby, and we were ready to charge off into the night...right after I applied makeup over the remaining bruises.

Seth drove for two hours, entertaining Gideon's half-assed directions. I practically leapt from the car as Seth parked off a desolate road. His job was done until we called him. A weight lifted, just knowing he was safe. Now, we could focus on Gabriel's safety.

Waving good-bye, we walked across the road into the woods.

"How far is it?"

Gideon slowed his pace, moving to my right. "Three miles."

"That's more than a skip and a jump."

He glowered, more than a little exasperated. "He couldn't drive us to the front door. They think your sister has locked herself in her bedroom, in one of her moods."

"But you took her car."

"Do I look incompetent?" He didn't give me a chance to answer. "I planned this to the letter. Everyone believes that her car is out for detailing. It seems a no-good soul scratched it."

By his expression, he didn't have to tell me I was staring at that darling soul.

"Thorough bugger, aren't you?"

He thought about it before answering, "Yes," with moxie.

"Since we have time, can I ask you something?"

"Always, my little titmouse."

I ignored that. We kept walking at a moderate pace and only spoke above a whisper.

"What's my sister like?"

"Shouldn't you know?"

Gideon realized his error as my breath wavered so minutely that a human never would have noticed. He filled the silence so I didn't have to. I noted the compassion.

"She is maybe like me. When she's happy, the world revolves for her. When she's angry, she thinks, as it revolves for her, so too shall it burn and weep for her. Since it doesn't, her anger flares out at her closest companions. Lately, it's even scorched the Members, who are growing weary of the toasty treatment."

"Why is she so angry?"

"Perhaps because the chosen one is supposed to be strong, but she couldn't do it. She's weak."

"Cautious, maybe. Ellenore was never weak."

Softly, he corrected, "Not as you knew her. She's very different now. The weak at heart always compensate with the most rage."

My heart wrenched in my chest. I could never express in words the pain I felt for Ellenore. She could have had so much, but she wasted it because she didn't believe it could really be hers without starting a vampire war. Don't get me wrong. The evil twin had to go down, and seeing her hog-tied in her own trunk was priceless. But part of me just didn't want to let go of who she was. Optimistic, possibly, that she could still be that person.

My companion took advantage of the silence. "I get to ask you a question."

Damn, I forgot the unspoken rule. Trying to throw him off, I confessed, "Yes, I'm wearing underwear."

Gideon's gaze raked the length of my body thoughtfully,

though his question surprised me. "What are your feelings toward my brother?"

"Whoa!" My strangled voice echoed through the surrounding woods. "What kind of question is that at a time like this?"

"A perfectly timely one. You're risking your life for him. Possibly, another meeting with the Mass. All for my brother. It's more than appropriate to ask."

"Well, I don't know how I feel about him. He's kind of a friend, and he's been helping me. I owe him."

"You owe him nothing. I refuse to believe this level of loyalty is propelled by guilt. What are your true feelings?"

I was angry for being put on the spot. He was a stranger, for crying out loud. "I don't know what I feel, okay? I haven't stopped to think about it."

"That, I absolutely believe."

What the hell?

In a loud whisper, I decreed, "I am not talking about this with you."

"Fine. But you will have to tell yourself, and even Gabriel, at some point."

"If he's not in a million tiny pieces, I promise to make time when the world isn't exploding. Right now, it's not a priority."

"When this is all over, make it one." Though his statement sounded like a command, it wasn't. "If you offer hope, only to snatch it away, it will break him." Gideon's pushy behavior was clearly driven by concern.

"You act as though he's a glass ornament." Taking care to watch each step over and around the cluttered forest floor, I pointed out, "If Gabriel actually has a breaking point, it isn't me."

Gideon's voice was sharp. "He has lost people close to

him. That makes him breakable. And you have more sway over him than I'm comfortable admitting."

My anger radiated. "Who has he lost, Gideon? Enlighten me. We've spent years irritating each other but no time actually getting to know one another, let alone stir up this great romance everyone keeps accusing us of having. Please, tell me about the man I'm supposed to be enthralled with."

He stopped walking. "Our family."

"Your human family?" I was shocked and felt foolish for not thinking of his human ties.

"Our only family."

I didn't know how to respond, so I kept my mouth shut as he recounted the details of their deceased loved ones.

"Our older brother, Lyle, died from a snakebite while farming when he was fourteen. He was a hard worker. When Gabriel and I were side-by-side, causing trouble, he was our father's faithful companion in the fields."

"That's a horrible way to die."

Gideon acted as if I hadn't spoken. "Three years later, Agnes, our eleven-year-old sister, ran into a flaming barn. She was trying to save our pigs." His smile was saturated in sorrow. "In the commotion, we didn't realize she had run in until it collapsed overhead. Her screams were as loud as the fire was high, and then there was nothing but the crackling of wood."

The peach fuzz covering my arms stood on end.

"We fought to get to her, Gabriel the hardest. His fingers were bled raw, his body covered in burns. She had been dead a long time before we claimed her small body in the coming light of dawn."

Completely sober, I muttered, "That must have been devastating."

"It wasn't until Ruby was lost that torment consumed our mother. Ruby was nine."

"What happened?" Someone had pushed *pause* on our mission. In the still of the woods, I listened to Gideon's story as if it were the only thing in the world. I'd caught a glimpse into his heart, and it left mine feeling as though someone was pounding an empty cooking pot with a mallet.

"Ruby was sick. Nothing could be done. It was the nineteenth century. After her burial, our parents grew apart from each other, then from us."

"Did they recover?" I was sure the answer would be yes.

"As years passed, our father showed improvement, but Mother was heartsick. She deteriorated at a frightening pace. He made us leave so she could wither in privacy."

"And that was it? They sent you away?"

He nodded. "Until he called us home just after our twenty-third birthday. We expected it was for her funeral. We were met by a horror far worse."

What could be worse? Not wanting to ask, I found I had no choice. My voice was soft yet persistent. "When did you die, Gideon?"

"Five days later." He smiled, but it was sick, anemic. "Our parents had found a way to cheat the Grim Reaper. Mother befriended a cauldron of vampires—a ruthless nest of the undead—and made a deal to save us all. Father disagreed, but her rapid improvement and newfound hope was enough to sway him. Gabriel and I walked right into their trap. Were taken against our wills to see the Cypher."

I blushed, though it had been a Cypher from long ago, not me.

"Soon after, they turned us."

"Why did they want you?" This was a serious question. Vampires didn't create vampires for any other reason than business. Not in the last two hundred years. The Cypher's revelations would have been the true catalyst for Gabriel and Gideon's change.

He shrugged. "We didn't have time to ask."

"Did your parents recover?"

"Maybe in Heaven. They, too, entered a trap." He smiled again. This time, it cast a wicked shadow.

"What happened to the vampires?"

"We killed most of them. Burned their ashes, buried our parents, and left home." He forced a laugh. "It was a busy evening."

I was speechless.

We continued walking, silent until Gideon cleared his throat. "I noticed you took a swim earlier."

"You saw that?"

There was a hint of satisfaction. "I don't miss much."

"Good to know." Rubbing my hair, still surprised by its new length, I defended my actions. "That little girl needed help. It wasn't a big deal."

"To you. To the rest of us, it was exceptional. Unheard of, some might dare say."

I stopped walking. "Why? Seth asked why I'm so special." Raising my arms and letting them drop to my side, I asked, "So, why?"

Gideon made a show of his annoyance. "You don't think much of me, yet you expect me to tell you everything I know. You call me crazy, yet I know more than anyone else." His accusation was almost identical to Gabriel's. Apparently, I was giving the Vertiline boys a complex.

"Just tell me why jumping into a creepy pond to save a child is unheard of."

"Oh, that?" He shrugged. "I don't know. You must be some kind of freak."

I rolled my eyes. "Very comforting. Thank you."

He bowed from his waist, dramatically snapping his body upright. "How else may I serve you?"

"Is that an offer or a threat?"

He cracked a smile and I couldn't help but laugh. It was short-lived as we arrived at our destination.

# Chapter Thirty

A clearing formed, giving way to a huge complex. It was the epitome of wealth. The monetary equivalent could have sustained countless charities. This was Ellenore's house? A township could fit inside the monstrosity festering over the otherwise beautiful landscape. The walls were shiny and dark. I didn't recognize the material. It didn't seem to have a traditional front or backyard. Rather, the manicured structure bucked against the natural setting with the loaded thrills and distaste of a zoo animal's habitat.

"This is her house?"

"One of them."

Well, la-di-da. What the hell did she need my soul for? Her material life seemed more than adequate. Luxury had always represented happiness to Ellenore. Maybe she'd finally realized that money couldn't buy life. I could only cross my fingers. Wait. Should I cross my fingers now that she wanted more? More being my soul.

Gideon grabbed my wrist. "We need to enter through the porch attached to her bedroom. Once inside, there's a hidden staircase in the linen closet right outside her bedroom door. You will find Gabriel in the basement."

"What about you?"

"I'll enter through the front door and act as a diversion." Almost bragging, he noted, "I'm very good at that. Once you've had enough time to find the door, I will make my way over to help gather my brother. Questions?"

"I feel like I'm geocaching for your brother. Is the basement smaller than the rest of the house or do I need coordinates to find him?"

His eyes grew wide, letting me know he thought my question was a waste of time.

"Never mind. I'll use his cologne as a reference."

"My brother doesn't wear cologne," he muttered offhandedly.

"Are you serious? He wears *awful* cologne. It smells like a pile of rotten fruit in a heated, airtight room. It's so completely horrible, it makes my nose want to crawl up inside my skull."

He grinned as though he were the cat who ate the canary. "Then he's playing with you. Gabriel would never smell like that on purpose."

Dueling emotions stirred deep in my gut. Gabriel had subjected me to that poison on purpose? *For years!* What an asshole! I hoped he wasn't dead already because I wanted to kill him myself.

Suppressing his amusement, Gideon asked, "Any more questions?"

"One." I forced myself to release the mounting frustration and focus on our mission. "How will he know that it's me and not Ellenore?"

"Do you make it a point to underestimate all vampires or just my brother?"

I didn't waste time arguing. I walked away.

Finding the porch and infiltrating Ellenore's bedroom was easy. Once inside, I couldn't help but snoop. Hey, not a lot! Her room was reminiscent of the one she had while we were growing up. There was an overstuffed mattress sprawled across a queen-sized frame, every bit of the material covered in lace and floral prints. Surprisingly, she still owned the turquoise baroque companion loveseat to the chair she'd given me. The one her husband had sat in during the reading of his soul in my spare room.

The walls were a bashful shade of pink, sprinkled with dark picture frames. Unable to stop myself, I inspected the photographs, secretly hoping to see my face staring back. But I was met with disappointment. They were photographs of famous monuments. Places Ellenore had visited, I presumed.

Her closet was crammed with the latest fashions. She hadn't even taken the time to remove most of the price tags. Shoes lined the bottom of the closet walls. They looked as though they were in danger of marching right out of the room. Ellenore never took care of her things.

I peeked behind another door to find a much smaller closet filled with organized men's apparel. It was the only evidence that a man had been given clearance to enter the gaudy sanctuary. Hell, as a woman, I didn't find the place very comforting.

I hadn't forgotten Gabriel. Time was limited, but I figured he wouldn't begrudge me a few moments to dump Ellenore's expensive perfume on the floor on my way out.

Nothing rustled as I listened through the door before opening it, staring into the hallway. As Gideon mentioned, there was a hidden spiral staircase in the linen closet. It was a tight squeeze. And I was proud of myself for remembering to close the linen door before descending the steep metal stairs.

The air shifted as I carefully regarded each step. The warmth of the main floor had vanished, replaced by a relentless dampness. My nose crinkled while my brain listed all the types of mold spores I was probably inhaling.

The room at the bottom of the stairs was six by six. The floor was nothing but dirt. It literally looked as though someone had taken a gigantic shovel and dug a large hole in the ground under the house. With the aid of a wall-mounted lamp, I could see wooden beams holding the ceiling in place, which gave me peace of mind that the whole damn thing wouldn't cave in.

There was a door next to the oil lamp. When I opened it, I couldn't help but find myself impressed by what lay on the other side. Gideon's earlier reference to it being a basement was misleading. It was a full-blown house. The furniture was conservative, the decorations minimal, and the windows...absent. Perfect for a vampire and his or her twenty closest companions. The place was huge. How was I ever going to find Gabriel?

I spotted two hallways, one on either side of the grand living room, both plagued by a row of doors. It would have been nice for Gideon to mention which room Gabriel was being held in.

In a bid to stop wasting time, I slowly tiptoed down the hallway to the right, taking a moment to notice the huge tapestries hanging on the walls.

The rooms were silent. A few of the doors were cracked, but all I found were bedrooms that reminded me of swanky hotel rooms. Halfway down the hallway, my hand accidentally yanked the edge of a tapestry free, uncovering a hidden door. Quickly, I ran down the rest of the hallway, swooshing the material aside, uncovering a total of four doors. I opened one to discover a dirt-floor room with dirt walls. It was completely contrary to the civilized rooms.

I forced myself to focus my thoughts on Gabriel's soul. Not on what it had said, but how it had felt. Remembering the feel of it in my chest, rolling it around, trying to reshape the foreign puzzle piece. Each had its own shape.

*Where was Gabriel's shape?*

Closing my eyes, I surrendered my instincts to the hollow space in my chest. Without delay, a tingle crept into my chest, tugging my body forward. When I opened my eyelids, I stood in front of a door at the end of the long hallway and turned the knob.

Gabriel's slack form lay on the ground. He was on his side, back turned toward me. No movement. I wanted to run to his aid, but he could be sleeping, which would pose a danger if I startled him. Worse, he could be consumed with hunger, waiting for an idiot with a new haircut to fall into his arms for dinner.

I inched into the room. Each step closer brought a new prayer to my lips. There were still no signs of life. I decided that it was best to shuffle along the wall until I could see his face. There wasn't a lot of space between us, but it was the most I would get.

"Gabriel?" I whispered.

Nothing.

As I reached the far wall, partly gripped by the primal need to run, I had a clear view of the front of his body. The light from the hallway was dim, though it was apparent that the trivial wounds I'd inflicted days ago were gone, replaced by a fresh barrage of bloody marks. Nothing life-threatening. Maybe Gideon had been telling the truth. Gabriel was probably hungry and pissed but otherwise unscathed.

Keeping that in mind, I kneeled in front of him. My knees nestled into the dirt as I leaned closer.

Softly, I announced, "Gabriel, I'm here."

Gideon appeared in the doorway. "Get away!"

Gabriel's eyes snapped open. My efforts to scramble backward on my ass were thwarted by his icy, dead hands latching around my wrists.

A scream slipped from between my dry lips.

# Chapter Thirty-one

Gabriel had caught the idiot!

"If you scream again, he will rip your throat out."

I froze. Gideon was right. If I fought or showed resistance, Gabriel's predatory instincts would take over and any chance of survival would be extinguished. If I remained calm, his senses might awaken in time to *not* rip my throat out.

His eyes were raging emerald wells, a deadly fusion of undead primordial cravings. And his breath was shallow, purely manufactured to lull me into a false sense of security. It willed my pulse to slow. To release my tense muscles and anxiety. To give up the fight.

While I pretended to be a mannequin, Gideon slid gracefully across the room until we were separated by no more than three feet. I thought he had a great plan of action or wise words that would help me not die. Instead, he whispered in a singsong voice, "You should have waited for me."

Matching his tone, I replied, "Don't point out the obvious. Get him off."

Gabriel's hands were stronger than metal shackles around my wrists. Because I hadn't struggled, his grip remained firm rather than bone-crushing.

Gideon seemed to be thinking up a Plan B. Mental note: think of Plan B before it becomes Plan A.

*Ugh.*

Those green orbs drank me in. If that weren't bad

enough, Gabriel ran his chin the length of my neck. His nostrils flared, inhaling my scent as if I were the last Twinkie on Earth. Not comforting.

After waiting for Gideon's miraculous plan that never came, I thought of my own.

I spoke low, as one might to a man on a ledge. "Gideon, he's your brother. Feed him."

He had the balls to look at me like I'd said, "Gideon, let's do a revival of *Gypsy*. That might cheer him up."

"He won't want my blood."

"Why not? He might rip my throat out."

"Yours is more...satisfying."

"Tasty. You were gonna say tasty, weren't you?"

He shrugged. "Yes, but this isn't an appropriate time to argue. We don't have much time."

"It's your neck or mine, and he's *your* brother."

"But he's made his choice. He hasn't even acknowledged my presence—which, I would like to add, makes me feel like a third wheel."

*Oh, come on!* "This is not a therapy session. Get over it."

"I don't blame him. If I had you, he wouldn't be a choice, either."

"Nice, Gideon!"

Raising my voice was stupid. Gabriel's eyes widened with anticipation the instant my temper swelled. Gideon was right. I was wasting time that we didn't have.

"Fine. Gabriel, drink what you want, but keep in mind that I'm not a juice box. You can't have it all. Gideon, leave the room."

"Why?"

"Because you're pissing me off."

"I should be here in case he tries to squeeze the box."

"Don't get cute. I'll take my chances."

He didn't look happy but left. "I'll wait in the hallway."

"We'll be out soon."

Once he was gone, I realized the predicament I'd put myself in. It wouldn't help to cry about it. Even though I was scared, I'd made my decision. If it was my time to die, fine. At least my sister wouldn't get my soul. Bitter, but true.

Gabriel's grip grew stronger. And strangely, as I studied him, my better judgment drained to a mere blood-curdling scream in my head. Ever so slowly, I stretched out beside his heaving form, leaving barely a breath between us. I stared into his face, letting the anger and fear float away.

Feral energy vibrated within him, yet he hadn't acted on it. He just stared back. There was control in him, after all.

Time ticked by. We continued staring into the other's masked face. Soon, I began to see the separation between the man and the vampire. His eyes were able to focus on more than the pulse in my neck. The vampiric discs drained into his human irises. I instantly relaxed when he began to blink. Until my fists unclenched and my toes uncurled, I hadn't realized I'd been bracing for the feast.

A flash of fear entered my mind. I was dressed like Ellenore. Maybe Gabriel was too busy fighting the urge to notice. Or had he been waiting to strike, cultivating my fear before he fed?

He pulled me into his body before I could protest. Another sick feeling swam in my gut, swelling my chest with dread. I was ready to kick and plead my case that I wasn't Ellenore. And maybe I wasn't Myranda, either. I was Ell, a hybrid of two beings, built from a flimsy legacy of horror and obligation. And I wanted to live, damn it! To become more.

My hands found his chest, ready to extract his soul and defend my life. But...he was more interested in cuddling?

His strong arms swept me to his chest, forcing my hands up around his neck. This time, when he brushed his face through my hair and inhaled, I didn't feel like a snack pack. I didn't feel disposable.

"What have you done to your hair?" he inquired in a husky, dry voice.

Go figure! He couldn't fish up a compliment to save his life. He almost sucks me dry and focuses on the one thing I want to ignore. To be optimistic, he didn't rip my heart out.

"How did you know it was me?"

He refused to release me from his firm embrace. "To a human, you're identical. To a supernatural, you smell different. She lathers herself in factory chemicals and dishonesty. You are a flower petal on the tail of a fresh storm. Your eyes are slightly different shades. I catch myself falling into their depths, marveling at the complex web of emotions they express. Hers exude regret and I want to recoil."

"Oh," I breathed.

I wanted to remind him that we didn't have time to snuggle as he whispered the sweetest words anyone had ever dared speak to or about me. But I was more than content lying in the dirt with my head resting against the muscular topography of his chest. Was this considered cheating? Technically, I wasn't dating Seth, though he had expressed major concern over my work-in-progress relationship with Gabriel. Earlier, I had wanted Seth to be my boyfriend. That hadn't changed.

This was some bullshit.

Taking Gideon's advice, probably at the worst possible time, I blurted, "I like you, but I like Seth, too. I have feelings for both of you and that royally pisses me off."

And that was that. It was out there. Take it or leave it. React or ignore it.

Curling me securely into his shoulder, he combed his fingers through my short hair. "Why does that piss you off?"

It was funny to hear Gabriel use that word because he tried not to use profanity whenever possible, though I'd heard him curse like a pirate on more than one occasion.

I smiled but didn't lose sight of the conversation. "I've been alone for so long that I talked myself into thinking it was the right thing. Then you go and prove you're not a total asshole the same time I meet Seth."

More to the air than directed to me, he mused, "The turmoil of the living."

"Don't blame humankind. This dilemma is one part human, two parts vampire. The proof is in the statistics."

A faint chuckle vibrated through his chest. "I'll try not to blame the whole of humanity." Clearing his throat did little good. Each word sounded as though it drew blood as he choked them out. "I'm trying to say, it feels good that you feel something for me...other than derision. We'll figure the rest out later."

"How much later?"

"When later becomes now."

Sarcastically, I muttered, "That cleared everything up. You're starting to sound like your brother."

"You sound like you've already spent too much time with him."

"A little less wouldn't make me tear up."

Lost in a maze of thoughts, I hadn't noticed Gabriel shift onto one elbow so that his face hovered above mine. "Answers are subjective. It's enough that you feel again." The ends of his hair tickled my eyelashes.

"Been keeping tabs?"

"For a long time. You were vibrant in the beginning, like

a new color. Then you shut down until you were in a blackout. You became an echo."

"A ghost," I corrected.

"But the ghost is gaining solidity. Life animates you, once again. I've helped torment you for good reason, but that's over now."

"Why did you do it?"

"You refused to feel joy or love, or even curiosity, but your anger never wavered. If you could be passionate enough to hate, there was hope."

"Did your experiment work?"

"We'll see." Expectations lurked behind his eyes. None he was willing to share.

I didn't call him out because I was betting that, as I waded into some heavy emotional baggage, he was doing the same.

We kind of had eternity to figure it out.

The mood shifted and I wondered whether he might kiss me. A shard of hope twinkled in my eyes. Instead, he hoisted me to my feet.

"I'm undecided about your new haircut. However, the clothes are a blessed change of pace."

"From what, my usual rags?" I spat, trying to suppress my annoyance.

He laughed, calling attention to the stiffness in his shoulders. It made me ache for him. A ghost pain of empathy. Thank God, nothing appeared broken.

Gabriel dusted off his clothes to the best of his limited ability. He must have sincerely adored every inch of me—even the haircut—to willingly canoodle in dirt, his archnemesis.

I decided not to mention that I located his soul using

supernatural GPS. That would remain a secret. At least, for now.

We escaped the small chamber and found Gideon pacing the hall, back and forth. "It's about time."

The air turned frosty as the brothers faced off.

"I'm not happy with you right now, Gideon. It would be smart to control your temper."

"Don't blame me. Worse things would be happening if I hadn't played my part. The Mass want your blood. Not even baby Jesus served as an appetizer could sway them." Cocking a brow, he added, "I've learned things that might blow a little wind up your skirt."

Gabriel eyed me nervously before his well-honed mask of ambiguity cloaked his features. Between gritted teeth, he told Gideon, "We'll talk later."

The lunatic waved him off. "Promises, promises."

Damn. I thought I was in the club. Obviously, they were still keeping secrets. Screw it. I kept quiet because we needed to sneak out of the compound alive.

Emerging from the hidden chamber, Gabriel walked into the bedroom first. Gideon and I reached the door when an unfamiliar voice addressed me—or rather, my sister.

"Mrs. Grant, it's good to see you dressed and about. Would you like dinner?"

While I froze with my back to the young man, Gideon just stood there, picking at his fingernails, nonchalantly waiting for me to reply.

I turned to face the vamp, quickly channeling one of my sister's personalities. I settled on "privileged hag."

"Excuse you?"

The guy, not much older than twenty in human years, tensed. He immediately adjusted his approach, speaking with less charm and more caution. "Dinner. Would you like dinner, Mrs. Grant?" He stumbled over his words.

"You offer me dinner when my ass is already the size of North America? Do you enjoy causing misery?"

"No! No, Mrs. Grant." He was scared. "I only wish to cater to your needs. Those are my orders."

"From my husband?"

"No, Mrs. Grant, from Alexi. She's hunting this evening and gave strict orders. If you were to emerge—I mean, leave your room early this evening—I was to care for any want or need before the ceremony."

"Ceremony?"

"Alexi and Drew have worked very hard to prepare everything as requested. I assumed you knew it was tonight."

"I know all about the ceremony." I didn't even have to pretend to be angry. "Do you think you would be privy to information before me?"

"No."

"Because you know what happens when you assume. You make an ass—"

Gideon placed a hand on my forearm. *Right*. Didn't want to blow my cover.

"How long before the ceremony?"

"An hour, Mrs. Grant."

"Perfect. Since I obviously look like a hideous spotted cow in this outfit, I have to change. Again! Leave us. You've done quite enough."

The poor guy looked stricken. "I meant no such thing, Mrs. Cow—Grant! Mrs. Grant. I apologize for everything I've said to offend you."

I had turned my back so he couldn't see the smile looming on my lips as I heard him add, "I'm sorry for being here."

"Dismissed!"

With that loud command, he immediately disappeared to wherever vampire flunkies go to cry.

Gideon smiled. "Impressive."

"I did live with the prima donna cow for years. It was easy. This was easy, not actually living with her."

We walked into the bedroom to discover a wiry-thin woman standing over Gabriel's limp body while a man sat on his back.

# Chapter Thirty-two

The pallid-skinned beanstalk staring at us was no less than six feet tall, dressed in jeans, a bright-pink T-shirt, and black leather boots that stretched all the way to her knees. Her hair was blonde with spiked black tips. Definitely hard to ignore.

The male remained crouched, ready to fight Gabriel. *If* he were to gain consciousness. The lanky man wasn't taking any chances. He wore head-to-toe black. It must have been easy living a stereotype, never having to worry about fashion trends.

The woman stalked closer. "Gideon's right. That was a very good impersonation of your sister." She had a heavy Southern accent.

I spoke, borderline outraged by her boldness. "Who are you?"

"Alexi. That's Drew." She pointed to the surly-faced man.

"Well, tell Drew to get his lame, dead ass off my friend."

"I don't think so. Gabriel is a very dangerous vampire."

"Apparently not, because he's the one who's unconscious."

"We were able to sneak up and drug him while his attention was on your little show in the hallway. It's hard to tell how long the effects will last. It's different for all of us, so Drew will stay exactly where he is."

"What do you want?"

She laughed. "What a silly question. You, of course."

I had never heard an evil vampire use the word "silly."

That, in its own right, was kind of silly. Didn't the really evil ones stick to scary, hair-raising words?

"Then take me and let him go."

"No, no, no, honey. He is officially a problem. For that matter, so is Gideon." Her brows scrunched. "What happened, honey bear? You lose interest in the game? Your attention span has always been shorter than a dog's snout. Or did you find more interesting players?" Jealousy boiled beneath her overly rouged cheeks.

He addressed her with a smooth temperament. "Alexi, you're a pure Georgia peach, but I was in it to have a little fun. I would never cause my brother real harm."

Her Southern charm dissolved. "Then you'll be judged with them. I won't be able to help you."

I had to speak up. "Who are you referring to? My sister, the Mass, or the Members? There's a maximum number of players in a game for a reason, and this game is definitely at full capacity."

"Don't get smart with me, girl."

"But I never went to college. I have to make up for it somehow."

"Shut up!"

"You still haven't answered my question. Who's involved in the ceremony and why are people being judged?"

She smirked. "You'll find out soon enough."

I was trying to egg her on. Under my breath, I said, "Why waste my breath? Like you know anything."

"Don't pick a fight with me, False Cypher." She closed the distance between us, glaring all the while. In my face, she snarled, "I'll mess your face up a lot worse than those Mass boys."

"Is that what happened to yours?"

She slapped me so hard I hit the bedroom door and slid to a sitting position on the floor.

While I worked on feeling my jaw again, Gideon stepped between me and Satan's lap dog. He held his palms out, signaling peace. "Alexi, so harsh. You never make a good first impression."

"Like I care."

"Tell me where the ceremony is and we'll be there. Only, stop acting like the woman you hate to be. It hurts me to watch."

God as my witness, the crazy chick melted right into him. I guess it really does take one to know one.

"I don't want to be the hard-ass, Gideon, but I have to be. She made me do it." She pointed at me as if I were the bully.

I blurted, "Oh, yes. I'm the ringleader. Chaos ensues wherever I go. Woe is me. Hark, I am a hellion."

Gideon rolled his eyes, acknowledging that I was being a smart-ass and that it had gone unappreciated. Gabriel would have gotten the humor...had he been conscious.

*Maybe not.*

Stubbornly, I apologized. It killed a part of me to do so, but I'd lost sight of the situation. If it helped, I could control my temper.

Gideon turned back to Alexi. "See? She's sorry. Now, tell me where we need to be and we'll go. But don't compromise the flower that you are just to make us go where we will go willingly just for you."

What a mouth! It was jarring to see him transform from a loon to a sophisticated lunatic. I was convinced mental illness ran in their family. Worse yet, Alexi was drooling over him. What issues did she have?

She swooned, with stargazed eyes. "That's all you had to

say, baby. Are you mad?" She purred, "Don't be mad, honey bear."

*Gag!*

"You are a goldfish in a sea of carp. I would never treat a charm with such disrespect. Tell me what you know and we'll rendezvous later."

"You'll bring her sister back?" Gracing me with a scowl, she said, "She's a handful, like this one, but she has to be at the ceremony, too."

"Of course. I knew it would take mere minutes for you to figure out my plan. I'll fetch her at once. Where is the ceremony?"

"In the rose garden, two miles past the south wing."

"Until then, passion opossum."

She blushed.

Give me a break!

Her girlish charm was a memory as she turned to Drew, barking, "Get off him, now! Let's go." And out the back door they disappeared.

As Gideon helped me off the floor, I mumbled, "That girl's a psycho."

"Those are the keepers." He winked.

"Don't wink at me when you say that."

I'd been called a lot of things, but never a psycho. Okay, I was sure some colorful phrases flew after the fire, but other than that, nada.

# Chapter Thirty-three

Gideon escorted us to the rose garden. Once he was done "securing the area," he left to gather my sister and tell Seth he had a longer wait than we originally planned. It made me nervous to split up. I hadn't overlooked what to do with Ellenore, but Gideon had been adamant that she not travel with us. Was it a safety precaution? Maybe there's an unspoken rule that makes riding with your hostage a faux pas. Anyway, I decided to ask.

"Why didn't we bring Ellenore with us? It would have been easier in the long run."

"Ride in the same car with that mouth? I thought you had suffered enough, my dear."

"Oh Gideon, you know how to cheer a girl up. Go on. Get outta here."

Gabriel was still unconscious when Gideon deposited him on a small hill. Once we were alone, I started to notice some sluggish movement. He was waking up.

I sat closely, careful not to touch him. He looked kind of peaceful.

"Gabriel?" I whispered. "Wake up, sleepyhead."

His eyelids opened drowsily and his head rolled sideways, following my voice until he was staring at me. I met his grouchy face with an amused brow lift.

"Don't call me that."

"Sleepyhead?"

"Yes, that. What happened?"

"It sucks to be the one in the dark, doesn't it? Who's

drugged now? Karma, bitch." So I indulged! Sue me. I'd sold the deed and banked the money to earn the right and I didn't plan to pass up the opportunity.

Sounding worse, if that were possible, he asked, "Drugged?"

"Quite." I refused to hold back the humor in my voice.

He sat up groggily, studying our surroundings. I filled in the gaps and he didn't look happy, especially when I told him the part about toothpick Drew sitting on him.

"This is exactly what happens when my brother gets involved in my affairs."

"At least I was included this time. Didn't miss a bit of fun."

"There's a reason why you usually 'miss the fun.' You have a tendency to escalate a situation. You and Gideon together make the end of the world seem like a church meeting."

"And we do it without breaking a sweat."

"This is serious. We're in the very place you shouldn't be."

"I'm aware, but it was either show up willingly and try to stop it or hide for the rest of eternity. Which would you choose? Oh wait, you were too busy sleeping to make any decisions. I forgot."

Lying back in the grass, he covered his face with his arms, letting out a long breath. "You're exasperating."

"No, I'm right, and that pisses you off."

"It does not piss me off." He removed his arms to show the expression on his face. "I'm frustrated because you're right." There was that thousand-dollar smile I hadn't thought I'd get to see.

"Well, look at that. You always talk about my demeanor,

but I think a drug cocktail has done more than a little good for yours."

He countered, "A temporary fix, but I don't think either of us needs to commit to bad habits."

"What's bad? A little comatose time between friends?"

Of course, I was joking, but somewhere in my mind it started to sound like a pretty good idea. Maybe I could sleep through this turmoil. And when I woke up, I would find out that everything had turned out just dandy without me. No more sister issues, no more Cypher interventions, no more creepy meetings, and no more Mass. Or I could drug them and ship them to Australia before they all woke up.

*My deepest apologies, Australia!*

But first, I'd leave my sister soulless and give the Mass a sunbath. And the Members? I would burn down their homes, vacation homes, retreats, timeshares, outhouses, and birdhouses. It would be particularly satisfying when they woke, realizing they'd been duped as thoroughly as they had duped me.

Gabriel noticed my dreamy gaze and commented dryly, "Don't."

"Don't what?" I retired my evil smile and played coy.

"Whatever you're thinking, don't."

"What do you think I'm thinking about?"

"Most likely, the next thing you'll burn down if this evening doesn't go the way you want. So don't."

*Wow.* Vampires couldn't read minds, but that was freakishly accurate. He knew me a lot better than I gave him credit for.

"Fine," I mumbled. "But just for the record, I would never burn down a birdhouse."

Okay, he definitely wasn't a mind-reader. He looked on quizzically. "You are a strange woman."

Sitting under the moonlight, listening to Gabriel refer to me as a woman instead of a Cypher, really marked how times were-a-changing. I was in *wowza* overdrive. But I couldn't ponder the whole Gabriel vs. Seth thing again. These two men were already responsible for my mind not being tip-top in the face of impending doom. I should have worried more about the threats on my life than being sidetracked by a choice I might not live to make.

Gabriel eyed me sympathetically as I closed my own to regroup. We sat quietly and waited for the rest of the pony show to arrive twenty minutes later.

Alexi and Drew did not disappoint.

"You're awake." Alexi sounded dejected as she stood over Gabriel, straddling his legs. He seemed unfazed, though I guess he was less than enthusiastic about her looming stance than he let on.

"I am." His voice was smooth. Not a hint of embarrassment.

"Too bad. I was hoping to do this the easy way."

My brows scrunched. "Do what?" Ask a stupid question...

She simultaneously collapsed onto Gabriel and unsheathed a knife from the top of her boot. As I hopped to my feet, Drew pounced with such force, our entangled bodies landed a good ten feet away from Gabriel and Alexi. My lungs struggled for air while he pinned me to the ground. I tried to wiggle free. He purposely squeezed my bandaged shoulder. I fought every bit of will not to scream out in pain.

"You're not going anywhere, Cypher." He dropped his head so our noses touched. "Too bad we can't do this naked." Drew's hips ground down on mine.

"You know what? You may be dragging me to a soulless

afterlife, but I have standards." I didn't know whehter it was his laughter or that he hadn't moved yet that disturbed me more.

"Lex, I wanna keep this one!"

"She's not yours, Drew! Keep it in your pants, damn it, and get her to the circle."

Alexi sounded tense, probably because she was exerting every ounce of strength trying to pin Gabriel to the ground. She pierced him in the stomach with her knife. At least it was a good distance from his heart. His pain wasn't apparent right away, but there was a growing tension around his eyes that most people wouldn't have noticed.

As we both lay on the ground, staring into each other's eyes, I decided that I could sell my soul if I had reassurances that Gabriel would make it through this alive. Er, undead. Animated.

What could I say? The bastard had grown on me.

"What's with the two-timing? You made a deal with Gideon. We got to the site on our own."

Alexi shifted impatiently. "Gideon ain't here, and I'm not risking my hide."

"Your hide?"

She spoke slowly for my benefit. "If you escape on my watch, that's my hide."

Gabriel tried to relax under the woman. "You're making this more difficult than it should be."

"Don't talk to me, boy." And then she twisted the knife enough to make him flinch.

"Hey, Alexi! If you call off your dog, I'll go willingly. No tricks. No fights. But you have to leave Gabriel out of this. He's just doing his job."

Gabriel clenched his jaw. "Don't," he warned through fanged lips.

I ignored the pleading in his eyes and the warning in his tone.

"What do you say, Alexi?"

She eyed me suspiciously. "Why would you go willingly? To save your sweetie pie here?"

"He's not sweet enough to be my pie slice. Gabriel's got a lot of girls, but I've never been one of them."

Her gaze shifted from me to Gabriel, who was still lodged between her and the ground. "If you ain't doing her, why do you want to save her?"

He fought to answer without showing the wear of her knife scraping against his internal organs. "I was appointed by the Members as her bodyguard. Nothing more."

Finally, he'd made a smart move. Although it was good to leave out the part where he volunteered, it kind of hurt to hear the "nothing more" part. Don't ask why I made my life more difficult than it had to be. He would have said anything to keep the situation from escalating, but his nonchalant tone felt like the knife was chafing *my* organs.

Alexi peered through squinted eyes. After a few moments, she ordered Drew to stand down. To me, she charged, "Gabriel stays with us until you're safe in the circle."

I couldn't help but snort. "I don't think 'safe' is the best description."

"Secured, then. When you're secured in the circle, I'll let him go."

"Promise?" I asked as I stood and dusted off my pants.

She smiled. "On my mama's best mock apple pie."

"That's reassuring," I replied sarcastically.

"Take it or leave it, honey."

"I think I just bought a bunch of crackers and a pie shell."

Alexi tugged Gabriel to his feet as she stood. She

removed the knife, stroking it restlessly in her hand. "That way," she ordered, pointing to a narrow trail through the bushes.

I didn't like how closely Drew walked as I was ushered down the path. I couldn't run anywhere but forward, anyway. The path was thin and the sticker bushes were thick. I was walking to my doom and had to put up with a pervert staring at my ass. The universe really was laughing at me.

The bushes suddenly ended. I stood in a moderately large clearing. There was an honest-to-God circle, complete with candles, incense, and pentagram. How trite. I was sure blood-letting would be involved, too. I searched for the animal sacrifice before realizing it would probably be my blood splattered all over the grass.

I was the chicken.

"Get in!" Alexi balked.

"Shut up. I'm going." I may have sounded tough; however, I was starting to wish for feathers and wings. My steel nerve quickly vanished as the reality of the situation slammed into my brain.

A small hum vibrated over my body as I crossed the line into the circle. It was worse than the feel of goose bumps on freshly shaved legs. The sensation of bugs crawling over my skin intensified.

"I'm in. Let him go."

"If he tries anything, he's dead."

"I'm sure he'll take your warning seriously."

I sure had.

She removed her hold. "Go," she demanded, no different than if she'd shooed a nosy dog.

"I want to watch," he said calmly.

"Gabriel, go. I appreciate everything you've done, but I

don't expect you to risk your life one more time, especially when this is kind of inevitable." I cursed myself silently as I fought back tears. This was really it, and I was rejecting the only help I had. My only hope... "Just go. Whatever happens, I'll be fine."

A lie, but I wasn't sure what was going to happen and didn't want him to watch if it was something awful.

Gabriel was almost arrogant, if you could imagine, retorting, "I may not be able to help you, but I won't abandon you."

Go figure. He was able to make a sweet pledge sound like a sentiment from a spoiled brat sent to the corner for timeout.

"Fine! It's not like I can kick you out. It's not my little soiree."

"No, it's mine." Ellenore appeared in the clearing.

# Chapter Thirty-four

Ellenore's burnt sienna dress hugged her body from shoulder to ankle as the neckline plunged between her breasts. The material whipped and curled around her body, lapping at the air. She moved forward gracefully. *Which was nothing like my sister's natural gait.* She had always walked with confidence, but never with such a sensual undertone.

She stopped on the outer rim of the circle. The dress swayed but never crossed the barrier. It was as if a true wall separated us, one that could physically stop anything from entering if the circle did not grant passage.

Ellenore smiled, head tilting to the side. "Hello, sister. You're looking well...for now." There was a new, unfamiliar layer in her voice.

"And you're looking especially sinister. Nice dress."

"A gift from a friend."

"It makes quite a statement."

"Oh, more than that. It was blessed to aid in the finalization of my permanent soul."

"So, it's not couture?"

"Sister, sister." She paced the circle. "You will not ruin my mood this evening. In just a few minutes, I will be whole." She turned back to face where she'd entered the clearing. "Priestess, the time has come. I'm ready." Satisfaction colored her rosy cheeks. "We're ready."

Humorless and flat, I asked, "Why wouldn't I be ready? I've dreamed of a moment when my wench of a sister would steal my soul as easily as my lipstick. I couldn't be more proud."

The smile vanished from her overly painted red lips as she marched closer, careful to remain on the opposite side of the perimeter. Her whimsy was lost as a more bitter side emerged.

"You will not ruin this for me! Do you understand? You have failed and I have won!" Her voice manifested into a snarl. "I'm warning you. Get over it."

As I met her venomous gaze, I noticed the strange color of her eyes: blue. The same blue I had seen when I looked into the eyes of the Mass. But our eyes were brown. What in Hell's poodles was going on?

Gabriel searched the small gathering for his brother. "Where's Gideon?"

Distaste sat on Ellenore's tongue as she snapped, "He declined the invite. I'm not very happy with the way he treated me. It's for the best."

"Miss Princess didn't like her time in the trunk?" I pouted my lips.

"Shut up!"

"Mistress?" The voice belonged to a much older woman, possibly in her nineties. The priestess. She wore a simple red robe, of course. Softly, she chided, "Do not let your temper dampen this event. She is powerless and that is a great victory. You have won. Be at ease."

Something laced her voice that made everyone physically relax. There was power in it, like an electrical charge. I used that awareness to hold on to the reality that she was a creepy bag of bones.

In my head, I created a mantra: *you have no power over me.*

Her presence made my heart slow. As she drew closer,

my panic began to fade. This was a kind woman, a woman who would never harm me. She could never be evil. What she was about to do was simply a remolding of nature for the greater good. She would ease my misery, removing the burdens that bound me to a life I never wanted.

The priestess wanted to steal my soul, but it would be okay, her essence whispered in my ear. It promised things. Laughter without the pain of wondering when it would end. Companionship without the fear of being called a monster. Knowledge that freedom was real. Serenity. She promised a life different from this one, and my tears flowed into the circle before I realized I was crying from the hope that she'd remove the burden that was my soul...

*That makes no sense.*

I blinked, startled, and immediately broke eye contact with the old woman. How could the permanent removal of my soul offer freedom? How could I find serenity if my soul was gone forever? It wouldn't free me. If anything, it would bind me closer as the Cypher forever.

I searched for Gabriel in the small crowd of conspirators. When I found him, he mouthed the word "witch." *The old woman was a witch.* A new dread filled my chest and I dared not look at her again.

Ellenore's concern broke the silence. "She fought the trance. What did you do?"

The priestess was flustered, at first, but composed herself. "Nothing. Her will is strong. She will not allow me to console her."

I ventured to gaze at the woman. "Yeah, real sorry your bedside manner can't cheer me up." I reverted my attention to the ground. I'd heard of how much power witches could wield. Hearing about it and being controlled by one were two very different things.

Not every witch is evil. I'd heard of some very nice ones. But the one in front of me, trying to impose her will on mine, was a scary witch, who deserved to have a house dropped on her. I wanted no part of this ceremony or her magic.

How had Ellenore become so entangled with her?

The priestess glared with a weight beyond her years. "You are correct, Ellenore. She does have a strong will, and quite the mouth, though it changes nothing. The ceremony is not lost, dear. Cheer up. We will proceed the hard way."

Ellenore smiled brightly.

"Peachy," I quipped.

Her smile wavered, though it returned as the priestess moved her away from the circle, signaling that she was beginning the ceremony.

The witch began her incantation. The language was unfamiliar. I thought it was nothing more than grandstanding for the crowd. However, upon finishing the incantation, she removed a jacket from a bag. My jacket. The one the Mass had stolen.

The tingling throughout my body grew dire.

Dropping to her knees, she held the jacket skyward. More pretty words slid free of her chapped lips.

My heart beat faster. A thin film of sweat enveloped my body. Each word brought with it a needle of pain, jabbing my skin until no expanse of flesh was left unharmed. The torture was unbearable as it mounted, sliding inside my ears and seeking out the whites of my eyes.

"Lady," I breathed raggedly, "I'm about to tell you where to stick your little sideshow act."

She ripped a hole through my jacket, which forced a gnarly gasp from my throat. As she pierced the material again, I felt the flesh rip straight down my spine. Each tear the jacket suffered brought forth fresh wounds. Swells of blood soaked through my clothes, across my stomach and legs.

I heard a deep breath that wasn't my own. Gabriel was horrified. But it was from my sister's throat that the jagged breath had escaped. *How odd that she would care now*, I thought as my flesh tore again.

Tearing skin could be heard as powerfully as a foghorn through the intimate clearing scattered with villains. No one dared move or breathe as the priestess's magic tore me apart, one strip at a time.

Suddenly, her incantation died.

"How do you feel, Cypher?"

I refused to acknowledge her handiwork. "Oh, did you start already?"

Everyone was right. I had a smart-ass mouth, and in situations such as this, it reminded me that inner strength carries its own magic. Use what you got, right?

The priestess grinned, exposing her perfectly aligned yet highly discolored teeth. "I enjoy your kind. It gives me a chance to spread my wings, so to speak. The weak break so soon, I barely have a chance to express with my art how much I should be feared."

The "little old lady" act was completely gone. This one knew how to cause pain and wanted to show off her talents.

"I always get stuck with the overachievers."

Without warning, she rose to her feet, her voice booming into the night sky. "Spill forth your essence. Use this offering as a vessel. Fill her with your fear, your spite, your torment, your guilt. Be light as she becomes lead from your wrath. Let her sink so the Grand Mother may soar."

I was knocked to the ground in the middle of the circle by...nothing visible. I searched, wide-eyed, to locate my attacker as I crouched on my knees. A devastating pain doubled me over. My forehead rested against the ground. The grass brushed my face. It smelled rich and wild, with an edge of sorrow. *How could grass exude an emotion?*

My knees and shins were tucked tightly beneath my body. As the pain escalated and multiplied, my fingers dug into the earth, ripping through the grass. A wave of seasoned emotions crept up my body, expanding the meat it touched until the pressure threatened to split me open with the ease of breaking a piñata. These emotions had traveled into my pores from the earth at my fingertips. They belonged to something greater, as if a million souls sought to fill my body with their sins in order to free themselves.

I couldn't breathe. I lifted my head in search of air but there was only sorrow and rage to choke on. It crushed my chest until I grew dizzy. When I tried to stand, my legs gave out time and again, dropping me to the ground. I writhed on my back, forcing my chest up, forcing it to inhale something that meant life.

My parents' faces came to mind. The way they laughed anytime I told an unexpected joke. Their combined love for a good puzzle, and how their eyes twinkled when we'd add the last piece. Their dismay at discovering that humans weren't at the top of the food chain. The tears they refused to shed as they hugged me good-bye...

I ached to see my parents one more time.

Horror plastered everyone's faces. All but the priestess, who merely watched with indifference.

Ellenore decreed, "This can stop, Myranda. Give up. Bend to the priestess' will."

"No," I rasped.

My sister sighed. "You have always been such a pain in my ass!"

I wanted to respond, to give her a smart-ass comment that would fry her temper. I screamed instead. Hair wrung with sweat, face drowned in tears, I fought my own body, willing it not to explode, though I could feel it trying to. My breath was quick and shallow between screams.

"That's enough!" Gabriel ordered. "If you kill her, the grave will claim her soul."

Just like that, the pain ceased. I relaxed on my back, not having the strength to stand or sit up. The pressure was gone, leaving me deflated, empty. I stared into the night sky, unable to blink. It demanded too much energy.

I murmured, "What was that?"

The priestess stood outside the circle. "The pain of the Earth, my dear."

I swallowed hard. "I promise to recycle from now on."

"Time is running out," the old crone barked. "Do you concede your soul?"

I was tired beyond the definition of the word. "I put up a good fight. I've tried and you keep knocking me down. I'm so tired. I've been tired for years. You're just going to keep trying to break me until you win."

She looked very pleased and eager. "Yes."

"I guess...you'll have to suck a bag of rotten eggs, because I'll die before I let you win."

Electricity gathered in the air as her anger swarmed the circle. It buzzed in my ears like a nest of murder hornets. The crone was fully outraged.

I would have laughed if I'd had an ounce of energy left to spare.

"You lay there, half dead, yet maintain such confidence that you are stronger than me? I find that quite entertaining."

"Really? I just find it to be a fact."

"You test my patience."

I mustered enough momentum to sit up. "You test my ugly meter."

Someone in the crowd snickered and then I heard Alexi snap, "Shut up, Drew."

"When Ellenore has the soul she rightfully deserves, I will kill you *very* slowly."

"Pinky swear?" I held up a finger, but it wasn't my pinky.

"You should show respect where it is due." The priestess, not taking my prodding lightly, recited something quick under her breath and extended her hands toward me.

A bolt of lightning struck the ground, the power shooting me into the air so hard, I thought it would heave me across the country. As it turned out, there really was a mystical wall around the circle because my body crashed right into it. I bounced off, landing on the scorched earth directly over the strike.

Something inside had to be broken. Drenched in unimaginable pain, I lay, face down, unable to move. Fresh blood gushed over my skin.

Voices whispered, "Is she dead?" "Is she broken?" "Is the ceremony over?" "Did something go wrong?"

*Yeah, my life.*

# Chapter Thirty-five

The priestess hushed the chatter. "She is alive. The ceremony continues. Ellenore, take your rightful place beside your sister."

"I'm not going in there."

"Do as I say, child, or the ceremony is for naught."

There was a sloshing sound, and then I heard hesitant footsteps as my sister crept close enough that I felt the grass bend next to my arm where she stood.

The instructions continued. "You must touch her in order for the completion. Wipe the blood I have dowsed on your chest and smear it across her back."

"No. What if she takes her soul back?"

"She is unconscious. Do as I say! You both try my patience. Let this be done."

The dress wisped across my arm as she squatted, touching the back of my neck. I felt warmth not from her hand, but from the blood she smeared across my back.

"Nicely done, mistress. Let us continue."

Those words seemed out of place. Why would she call my sister, of all people, mistress? Someone so powerful answers to no one. My sister had to be paying big money.

Ellenore sounded upset. "What are you doing?"

"I must reseal the circle."

"I don't like that idea."

The priestess replied venomously, "It must be done. Silence."

"Yes, Priestess."

The priestess paced the full circle. I knew it was sealed when the footsteps quieted. This was my chance. I was hurt, but life had been flowing back into my body as I listened to them squabble. I knew I could move. "Attack" was all my mind understood as I reached around and snaked Ellenore's ankle. The action knocked her to the ground, and I was on top of her quicker than the hag could send down another lightning bolt.

"Priestess!" She squealed.

I spoke between gritted teeth. "What hurts me will hurt her, Priestess. Patience is a virtue. But I'm sure you lack any real virtue."

Everyone moved to the perimeter of the circle to watch. You would have thought it was a mud wrestling cage match from some of the expressions. I'll give Gabriel credit. He just looked stricken.

"Don't hurt me, Myranda!"

Pawing her throat, I leaned in close, our faces almost touching. "What's the secret word, Ellenore?"

She spoke so low, I could barely hear her answer. "I'm sorry. I'm so sorry."

I whispered back, "Why should I believe you?"

As I stared into her contorted face, the blue ocean of her eyes wavered to unmask a touch of brown. Before I could blink twice, the blue sponged it right back up.

I was frozen, my death grip holding firm. Now, my voice had turned uncertain and breathy. "What was that?"

The brown filtered back, though the blue never truly receded. Ellenore whispered in my ear, not of childhood secrets, but trespasses on the natural world.

"I didn't mean to do it. She recognized me at the party and knew my soul wasn't mine. She offered to help us. But it was like she could see into me, what I really wanted and...

She made me want it more. I can't take back what I've done to you, and part of me doesn't want to. I am so sorry. I didn't know what she was."

The priestess moved as close as the boundary allowed without crossing over. "What are you doing?"

We didn't acknowledge the witch. I stared at Ellenore's unnatural eyes. "What's happened to you?"

"I don't know. She knew my desire, and somehow being close to her made me want to make it real. I think she's inside my head. Help me."

"That's what she tried to do to me. She was reading my desires, but it didn't make sense. I think it's because you and I were standing too close together. She was trying to control us both at once and it kind of merged together in my mind when she had me in the trance. That's what broke it."

"Why can't she control us in the circle?"

"It must block everything except for her magic to do harm."

"But she can cross through the circle at any time."

"No, she can't. It was made for us, not her."

"How do we stop this?" Desperation laced her being from the inside out.

"I have an idea. Do you trust me?"

Ellenore paused. We stared at each other silently. I released a breath when she nodded.

"After everything, you trust me in this?"

"Yes." Tears streaked her cheeks.

"Then hug me, for old time's sake."

She gave me a funny look before giving in to the embrace.

"What are you doing, Ellenore?" the priestess demanded, pacing the invisible wall.

We stood slowly. I dusted the dirt from my clothes while Ellenore straightened her lively dress.

She whispered discreetly, "Hold my hand."

I was just as discreet. "Why?"

"The dress needs to touch you. It's blessed, remember?"

I clasped her hand in mine as I stepped in front of her to face the priestess. "We've discussed the matter, my sister and I. Continue."

"With the ceremony?" she asked, flabbergasted.

"No, with your recipe for pea soup. Yes, the ceremony."

"Why, all of a sudden, have you changed your mind? You were so adamant that we would never win."

"I was being selfish." I smiled at my sister as I spoke to the old crone. "She's my sister. What can I say? If one of us has a chance at a decent life, well..." I made eye contact with the priestess again. "She's got more than I'll ever have. If one of us can be happy, let's do this. You can't win if this is what I want, too."

I was scared, and if the sweat on Ellenore's palm was any indication, she felt the same way.

"Finally, you are making sense, girl." The woman walked back to her bag of tricks. "The ceremony continues. Everyone, stand back from the perimeter."

Gabriel stepped in front of her. "This is not what she wants." He turned to Ellenore. "How can you live, knowing you sold your sister's life for self gain?"

*Come on with the heroics!* Where was he when Mother Earth had been ripping me a new one?

"Gabriel, it's okay. Ellenore and I talked it over. We had a sister moment. I know you mean well, but back off."

"No!" The anger in his tone matched the pleading in his heart.

I would have to play the sap card to calm him down. "Gabriel, it's hard to accept, but this is what I want."

The priestess began her incantation without a second glance in his direction. With her words, we felt a terrible prickle of power growing, thickening the air around us. The wind whipped our hair and tousled our clothes. As we watched, we realized the wind only affected us. Everyone else was as still as death.

Everyone except for Gabriel.

"Don't go through with this, Ell!"

Wow, I was impressed. He was quite shaken, from the tips of his toes to the ends of his hair. Gabriel had verbalized his feelings in the basement. To see them at work, however, was overpowering.

But he needed to cooperate.

"It's okay, Green Bean. Everything will be peachy. I'll be the same person, no matter what happens." My words were soft, intimate, like no one else existed. Funny, considering we had quite the audience.

He stared at me blankly. "Green Bean?"

"Yes, Green Bean. Don't cause more pain when I've already made my decision."

His expression turned to recognition, then to admiration. He hadn't thought I could pull it off. Well, shame on him! I had a few surprises up my sleeve.

I smiled wistfully. When the priestess lowered her head in prayer, I winked at him. An unmistakably idiotic mistake. The world had narrowed so much that only Gabriel filled my vision. We were in a private moment, but our public audience took notice. Alexi, having glimpsed my slip-up, yelled for the priestess to stop the ceremony. Luckily, the crone had just finished her last words, clapping her hands together so loudly that Alexi's plea was drowned in a wash of power.

The ceremony was finished.

Alexi ran to the old hag. "Priestess!"

She turned to Alexi with unforgiving eyes. "Shut up!"

"Mistress!"

Mistress?

"Shut up!" She drank from a cup and spit the liquid onto the edge of the circle. I felt a wobble through the air, and soon the old woman stood beside us. Quite a surprise.

"Well, hell, why didn't you do that earlier?"

"I dared not enter until the ceremony was complete. Had I breached the wall prematurely, it would have spoiled the entire event. But now..." The smile on her face was truly bone-chilling. "Now, you both belong to me, and no one beyond the pentagram's barrier can stop me."

Ellenore looked completely puzzled. "What do you mean?"

The hag spared an expression of pity toward Ellenore before explaining, "You stupid, stupid little girl. I made you act on what you wanted most. You had no idea, and I had no idea how easy it would be."

It was my turn to ask the questions, seeing as how Ellenore's were leading nowhere. "What was easy? Helping Ellenore 'secure' my soul for her own?"

"No." She stopped to ponder her answer. "Well, yes. That was easy. But I did not go to all of this trouble to help a stranger find what she believes to be true happiness."

"What's in this for you?" *Nothing good.*

"Your soul is secure inside her body now. She would be useless without it. I am claiming her flesh and newly acquired soul. As you can see, I have grown old. How can I allow this power and knowledge to die from something as foolish as mortality?"

"You want my sister?"

She smiled. "She is so easy to control. And she does have quite the life. Have you had the pleasure of meeting her husband?"

"I have."

"Then you realize how priceless he is. I can sense it in the air that animates him. His power, too, will be mine. It was all so easy."

I stood in front of Ellenore. "How do you plan to take her over?"

"By doing this." She reached around me and grabbed Ellenore's arm. "Yours will be mine and mine yours. Your blood will beat through my heart and mine through yours. Your soul will fill my body and mine yours. Your—" She stopped, gaping in horror.

"Didn't get very far, did you?" I smiled sweetly.

She paled. "What have you done?"

"Nothing. It's what you didn't do. You see, Priestess Buzz Kill, you only re-secured my soul as my own."

"No!"

"I'm afraid so. When she and I hugged, I took my soul back. You can't secure it within her if it isn't there." I gave her my best pity smirk. "I suppose you didn't think about that potential outcome."

The priestess was dumbfounded. "I... Ellenore would not have given it up easily. I made sure of that."

"I'll give you an A for effort. The pain of Mother Earth is a mother, but not the sweet kind her name refers to, let me tell you. And the lightning! That was a once-in-a-lifetime rush. Better than a roller coaster. The flesh-tearing...I can't forgive. Call me crazy, but that sucked. And you ruined my favorite jacket."

She cautiously backed away, closer to the edge of the white ring. "I have failed."

"I was trying to be nice about it, but yeah, you're a big loser."

Ellenore took her place beside me as she spoke to the old wretch. "I'm responsible for the abominations in my heart, but you made me act on them." Tears streamed down her face. "You exposed my worst fears to the one person I tried so hard to keep safe from them."

I touched her hair. "Don't cry in front of her. She doesn't deserve to see your tears. We're done crying."

Ellenore straightened her posture and wiped the tears from her face.

I took that time to stalk the priestess.

"You've hurt me and my family. You tortured us, and I'm not a forget-and-let-live kind of person. You won't find forgiveness here. But you will find your mortality. In fact, much sooner than you feared."

"Do you think I will let you harm me?"

"To commit harm in the circle is to endanger all in the circle. That includes you, you freaky rotten prune."

Alexi and Drew rushed the barrier. The minute their bodies made contact, they were flung out of sight with a ball of light. Gabriel grabbed two vampires and ordered them to find and detain the deranged duo.

I turned my eyes to the priestess. She finally looked as scared as I wanted her to be. It helped that I was feeling particularly scary, and that it was all about to crash into her.

"You can't kill me!" She shrank back.

"I think my soul will forgive me."

As I knocked her down, Gabriel yelled, "You still have your soul!"

Right. I couldn't take hers if I had a no-occupancy sign in my chest.

"Thanks for the reminder, Green Bean!"

Before he could answer, I flung my soul into Ellenore, ignoring the pain that would ensue. The ball of energy hit so hard, she was thrown from the circle with a zap. I felt the electricity as she barreled through the invisible force field. I'm sure it wasn't a pleasant ride.

Without thinking, I planted my palm on the old woman's chest. "Your soul is mine," I snarled.

"I chose the wrong twin," she whispered, awe-inspired by my savagery.

Because Ellenore's body had breached the circle, the magic was broken, enabling Gabriel to toss me Alexi's discarded knife. The hilt of the blade rested in my palm. If there was any other way, I would have taken it.

"You've probably done more harm in your stolen lifetimes than any creature walking this Earth," I concluded.

"Certainly, dear. It is the way of the wicked."

I drew her soul inward, watching the light leave her eyes as her lids drooped and her body sagged, transported to that state of metaphysical unconsciousness. That hollow space delighted in the feel of her soul, even as it disgusted me to have something so tainted inside my chest. I immediately blocked what it yearned to tell me. Oh my, the priestess had been busy and her soul was a chatterbox. It needed to brag. I caught a glimpse into her past long enough to know exactly how she would spend her future, if given the deranged opportunities her soul sought out.

This soul wouldn't hurt to return. It was putrid, having wasted away centuries ago. I shoved it through that one string of Silly Putty. Her chest heaved with a sigh as her eyes opened. I thrust the knife through her dusty heart, hoping she felt her death with every part of her being.

Leaning into her ear, I whispered, "You should have tried the 'give a penny' approach rather than always taking one. And I'm glad I burned your house down. It was ugly and creepy, just like you!"

"Stop touching her!" Gabriel wrenched my body loose.

We fumbled backward to the ground, the knife left wobbling in her chest.

"Why?" I yelled as I lay on top of him, my back pressed against his chest.

"I've heard stories of witches. They'll do anything to save themselves. I don't trust this one not to do the same. Touching you gives her more power... Can you get off me, please?"

"Oh!" *Embarrassing.* "Sorry." I rolled onto the grass. His ribs were still healing. I'd momentarily forgotten his injuries. "Did I cause more damage?" I touched his abs before I quelled the urge.

The barest of a smile graced his lips. "If I don't look upon your face right this instant, my heart won't believe that you're here."

Voices yelled warnings behind us, but it was too late. The priestess was officially a party pooper.

# Chapter Thirty-six

She had me by the neck, quickly squeezing the air from my body. Seriously. I could feel every bit of oxygen being artificially drained from my cells, not just my lungs.

"I win." The old bag of bones was foaming at the mouth.

Gabriel tried to rid me of her, but her body had taken on a translucent quality. His hands swished right through her as though she were made of fog. When that failed, he grabbed at my arms, but discovered the same outcome. She had cast a spell that traveled between us. Only, I could touch her as sure as her hands were solid around my throat.

I dug fingernails into her arms.

She laughed. "I will have my way. It is my due."

Flat-palmed, I punched her right in the nose. She cursed and released my neck. Air flowed into my body.

"You ain't gettin' your way with me, lady." I stood, looming over her frail form wallowing on the ground as she held her hands over her nose.

Again, Gabriel held the knife out. This time, I took a different approach. Without warning, I dropped to her ragged form and snapped her neck. Only then did I plunge the silver blade into her chest a dozen times. As a precaution, I twisted it into her heart and left it there.

I knew what had to be done next but hesitated.

Taking action, Gabriel ripped her head from her neck in one gruesomely smooth motion with his otherworldly strength. After enduring an awful, squishy noise, accompanied by the unforgettable sight of Gabriel holding the severed head by the base of her bloody spine, he dropped it on the ground. Disgusted, I kicked it far away from us.

I stood beside Gabriel and muttered, "Teamwork makes the dream work."

But it wasn't over. Although the body lay motionless, the surrounding earth quaked to the tempo of a dying heartbeat before it succumbed to silence. Death, at last. A putrid stench rose from the corpse, along with a smoldering, dark cloud. We witnessed the body transform to ash, wilting into the ground with a finality the priestess had reared against with her last dying breath.

We let the sight sink in.

Remorseless, Gabriel pulled me away from the scene. "I've never seen that before."

I searched his face for any clue to what he was feeling, but only picked up on curiosity and, in the background, satisfaction.

Wiping my bloody palms on my pants, I tried not to sound completely disgusted with myself when I said, "That old trick? I picked that up years ago when the Christmas lines got too long."

Ben appeared in front of us before Gabriel could laugh. "I'll gather the others and get rid of the...dust. We've taken Alexi and Drew into custody and will deliver them to the Members." He was trying so hard to be professional.

Gabriel nodded. "Thank you. You've done exceptionally well this evening."

Had he? It seemed as if we had done all the work while the Members' people arrived just in time to take all the credit. They literally arrived to pat themselves on the backs.

*Whatever.* Ben needed this win.

His smile was brighter than a flashlight. He was trying his hardest to prove himself and was succeeding. Gabriel never gave undue compliments, especially if it was just to make someone feel better. Ben looked as if he would implode with excitement right where he stood.

"Thank you, Gabriel." He said it with such heart. And with that, he turned and began gathering everyone to move the prisoners.

Gabriel shifted his attention to me. "Would you like to go home?"

That was the best question I'd heard all night. I was so ready for a shower and maybe a snack while I sat on the rickety porch swing. "That sounds great, but remind me to wash the sheets on the couch before I go to bed."

He shifted his gaze to the grass. "No. I meant, do you want to go to *your* home?"

"Oh..."

*No, I didn't.*

Why didn't I want to go home to my own bed, or my own porch, or my own snacks? Because I didn't feel safe anymore, damn it. Before, I was my own worst enemy. Now, I had corporeal enemies with the power to curdle my blood. I didn't know how to answer Gabriel, but I definitely didn't want to say all of that out loud and sound like an ungrateful jerk. Especially while I thought I might puke from what I'd just done.

Thankfully, he saved me from having to share my answer.

"Actually, going home may not be wise. Let's make damn sure the Mass are out of the picture before we take unnecessary risks. You're stuck with me and the farmhouse awhile longer."

I wanted to tell him not to pamper my fears, but he

walked away. No major moment. No, "Oh, I can see that you're a mega scaredy-cat and I'm calling you out on it." Nope. He left to oversee Ben's progress.

Ellenore wandered over, but I noticed that she wouldn't —or couldn't—make eye contact.

"I'm sorry, Myranda. I'm sorry that what I feel made this entire nightmare possible."

I found I couldn't look at her, either. "Call me Ell."

"I didn't mean for this to happen..."

"You think my life and my afterlife are expendable just because I can't use my soul."

It wasn't a question, but she answered anyway, choking back a sob. "Sometimes, but I don't mean to. I don't want to feel this way." Her silent tears hit the blades of grass, running like splinters into the earth to hide.

"We can't control our feelings. If I could, I would hate you right now."

"But I didn't know what she was." Her voice rose.

"Not for that." My own tears would have glistened in the grass had I let myself cry, but I didn't. My voice was husky with the need. "You took Mom and Dad from me. That was before the witch. You had control over that, and you took them when I was scared and lonely and needed them."

"I'm sorry."

"Don't apologize. I can't accept it. Maybe one day, but right now I need to not be near you. I can't look at you, and I can't talk to you anymore. Maybe later," I hoped out loud.

Her heart sounded broken. Between sobs, she asked, "Do you want it?"

The "it" she referred to was my soul.

"Keep it. I'll come for it when I need it." The words escaped my lips like a soft warning.

That was it. I could hear Nick's confusion and sincerity as he ran to her. I walked away. He had missed the entire show. Lucky him. But I was glad to hear the affection in his voice, because she needed someone to love her unconditionally and it couldn't be me.

Not anymore.

I was betting the priestess's presence had something to do with the grim personal feelings I'd read from Nick's soul concerning Ellenore. Had the witch been allowed to inhabit my sister, Nick would have grown to despise her wickedness. Now, their love had a chance. And he did love Ellenore. I only hoped that she could realize how valuable love was. Maybe she wouldn't throw it away a second time.

Gabriel escorted me back to the farmhouse. I was silent the entire trip, and he didn't try to interrupt my quiet trance.

Hours passed. It was almost dawn when I mechanically left my shoes at the door, took a shower that I barely remembered, dressed in clean sweats and a random shirt, unwrapped a store-bought muffin, and sat on the porch with my legs dangling over the edge. I turned the muffin over and over in my hand, uneaten.

I was left on my own for a while before I heard the screen door open and close. Gabriel had changed into a pair of black pajama pants and a gray V-neck shirt.

He leaned against the house, behind me.

"Are you okay?"

"I'm alive, soul intact."

"I know. I'm asking if you're okay."

Disheartened, I answered, "Peaches n' cream."

"Always dodging."

"'Till the end..."

"Can I sit next to you?"

"No."

The wood shifted, though he only ventured a foot closer. "Why?"

"I don't want you to see me cry again." And I was crying. I had tried not to, but when you hold back for so long, you either let the pain kill you from the inside or weep it out, like exhuming a poison.

"Do I not deserve to see you cry, either?" He was noting how I'd refused to cry in front of my sister. "Am I so low that I'm forbidden to see your tears and wipe them away when you don't have the heart to do it yourself?" Something in his tone had changed. It bordered on fear, as if he thought he didn't matter to me, after all.

"I didn't mean it like that."

"Then give up your shields, Ell. We're both tired. I know you want to hide from the world, but please don't hide from me."

"I'm not hiding."

"You've hidden behind this armor of yours every day for four years. Do you realize how long it actually took before we noticed something wasn't right with your abilities?" His voice drifted closer. "You cloaked your emotional and physical pain that well. It took us even longer to uncover your secrets, and only when your sister dropped the information in our laps. That was a long time to be alone." He was directly behind me. He had moved with that vampire silence, distracting me with his voice.

"I didn't think I was alone. I had Ellenore."

The arrogance I had come to know so well over the years shoved Gabriel's sympathy aside as he noted, "I'm sitting down. It's my porch."

"Fine. Take the muffin you bought while you're at it."

"If you're going to waste it, I will."

And damn if he didn't take the last blueberry muffin right out of my hand and start eating it.

"This is the first time I've ever seen you eat food. And steal."

"You offered it. And yes, I eat. I'm not that old-fashioned. There's a lot that I'm happy to do without, like fast food and meatloaf, but there are some things I'll never give up."

As I laughed, he took the opportunity to wipe my tears. "Are you okay?"

I shrugged, unable to speak as my throat tightened.

"No one expects you to be."

"Apparently, everyone expected me to be a freaking moron who'd just drop dead on command."

He pondered my words. "Some did. That's not what eats at your heart."

"You know why I'm upset. I don't need to say it out loud."

Gabriel's tone hardened. "I'm trying to help you come to terms with this."

"I'm trying."

"And I'm trying to make you realize that you don't have to do it alone. Your sister—your only friend—tried to steal your soul and didn't mind that the byproduct might be your death."

"That's not what bothers me!" I yelled, shocked by the echo it produced. I just wanted to pity myself, which was unlikely to happen with Gabriel in my space, trying to be nice.

"Do you support back-stabbing and attempted murder? I'm sorry. I didn't realize."

"Stop it. Of course it bothers me, but—"

"What?" His voice was softer, waiting.

"She stole them." Great, I was crying again.

"Your parents."

I hopped off the porch and whirled to face him. He wanted to see my pain? Well, it was about to consume both of us. I would have screamed if my voice had let me, but it just came out strangled.

"All these years, I lived with the pain that they couldn't love me for what I'd become. For what I am. But I was able to live with it because I had saved Ellenore. You should have seen her fear when she was chosen. Even now, that memory, the look on her face, shatters me. Had she become the Cypher, I would have lost every part of her forever."

My voice gave way to a scream, though it crackled under the stress. "I didn't do it to be the martyr! I did it because I would have died, anyway, if I'd been forced to watch her life be stolen away, to watch her become what I've become. I did it because I was selfish! I didn't want to lose my best friend. And after everything, she thinks I did it to show how much better I am than her? And then she stole them..."

I dropped to my knees and my voice was nothing but a broken sob. "All these years, I've lived with this pain that they hate me, and the one person who knew that pain was the same one who caused it. Why?" I searched Gabriel's eyes for an answer. "Why would she hurt me so badly? How could she do this? And knowing everything, how can I still love her? That's so screwed up. I just want to hate her. It would be so much easier." I inhaled desperately, as if I'd never breathed before. "I feel like I should be dead."

"There are days when I feel like I should be alive, but that doesn't make it so." Gabriel approached as ragged sobs jolted my body. He kneeled in front of me. Grabbing my hands, he drew me to his chest, wrapping his arms around me.

And I cried.

All those years, I thought I was sad and pathetic. But I

was angry, and that anger had turned into an inner rage feeding off itself. That's the truth Gabriel wanted me to see. I had shut everyone else out to punish myself. And though Ellenore had screwed me over by lying, the lies I'd told myself were much more damaging.

# Epilogue

I needed a vacation. It took me by surprise when Seth was ecstatic to arrange it. And Gabriel proved to be much more than my greatest expectations. He even stood up to the Members when they initially denied my vacation request. Since rumors escaped concerning me and my sister, the Members want me working more than ever. Gabriel tactfully mentioned the repeated sacrifice of my soul for "the cause," and wasn't shy about reminding them of the ruin my temper was capable of. Apparently, unhinged, destructive employees are allowed vacations.

I haven't spoken to Ellenore or my parents. I don't know what to say to Ellenore. We've wronged each other. And considering her silence as well, we both need time to heal. Maybe we'll find our way back to each other one fine day, away from the vampires and the lies.

My parents are another matter. Gabriel found their address and phone number, but I haven't used either. The information was written on a sticky note, hiding in the pocket of my new denim jacket. A gift from the Members, although I suspect that Gabriel had a little something to do with that. I will talk to my parents but, for now, what can I say? Ellenore's tampering was the cause of our disintegrated relationship, but the fear that they won't want me is still fresh and very real in my heart.

After spending a month with Seth, I've grown to like him more than I've wanted to. He felt awful about missing the ceremony—not being able to help—but that's life. I told him to get over it. I talk to Seth a lot, but some of my best epiphanies are found in his smiles. Every once in a while, though, I get this nagging feeling not to get too close.

Gideon has been missing since the night of the ceremony. Gabriel doesn't seem to be worried yet, since he's notorious for disappearing faster than a matching sock in the dryer. If he's still missing by the time I return, I've sworn to help find him.

I've also decided to redecorate my house and upgrade the security system when I get home. A measly latch doesn't seem as safe as it used to. And the old décor just isn't who I am anymore. I'm different. I am. I can feel it before I open my eyes each day. My soul is still on loan, but I'm letting go of the fear. I'm not afraid to see what I became because I look forward to who I'm becoming.

I've come to realize the world is built on crumbling families, bowed lives, and flecks of wrath and optimism blowing in the breeze like pollen. And that's exactly how it's meant to be: fire and ice, love and hate, tears and peaceful hearts. We all have to bide our time, raging against the world. That way, we can appreciate serenity when it comes.

And it does.

I'm figuring you out, world, one soul at a time. I just haven't taken you over yet because I've been too busy taking back my life.

I'm ready to have some fun.

## ABOUT THE AUTHOR

Please take a moment to leave a review online. Your voice matters. By leaving a review, you can help fellow readers discover books by Blakely Chorpenning.

---

Blakely Chorpenning lives in the American South with the best family a woman could ask for. When she is not writing genre and literary fiction, Blakely and her family laugh a ton, craft more than any human should, and enjoy the little things.

Visit Blakely on:

Her Blog:
indiscriminatewrites.blogspot.com

Twitter:
@bchorpenning

Pinterest:
www.pinterest.com/bchorpenning

Facebook:
www.facebook.com/blakelychorpenning

Goodreads:

www.goodreads.com/author/show/5394681.Blakely_Chorpenning

**Continue for an excerpt of 'Blood Lies,' book two in the Ell Clyne Series.**

BLOOD LIES

Book Two in the
Ell Clyne Series

# PROLOGUE

BLOOD LIES EXCERPT

If I could view life from a space shuttle, I would know what's behind the blind turns long before they're made. But, for as much money as the Members of the Allegiance (a.k.a. the Members) pay me, I think a NASA toy would be overlooked on my Christmas list to Santa. In fact, I would consider myself exceptionally lucky if I stayed off their radar for a very long time.

The Members are made up of the eldest vampires. They delegate, judge, and punish. You know, when they're not binge-watching 90s reruns. I found that out the hard way. Since my sister wanted absolutely nothing to do with being the Cypher -a job outlined by long hours in the company of vampires, reading souls to determine one's future capabilities, and the requirement to become quite literally soulless- I took the job. Turns out, there were a lot of hurt feelings over that decision. It wasn't as simple as ordering a new name tag.

As an identical twin, it wasn't hard to fool the Members with our dusty blonde hair and chocolate swirl eyes. If they didn't look too closely, they'd miss the dark hollows lining my eyes, brought about by endless nights of worrying for two. And maybe they'd never notice Ellenore's fake pout. The one she used while pretending that being special was a good thing.

I became Ell Clyne and Ellenore assumed my identity as Myranda Clyne. It was the best of a broken plan until Priestess Buzz Kill influenced my sister's wishes two months ago, creating a power-hungry, backstabbing twin looking for a permanent soul: mine. Because no one can possess two souls simultaneously, the Cypher's soul flies away somewhere so he or she can "read" borrowed souls. When Ellenore's soul flew away, I did what any good sister would do. I ripped mine out and flung it into her chest because the only way to get back her original soul is through death. Seeing as how Ellenore wasn't looking for a quick reunion with her own soul, she and her witch dug up an ancient ceremony to steal mine. Some sisters are never satisfied, which is why we're not on speaking terms. That, and the fact that she's responsible for the nonexistent relationship I have with our parents.

Encouragingly, she didn't get my soul. It's still on loan, but I can take it back whenever a fart blows wrong on the wind.

Destruction and injustice happened to find me all at once, which is why I took a two-month sabbatical from work, my interpersonal turmoil, and Mission, North Carolina, all together. I needed some time to work on my psyche. It took a beating, along with my body, but I've been recovering. A lot has been accomplished away from reminders of my life. A lot answered. I only have one looming question left.

Am I ready for more?

## CHAPTER ONE

BLOOD LIES EXCERPT

Turning the key, I swung my front door open. Evaluating the house with a post-vacation attitude, I realized that small miracles can be tailored to fit a hot mess.

I'd mentioned to Gabriel how unsafe I felt in my house after the Mass, a bunch of vamps on steroids, broke in twice to abduct me, succeeding the second time. He offered to oversee the home improvements while I was vacationing, which consisted of replacing locks and upping my security system. As I stood in my living room, I found myself surrounded by luxuries like a forty-eight-inch flat-screen television, thick bronze carpeting, and new paint. Holy hell, even the damned walls hadn't escaped his wrath. They were still white, but I hadn't realized until I saw the fresh paint just how zombie rogue the old paint had gotten.

The edge of my lip scrunched at the thought of being too void in my own life, not too long ago, to notice crusty paint.

The small things were seen to, as well. There was a magazine rack next to a plush, sage sofa, kind of tucked under the new oak end table. Admittedly, it was much better than the old holder... The floor. Lively potted plants lined my windows, giving the house a breath of life that was missing before. And, as I started to drop my jean jacket on the chair, I noticed the fancy iron coat hooks fastened on the wall to my left. A little reluctantly, I surrendered to the hooks, not wanting to disturb the clean aura my house had spontaneously adopted during my absence.

Would my home recognize me? Would I have to sleep outside with the strays, like the dirty mofo I was? Did Gabriel think changing my surroundings would inevitably change me? Not likely! I dropped my bag in the middle of the floor rather than kick it toward the wall where it would have been out of the way.

Dirty mofo for life.

I didn't fail to notice that the stacks of boxes—the products of late nights alone with infomercials—were missing from the doorway between my living room and kitchen. Not one had withstood the wrath of Gabriel's need for infinite space and empty surfaces. Now my brownies would never be evenly spaced and I could forget about the perfect chemically enhanced smile.

The new, state-of-the-art lock system didn't slip my attention. There was even a panel displaying a bunch of numbers attached to the wall next to the light switch. I'm sure it would take months of obscene phrases and a lot of false alarms to become besties, but the safety it promised would be worth the aggravation.

Before I had a chance to explore further, Gabriel stepped into the living room from the hallway. Unable to stop myself, a whirlwind of emotions swept my lips into a smile. Gabriel was six-two and built like a brick house. That's what happens when you make a vamp out of a Texas farm boy. Eternally toned muscles. Not as prominent as a weightlifter's, but more than good genetics. His midnight brown hair shifted under a new hall light, hints of highlights catching my eye. And those emerald eyes... Carelessly overlooked for years while I wished horrible things upon his person, like actual death or inescapable reality TV reruns.

He wore a muted pinstripe dress shirt. Something was out of place, though. Gabriel's cuffs were rolled up just below his elbows, and the material was wrinkled, which was a little *too* casual for his M.O. His black slacks also lacked the extra starch and hangar look. To the average eye, nothing would seem askew, but my eyes knew better. He still looked damned good, just a little off the mark from his usual polished style.

My vacation had been great. Spending more time than imaginable with Seth had completed the experience, but to see Gabriel... It gave me a sense of familiarity, like I was really back in my life. While that used to be a bad thing, I was looking forward to the positive changes I wanted to make, like having friends and a life outside of being the Cypher. One outstanding bonus of being the Cypher meant that I had an immortality rating much higher than a normal human. I would never die from old age or sickness, but I better watch out for homicidal maniacs. All the more reason to stop sulking and start living.

Not long ago, Gabriel had been nothing more than a fellow employee. He worked for the Members, too. I was forced to see him on a nightly basis because he was the guy in charge of escorting the Initiates to my house for their soul readings. That was that. Through all of my soulless troubles, however, he'd proven to be much more. Now, I considered him a good friend. Not too long ago, I considered acting on feelings I'd tried hard to ignore, but it wouldn't work for either of us, so what would be the point?

It was still good to see him. Comforting. I would've hugged him if the damned moment didn't promise a world of awkwardness.

He held his hands out to his sides, like the ringleader of a circus. "What do you think?" Gabriel had a spectacular voice. It wasn't too high or too low, but it demanded attention. He could whisper through a crowd and everyone would stop to listen. Not because of vampire wiles. Just his own power, I suppose. "Do you like it?"

"It's more than I expected."

"I started with a few items, but as the new things arrived, the old things started, well, sucking. So June and I turned this into an intervention."

June? I'd spent a little time with her over my vacation. How much time had Gabriel been spending with her?

It didn't matter. They had been doing something really nice. For me. No one had done something like this for me *ever*, so I refused to repay their kindness with jealousy.

"You know what? It's pretty livable." As my words trailed off, I sauntered past Gabriel, into the kitchen. In the back of my mind, I noted how sweet he smelled when he didn't bother wearing that horrid gigolo cologne to tease me. It was one thing to smell like a fly trap, it was another to cause irreversible damage to my olfactory senses.

"Against her better judgment, I didn't permit June to throw everything out. It is *your* home, after all. I tried to keep it within your...taste."

"Which is?"

He took a minute before answering. His mouth opened once as if to speak, shut, then finally opened, settling on, "Eclectic."

I squinted, catching him in his lie. "That's not what you wanted to say."

Gabriel rattled off, "A hoarder's dream. A city fine waiting to happen. A near-death experience. Better?"

Laughing, I shook my head. "Definitely not. Eclectic was better. Smart vamp."

"Smart *man*."

If I hadn't known better, I would have thought I saw a not so chaste glint in his eyes.

"Guess so." I brushed my hands across the glimmering new kitchen table. The white tile top was spotless. It was the perfect excuse to keep myself from staring to see if the glint was real.

"Like it?"

"It's shiny. Won't be for long. I'm not much of a housekeeper, but you've already figured that out."

The words had barely died in my throat when I caught Gabriel move out of the corner of my eye. He advanced so quickly I thought he'd either hug me or run right through me. Instead, he settled on standing unusually close. The inch of space between us was a godsend. Or the worst form of torture.

"When the time comes to dust, buy a new one."

"Right. The Members would love my excuse for that bill. 'Why the extra mortgage this month, Ell?' Oh, you know, dusty floorboards and a spider in the kitchen. Had to burn that evil down and start fresh."

His chuckle startled me, calling attention to the effect he was causing. My muscles were tense, my jaw set tightly in place. He was under the impression that one day we would be some sort of a couple, though he refused to indulge my curiosity with details.

Smelling the welcoming aroma of sage and spearmint waft from his hair wasn't helping, damn it.

Rehashing this was giving me a sense of Deja vu. I

couldn't quite grasp why. I had inadvertently read Gabriel's soul, along with Seth's, not long ago. However, all of the trauma left me with a sort of amnesia as to what I'd read. Everyone kept reassuring me that it would come back, but it was really starting to piss me off. Anytime it was brought up I kept getting a nagging feeling in my gut that no one, other than myself, really wanted me to remember.

Gabriel noticed my thoughtful expression and interrupted. "You don't like the table?" He asked a casual question, though his tone gave away the fact that he knew my thoughts had nothing to do with the table.

Lost in contemplation, I mechanically muttered, "Nothing's wrong with it," as I walked away, grabbed my bag off the floor, and proceeded down the hall to my bedroom to unpack. On the way, I managed a cheerier tone when I asked, "Do you have to work tonight?" This was my way of asking if *I* had to work my first day home from vacation. Because, without my Cypher services, Gabriel didn't have a full plate to keep him busy with Initiates.

His hauntingly bewitching voice drew closer as I tossed my bag on the bed and dumped the contents out.

"We both have a few more days. I'll make a copy of the schedule." With the end of his answer, Gabriel was leaning in the doorway, watching me unpack. "How was your trip?" His tone was neutral. No hint that he was fishing.

Not like I had anything to hide. He knew I'd been vacationing with Seth, a pointy-toothed friend. He also knew that Seth and I had been flirting with the idea of being more than friends, and seemed okay with that. Odd, but oddities were beginning to clutter my life like a macabre museum of doll heads. So unless it was a kick in the lady bits, I was learning to let things go.

"It was great. We stayed in the mountains with Seth's friends. June was even there for a while."

*But you knew that*, I finished pointedly in my mind.

June was a vampire. She was also inherently sweet. The inhuman equivalent to a puppy in a sombrero or a baby goat in pajamas. I didn't know her brother, July, at all, really. Just that he was a friend of Gabriel's brother, Gideon, and often visited June at work, which was my major haunt, Two Cents. It was a small sports bar owned by Danny Lynn, who chose the short straw and became my Member-appointed guardian.

I used to justify all the time spent there as simple convenience. Two Cents was only a few blocks from my house. In retrospect, I'd been completely numb to the world and it was somewhere to hide in plain sight.

"June informed me."

"Oh, she *informed* you? How sweet of her to keep you *informed*."

Damn, I sounded like a jealous twit, but I wasn't... Was I? If Gabriel registered my ill-meaning tone, he refused to call attention to it.

The thought crossed my mind that he'd been using June to spy on me. I liked June. I hoped she wasn't playing nice for a free slice of the pie. No, she wasn't the type. I refused to allow myself to ruin new friendships all because of a low blood sugar moment.

Crossing his arms across his chest, incidentally tugging his shirt in all the best places, Gabriel corrected, "She *shared* with me when I called to ask if July has seen Gideon."

"Mm," I offered in return as I recalled the short amount of time I'd known June, reevaluating how much I should really trust any new acquaintance. I realized I'd spaced out and left Gabriel waiting for confirmation that I was listening. Being ignored was one of his pet peeves. "I'm listening." Looking at me with a doubt-laden expression, I rephrased, "Has July seen Gideon? See, attention being all sorts of paid."

He seemed satisfied enough with my answer to shake his head. His words sunk in as he gravely stated, "No one's seen my brother."

Gideon is Gabriel's twin brother. It must be a cosmic joke to have us all intertwined in one another's lives, but that's the running theme. Gideon disappeared right before I left for vacation. No one panicked at first because he tends to walk just this side of the line between trouble and danger. Two months later, on the other hand, the red flags couldn't be ignored any longer. Gideon is a perfect storm, to put it nicely. He and Gabriel are as different as, well, me and Ellenore.

"Are we ready to send out the search party?" I asked.

"We?"

"Yes, *we*. Don't be difficult, Green Bean. I told you I'd help if your six-ways-to-Sunday crazy brother failed to reemerge."

I finished unpacking my clothes and moved across the hall with a smaller bag to put away my toothbrush and other toiletries. Gabriel simply changed direction, leaning in the doorway on his right shoulder instead of his left.

"And what do you suppose our course of action should be?" he prodded dryly.

"I don't have an official plan yet. I need more information first. And it would help if you could restrain this." I waved my hand back and forth in front of his face.

"What is *this*?" he asked, flailing his hand at a failed attempt to mimic mine.

"Your skepticism. So spill the details." When his eyebrow

rose, I quickly added, "Now, damn it." 'Please' would have been more appropriate.

He was more uptight than usual. It certainly showed when he started rambling off exactly how little he knew.

"He hasn't been home. Not once. No personal items were taken. He's made no contact with me or anyone I've thought to call, which have been many. And there hasn't been one sighting of him since the evening of your Soul Heist Ceremony."

"Is that what we're calling it now, a Soul Heist Ceremony? God, I was crossing my fingers it would earn a snazzy name I could put on a T-shirt or name a band. If I ever start a band. I have to know, is that the official terminology passed down by our ancestors or something special you picked out just for me?"

He started brushing his hands through his hair, which meant he was getting stressed out. Okay, not a good time to play.

"Sorry. Go on."

Notes to self: make T-shirt. Start band.

"That's all I have." The inflection in his voice made me suspect that wasn't the full truth. Gabriel was one to hold his cards close until the time came to show them or bluff like a Sin City crook. This must not have been the exception. Or, he really didn't believe there was anything I could do to help so why risk telling me everything, right?

"There's absolutely no chance he's just hanging out with some chick he broke out of the clink?"

He rolled his eyes before saying, "No," very curtly.

"Hey, bars can't cage love."

Could he blame me? I'd met Gideon and he definitely summered in Crazy Town. He may not live there, but I was convinced he used up a lot of frequent flyer miles visiting so often.

Even so, there was something about him that I liked. And seeing how he proposed the moment he saw me, I knew that if things went south with Seth and Gabriel while I simultaneously went insane and flying Hell piggies learned how to play Sweet Child Of Mine, there was a man out there willing to embrace me. Of course, there was no real interest between us, but I got a distinct feeling that he could be trusted. That's a rare quality, especially in a vampire. A peculiar specimen of a vamp who was unafraid to fly his freak flag high.

I walked past Gabriel, back into the bedroom. When I turned to face him after shoving the bags under the bed, he'd slid down the doorway to sit with his forearms resting on his knees. The back of his head slumped against the doorframe, eyes closed. Usually, Gabriel went to great lengths to disguise his weariness. To see his shields down so completely was a bad sign. In fact, I'd never seen him abandon the defenses every vampire perfects over time.

There had to be a very important something he wasn't telling me, that he most likely didn't want me involved in. But he had gone to great lengths to help me, and it was time to shove my goodwill down his throat. Very simply, he needed my help now as bad as I'd needed his two months ago.

And Gabriel was my friend now.

Unsure how to reply to his despondency, I sat with my back against the opposite side of the doorframe, resting my legs to the right of his because his six-foot-two frame demanded a lot more space than my compact five-four.

"You think he's in trouble?" Unable to or not wanting to respond verbally, he nodded, eyes remaining closed. "Okay, then. We find out where he is, kick some ass, and bring him home. That's the plan."

Upon that meaty nugget of genius, Gabriel's eyes snapped open. "That's the plan?"

"I'll give you a copy of the Cliff's Notes later. There'll be diagrams. Oh, and a pie chart! Don't worry, we can't all be pretty *and* smart." Staring at the line of his tense brow, my smartass facade faded. "You should have told me you've been this worried. I would have come home much sooner."

It agitated me that he'd been this upset and refused to let on one bit when we spoke on the phone quite a few times while I was gone. I felt terrible for having not known what he was going through.

"It would have been selfish to mention it. You deserved to be free of us, if only for a few weeks."

My head was in danger of vibrating right off my neck, I protested so hard. There was no arguing with Gabriel when he thought he was right, so I was forced to focus on what I did have to work with.

"Well, I'm home now. We'll figure something out. I'll take more time off if I have to." Placing my hand on his knee, I grinned. "I know, you must be wondering how I get so far ahead at work *and* make time to give back to the community. Hashtag blessed."

Finding and initiating a new Cypher is a very time-consuming endeavor. Unless I walked out permanently, I wasn't losing my position in the fanged community anytime soon.

Job. Security.

Gabriel placed a palm over my hand before I could withdraw. I froze under his cool touch. Instinctively, I wanted to pull away, to create more distance than an ocean or planet could provide. But a curious piece of my heart wanted to know what it would feel like to hold the calculating hand of Gabriel Vertiline. Though, technically, he'd merely rested his hand over the top of mine.

Feeling the air stifle around us, I listened as his voice traveled the short distance, like a dream that might turn deadly and real in a heartbeat. Gabriel Vertiline was no house cat with fangs. While he'd always refused to share specifics of his past -as had anyone I'd questioned concerning him, for that matter- I knew the man was a mask for the beast. It was the beast who drew me in, after all.

"You can't be a part of this," he insisted. "There are certain elements involved I don't want you exposed to."

Effectively ruining our intimate moment, I hastily retracted my hand. "I'm already involved, so get over yourself. I know there's more to this than you're willing to tell me, but I still want to help. I only stipulate that if this secret you're keeping starts to sneak up and bite one of us on the ass, warn me before it's too late."

Gabriel looked displeased, but he accepted my help with a brief nod before relaxing against the doorframe again. I didn't miss the subtle flaring of his nostrils, however.

"Good. I really don't want to argue with you, on this, the eve of my homecoming. It's a wonder you have any friends, at all. You're so high maintenance."

He raised an eyebrow. "You're the one bullying your way into a catastrophe."

"I am a persistent go-getter. There's a difference."

"Not in the least."

Hopping to my feet, I ordered, "Stop fretting before you thoroughly ruin those floofy clothes."

Gabriel was almost offended. "What's 'floofy?'"

"This." I pointed to his shirt. "All of this -the sulking man caught in his inner storm, the expensive labels framing his plight- is an ad for some floofy, high street shop where they brand their name across your ass."

Silently sifting through my answer for a satisfactory definition of 'floofy,' Gabriel came to life as he grinned slyly, interjecting, "I better get up, then. I would hate to think the only reason you would be staring at my ass is to read a label."

He laughed when I blushed. I didn't think it was that funny. And again, my attention was drawn to our closeness and how it made me more than a little self-conscious. I was leery yet comfortable. I never felt comfortable around people.

Most people.

Quickly walking down the hall, laying distance between us, I quipped, "Don't be ridiculous, Gabriel, I don't need a second reason to stare at your ass."

**PURCHASE BLOOD LIES TO FIND OUT HOW ELL'S ADVENTURE ENDS.**

## SERIES & SINGLE TITLES BY BLAKELY CHORPENNING

Ell Clyne Series

(YA Paranormal Fiction)

A Madison Lark Adventure Series

(NA Shifter Fiction)

Hope & Darkness Series

(Dystopian Fiction)

Sinners & Saints Series

(Vampire Horror Fiction)

Literary Fiction:

Tin Moon

(Historical Fiction)